THE HOUSE ON MORGAN STREET

A Novel by
Elisabeth J. Stafford

JECATHIA PRESS

For my father, my compass in all situations --
the finest man I have ever known.

For Ellen, my kind and loving grandmother.

For my husband, my true love, whose devotion has never wavered.

PROLOGUE

NORTHWEST SOUTH DAKOTA - AUGUST 1939

The warning cry of a black-tailed prairie dog broke the silence of early dawn. Standing on sun-cracked earth, the pup abruptly cocked its head and with lightning speed, slid into a burrow. The mystery of the hasty retreat was solved when the wind parted a patch of brush, revealing a pair of vigilant eyes. The eyes could have been those of a predatory animal, watching and waiting for the right moment to attack its prey. But with a second look, it was apparent that the eyes were human.

With clenched fists and an unsteady gait, the onlooker rose and walked to the weathered plank doors set into a rise of prairie ground. The open padlock swayed slightly, as the doors were released from the center latch and closed again. There were now three human beings inside the small coal mine, but two of them were unaware that the thick darkness had been penetrated.

The intruder, close enough to the couple to smell male sweat and five and dime perfume, silently moved forward, lost in the shadows cast by a kerosene lantern. The man removed his hat and placed it on a protruding nail, exposing a black eye patch -- a souvenir from picking coal during his homesteading days. He moved toward the blond woman lying on a work-scarred table. The sounds of passion and the creaking of an unstable table leg masked the scrape of the pickaxe, as it was pulled from a pile of rocks.

CHAPTER ONE

MAY 7, 1991 – ALMOST MIDNIGHT

Natalie

Just before midnight, a sleek, dark vehicle passed through the gated entrance of the Abbott mansion and pulled onto the cobblestone drive. I must have dozed for a moment, as I sat on the veranda, and the headlights caught me by surprise. Tired and feeling bedraggled, I hurriedly tried to smooth my unruly dark curls and attempted to apply lipstick before the limousine arrived at the covered entrance to the house. I stopped abruptly when the headlights lit up the porch. Preening like an insecure teenager wasn't the impression I wanted to make when Lydia saw me for the first time in a year.

Lydia Abbott is three hours late, most likely because of the heavy rain and flooded roads. The storm was fierce, and the gaslights along the walkway reveal fallen tree branches and luminous patches of hail strewn about the grounds. *I must have those branches cleaned up first thing tomorrow. Lydia wouldn't approve of the mess, I thought to myself.* I have been her property manager for more than five years, despite our strained relationship, so I understand her expectations well and make every effort to please her.

Although Lydia must have been tired from the flight and the subsequent drive to Coventry, she stepped from the limousine looking morning fresh. Her blonde hair was smooth and shiny, despite the humidity, and she was wearing an understated gray pantsuit with a blush pink satin shirt. A single strand of pearls

1

and matching earrings provided the final touch of elegance. As always, Lydia looked sophisticated and wealthy, but her lack of eye contact and unfriendly body language justified the anxiety that has been nagging me since our phone conversation of a few nights ago. A half-hearted hug was the best she could offer as a greeting, and uncomfortable silence followed -- until I finally spoke. "It's so good to see you Lydia. Let's get your damp coat off before you catch a chill. Are you hungry?"

"No," she replied in a voice that sounded exhausted, but tinged with irritation. "I'm too tired to eat. I just want to go to bed. Tomorrow will be difficult."

Lydia's designer suitcase, small enough to qualify as an overnight bag, was blatant evidence that she didn't plan to remain in Coventry for long. She never packs lightly, even for a weekend stay, but how she got everything necessary for her mother's funeral in one small bag is a mystery. I was about to enter her upstairs bedroom to unpack when she grabbed the suitcase from my hands and abruptly shut the door without a word of explanation. Confused, I turned around and moved down the staircase, until I heard her door open behind me. There was a sheepish tone to her voice when she said, "I forgot to ask you to come back in the morning before the funeral, Natalie. I may need some help dressing."

I took a moment to regain my composure and said, "Of course, Lydia. I'll see you about 8:30."

During our childhoods, we were inseparable, but I was from a family of Abbott servants, and Lydia was the daughter of Helen, the Abbott matriarch. Helen didn't approve of our relationship, and with her unrelenting negative attitude and damaging comments, our friendship eroded over time, until Lydia hardly spoke to me. As time passed, she became very aware of her place in the world as an upper class socialite, and she put me in my place as a fourth generation housemaid, even though I am now the city librarian. It took me years to get past the loss of Lydia, who was like a sister to me.

As I finally left the Abbott mansion at 1 a.m., it was clear that further discussion of our previous phone call and her vague request was off the table, at least for now. *It's a good thing that caretakers Hedda and Lyon will be in the mansion tomorrow. Being alone with Lydia in this dark, brooding house, with its unspoken secrets, is not something I look forward to.*

Lydia

Returning to Abbott House, my family home, is difficult. There are too many memories and so few of them are happy. ...and then there's Natalie. We were as close as sisters during our childhood years, but everything changed when my life took a new direction, and she remained mired in this provincial Minnesota town of 40,000 people. However, I must remember that Natalie comes from a long line of Abbott housemaids, so perhaps she is well suited to that sort of life. She's now the city librarian, but I'll always think of her as one of them.

It was annoying that Natalie had overstayed her welcome at the house after my arrival, but I understood her motivation. She was hoping to continue our telephone conversation of a few nights ago; nevertheless, her tenacity was a bit too apparent. Knowing Natalie well, I understand how to manage her. She has her weaknesses, and one of them is a thin skin. Rudeness will always send her running, but I have never shut a door in her face before. Her look of shock and surprise bothered me, although only briefly. Perhaps it was overkill, but I wanted her to leave.

The flight from San Francisco to Minneapolis was nearly four hours long but gave me time to think. Making the decision not to involve Natalie in my business was the right thing to do. Our phone call of a few nights ago was a mistake, but at least the information I gave her was minimal and vague. It's safer for both of us if I take care of the nighttime trip to the cellar on my own. The less she knows of my life the better, especially for me, and that includes my financial situation. It's an understatement to say that the trip to Coventry for my mother's funeral cost more than I could afford. Although I still look like a rich, upper class woman, thanks to my one remaining credit card, things are not as they seem. Unless something happens to replenish my bank account, I won't be able to make the minimum payment next month. The cost of maintaining my image and youthful looks is now beyond my financial resources. Designer clothes, nips and tucks, and regular visits to my dermatologist, with all of his youth preserving treatments, are expensive.

My efforts to sell Abbott House have failed. There were no real buyers, which hadn't surprised me. Those who are wealthy enough to support this money pit don't reside in Coventry -- not anymore -- and they don't want to. It was finally purchased for the price of back taxes by a company that will demolish it and build senior apartments. Any thoughts I had of making a profit were a fantasy, so I had to resort to an age-old answer to my financial problems – making a lucrative marriage. There were two men, both wealthy and well-known, who were ready to put a ring on my finger, but once they introduced me to their grown children, it was all over. There were incessant questions about my finances: "Ms. Abbott, do you have a trust fund? Do you have alimony, and does it end with remarriage? What is your family's estate worth? How do you generate your living expenses?" Such questions weren't easy for me to answer, due to my depleted accounts, so I had no choice but to walk away from the possibility of making a financially appropriate marriage. Embarrassed and branded a gold digger, I became a pariah among the A-list, but there is something in this old house that will change everything. Realizing that I must act tonight, I changed into the workout clothes concealed in the zippered pocket of my suitcase and navigated my way down the staircase and through the dark house toward the cellar.

CHAPTER TWO

THE CELLAR

—

Lydia

—

The thick, musty cellar air left me breathless and adhered to my face like a stubborn cobweb. And to make matters worse, the dim lightbulb hanging from a ceiling rafter didn't provide adequate illumination. Shivering with nerves and dampness, it had become apparent that lack of preparation could put a halt to my plans. This task requires a small ladder and a shovel, which are most likely stored in the carriage house, and I wasn't up to searching there at this hour of the night. Not yet ready to give up, I began to explore and spotted what appeared to be a rickety, wooden step stool propped alongside a shelving unit. The shelves contained some ancient garden tools that were lying askew and thickly covered with cobwebs. Luckily, there was a small shovel with a cracked handle in the jumble. While the step stool and shovel were far from adequate, they just might work.

Access to the crawl space required a bit of a climb, but putting aside my distaste for dirt that smelled like dead rodents, I was able to force myself over the stone wall. Working a shovel is something I have never done before. Nevertheless, I was about to begin digging when everything went black. Desperate to finish, I switched on my mini flashlight, and it didn't take long to conclude that without proper lighting, there was no use in continuing my efforts. Before I could make my way to the stairs, an awareness of subtle sounds emanating from every dark corner sent me down the unsteady step stool with the speed and agility of a teenager. With nerves that felt as though they were on the outside of my body, raw and exposed, I hurriedly moved toward the stairs. But before finding my footing, a whisper in the dark sent terror throughout my body like an electric shock. The sound was so soft as to be nearly incomprehensible and without a distinct origin. After convincing myself that the noises were only a figment of my imagination, a defense mechanism I desperately needed to trust, something brushed against my cheek, like a barely perceptible kiss. My mind ran wild with thoughts of bats and other creatures of the darkness. Panic set in, and I began to flee. I raced up the stairs as though I had been doing it all my sedentary life, only to feel my heart sink to my stomach when I couldn't turn the doorknob. There was no movement either right or left. Feeling trapped in this Godforsaken place, I began to scream. "Help me! Someone, anyone, help me!" ...and then I stopped and became very quiet, not wanting to give away my location to whatever or whomever might be lurking about. The house was empty, and there was no one to hear my pleas anyway. For what seemed an eternity, I pulled and turned the brass knob, and finally it was released.

Guided only by moonlight and memory, I ran up the stairs to my childhood bedroom and quickly locked the heavy door behind me. At that moment, I understood the need for Natalie's involvement. I must make sure she is on board as soon as possible, but not tomorrow, as I had promised. Knowing that she has an anxiety disorder, I won't tell her that I attempted the trip to the cellar myself and failed. She might want to know details, and if that happens, I can't be sure that she will agree to take on this task. I regretted my cool demeanor when I arrived, but after my experience in the cellar, any concern should be for myself. I desperately need what has been buried in the crawlspace for so long, and I must get there first. Now It's time for Natalie to do something for me -- after all we have done for her and her servant mother.

I slept in my clothes, which were still musty from the dank basement air and left the bedside light on. I was keenly aware that I had failed and grateful that this mausoleum would soon be no more.

CHAPTER THREE

WEDNESDAY, MAY 8

Natalie

Lydia had showered and was sitting at her vanity applying makeup like an artist painting a portrait. The light breakfast tray I had delivered to her room sat nearly untouched on the serving table in front of the bay window. There was nothing for me to do but quietly observe and wait. The tension was broken when Lydia spoke in an offhand manner. "Sit down, Natalie."

"Thank you, Lydia," I responded rather meekly and made a move to sit on her chintz covered four-poster bed, as I had during our childhood and teenage years. Lydia, obviously displeased, snapped her fingers and pointed to the arm chair. Forgetting that this cozy scenario is no longer part of our relationship, I had definitely committed a faux pas. I must be more careful in the future.

Despite the sharp reprimand, I found Lydia's grooming routine to be quite mesmerizing. She is a beautiful woman of forty-five who doesn't need much makeup to enhance her classic looks, or so it would appear. But having known her for a lifetime, there are small signs that her beauty has been preserved with some high-quality surgical interventions that were not performed by a mediocre plastic surgeon in a local strip mall.

After brushing her hair and laying out her stylish black funeral dress, I understood why I was asked to return this morning. The back of the dress had at least twenty tiny fabric-covered buttons that needed to be dealt with. She couldn't have done that on her own. Once the buttons were fastened and the dress looked perfect on her tall, slender frame, I again sat in the chair, hoping that she would engage me in a follow-up discussion to our phone call of two nights ago -- as she had promised. During that conversation, Lydia seemed quite desperate. The anxiety in her voice, so intense, so unlike her, was disturbing. But today, she was silent on the subject, and our discussion turned to the mundane.

As I fulfilled my "lady-in-waiting" role, there was an unmistakable tension in the air. We had sat too long speaking of ordinary things, and the atmosphere was filled with insincere words and nervous gestures. It was easy to sense that past resentments were rising to the surface for both of us. My fingers dug into the arm of the chair, as I recalled a particularly hurtful comment.

"There's nothing you can do about your looks, Natalie. How fortunate that you're so smart, because the kind of husband you would attract will never have money. At least you can get a job that will allow you to support yourself, even if you end up a spinster."

Lydia speaks in that finishing school manner that uses words from the past such as "spinster," but it doesn't make her remarks hurt any less. That comment was the defining, stinging moment of our long relationship -- not so much because I had been told that I was unattractive, but at that instant, I knew without a doubt that my childhood playmate had been claimed by the inevitable force of her social class, and I had been relegated to mine.

Edgy and trying to hide my discomfort, I waited for something – anything -- to lighten the conversation, but there was a strange emptiness, and the silence was growing. My eyes wandered about Lydia's bedroom seeking some relief, until settling on the familiar photograph on her desk. I felt a pang of emptiness, as I glanced at the smiling face of her handsome young father in his World War II military uniform. Lydia doesn't remember him, but she knows who he is. It's my greatest sadness that Mother had never revealed the identity of my father. "It's better that you don't know, Natalie," she would say in that voice that warned me to not to persist.

Needing to wrap up this uncomfortable scenario with Lydia, I asked, "May I do something more for you?"

She vacantly looked into the mirror and spoke in her languid finishing school manner, "Please have Lyon bring the car to the entrance at 10 a.m."

"Of course, Lydia. I'll speak with him right away. Are you coming down for breakfast?"

"No, I have eaten enough. You may leave now, Natalie. We are finished here."

Hedda will not be pleased that the breakfast she has been preparing since 5 a.m. will now go uneaten. Perhaps Lyon can deliver the food to the homeless shelter.

Although Lydia is a flawless woman to look at, her rough edges are on the inside, and they are as jagged and cold as an iceberg.

CHAPTER FOUR

THE FUNERAL

Natalie

Standing discretely off to the side of Helen's casket served me well, as I made every attempt to avoid looking at her emaciated corpse. Helen, like her daughter Lydia, had deprived herself of food for most of her life. Her primary caloric intake came from wine and bourbon, so there is no flesh to soften her once classic features. My involuntary glances were disturbing, but I couldn't stop. The body was a preview of what Lydia would look like in death. Mother and daughter were nearly twin-like in their appearance, if one could subtract the age and illness factor. After what seemed an eternity, I was grateful when the casket was closed.

The Presbyterian Church was older than Abbott House, and inside the cut stone edifice there was a musty odor mingling with the fragrance of spring blossoms. Musty church odor -- a mixture of stone, old wood and books -- has always appealed to me. Today, I was pleased that there was no air conditioning to dilute the scents of the past.

During the service, the buzzing of a flighty bee created a mild distraction, as it targeted the gray hair of the forty or so mostly elderly guests. Growing tired of dodging waving hands, the failed bee finally flew out the window. There was relief among the congregants, but I was rather disappointed. The buzzing insect seemed to be more alive than anyone in the room, including myself. Funerals often have the effect of creating a comatose atmosphere, as if we are all practicing for our own demise.

I wasn't sad about Helen's death, nor did it appear were any of the other somber and detached townspeople. During the past year, Helen had lived in a care facility, barely staying alive in the aftermath of a stroke. But in the end, despite her wealth, she met the same fate as my mother Grace, her housemaid. It's true that old age and death are the great equalizers.

Lydia

This funeral is quite boring, and for some reason, I am unable to do anything but think about the past. My mother Helen is gone, and I can't say it makes me sad or that I will miss her. She could only be described as an angry, unpleasant woman—and a drunk. Mother wasn't one of those alcoholic women who frequented bars, drinking and looking for men. She was the kind of drunk that rich women become, rarely leaving her house, spending most of her time in her bedroom. When she wasn't sleeping, she was tormenting everyone around her, especially Natalie's mother Grace -- and me. For some reason, she treated my dead brother Tice with kid gloves, but once he was gone—long dead, the result of a fire at our lake cabin—she never mentioned him again.

I know little about Mother's life outside her bedroom -- only what I have occasionally overheard from the Abbott staff when I was prowling around the kitchen. It seems that Mother Helen was born on a farm somewhere in South Dakota and came to live with her grandmother Marguerite Abbott and Uncle Ellsworth in 1939, after her parents died. I never knew her parents, my grandparents, but from what I overheard from listening to kitchen gossip, her father Thomas Abbott met a suspicious end, and her mother Bridget had hung herself. I dared not ask for more details, but Ellsworth sometimes mentioned that Thomas died in a mine accident and Bridget succumbed to influenza. With the discrepancies in information, it appears that something was amiss, so I took every opportunity to lurk about and eavesdrop on the staff, especially when they took their tea and bread in the afternoons.

Natalie and I left the church walking behind Mother's coffin. Although our relationship is on poor terms, I was still grateful that she was with me today. I don't know how she can stand living in Coventry. It occurred to me that her life must be as dreary as a nun's.

CHAPTER FIVE

MAY 8 – 11 P.M.

Natalie

Lydia has gone back to San Francisco, and I have the responsibility for something she wants taken care of secretly and in the dead of night, but with little information and few directions. Her promise of a call tonight may or may not be kept.

As I was lying in bed fighting sleep, the phone finally rang just before midnight. My nerves are on edge, and the ring seemed to become more insistent with each burst. I didn't pick up until I had counted twelve. Finally, feigning a casual voice that masked my nerves, I answered with a rather disinterested "hello."

Lydia's voice was surprisingly rattled and a bit tremulous. "Oh, God, Natalie, I was afraid that you weren't going to answer. Take a pen and paper and write this down. It's important to get all of the instructions correct." Again, Lydia didn't sound like the cool, confident woman I had interacted with during the past two days, nor like the woman I have known for my entire life. She went on for a minute or two with a whispered staccato speech that was difficult to understand. At one point, I tried to interrupt and ask a question for clarification when I heard another person in the background. The voice was angry and seemed to be male, but because of an unusual tone, I couldn't be sure.

"Get off the phone. Now!"

Curious, I asked, "Who are you talking to, Lydia? Who is with you?" She didn't respond to my questions or the person in the room with her. She continued to speak, which seemed to make the one with the mysterious voice increasingly angry. I sensed a frenzied scenario on her end, even though I wasn't present.

Again, I heard another hoarse, angry outburst. "Who are you talking to? Get off the phone you bitch! Hang up…now!"

Lydia continued trying to converse with me, but her last words, completely out of the context of our conversation, were obviously intended to deceive the person in her presence. She had simply given up trying to communicate with me in a straightforward manner, and instead, her words turned to a vague code.

"Yes, Leslie, that is all I have for you. What I told you about the painting will have to do, but I will call you next week to finalize our plans for the gallery date and…" At that point, there was a sudden, interruptive click, as though someone other than Lydia had ended the call in mid-sentence…and then there was nothing but empty silence hanging in the air like a deflated balloon.

Concerned, I raised my voice and said, "Lydia, Lydia are you there?" When I realized she was no longer on the other end of the line, I hung up, resigned and in a rather confused state about what she wanted me to do. But it didn't really matter. I have always done what she asked of me, so I decided to proceed with the information I had.

The raspy voice on Lydia's end of the line bothered me, but then I assumed that she must have a new boyfriend -- and a rather demanding one at that. As beautiful as she is, Lydia has never been lucky with men.

Tomorrow will be a busy day, because I also have to do something for my mother. She made a request that I've been ignoring since before her death. I planned to accomplish both tasks during one trip to the mansion, but that may not be possible. Right now, I badly need to get into bed. I suspected, and rightly so, that sleep would be elusive and brief.

Lydia

My phone conversation with Natalie had come to an abrupt halt. I think she found the whole thing odd and disconcerting, with him constantly interrupting before he finally disconnected us. He was venomous when he shouted, "You're keeping something from me, and I will find out what it is. You have no idea who you are dealing with, you bitch!" With that, he grabbed me by the shoulders and pushed me to the floor.

Through gritted teeth, I said in a firm voice that belied my fear, "Stop immediately! This is my house, and I will have you thrown out." He continued his angry, aggressive tirade but stopped short of slapping me with the back of his raised hand. I was relieved when he finally went downstairs to his cell-like servant's room off the kitchen. Locking my bedroom door and giving it a strong tug provided the reassurance of being safely sealed inside. He is becoming more antagonistic and dangerous. I need to find some way of getting this monster out of my life.

It's true that I am keeping a secret from him, and he knows it. Once this is resolved, complete separation would be wise. He is evil and capable of anything to get what he wants. It won't be easy to do what needs to be done, and that is why Natalie must be on board. I desperately need her help. I should have been nicer to her.

The stress of this situation calls for some wine. Although I had promised to cut back, denying myself is probably not wise right now. The wine cooler at the end of my walk-in closet has been well-used since I installed it several years ago. The best thing about it, aside from easy access to the wine it stores, is its lack of visibility to anyone entering my bedroom, especially a prospective wealthy husband. Rich men don't want a lush for a wife, especially one who drinks alone in her bedroom. Not that I am a lush, but I don't want to give the wrong impression.

The process that goes with uncorking a good bottle of wine and pouring it into a glass of fine lead crystal is something I have always enjoyed, but when I caught my reflection in the antique French mirror hanging above my dresser, the scene was a bit disturbing. I saw my mouth make a slight, silent smacking motion, followed by a subtle tongue thrust, in anticipation of my first sip. I have seen my alcoholic mother Helen make that same facial expression many times before she takes a sip of wine. With that thought, I made a vow to have only two glasses – but then changed my mind. Two glasses wouldn't be enough tonight, so I decided to have a third after all. A small indulgence can't hurt -- and besides, it might distract from thoughts of my unwanted house guest.

The wine never fails me, and after three generous glasses, I felt a warm, mellow glow and was finally in that sweet place. I hope Natalie was able to understand enough of my instructions during our disjointed conversation. Having known her for her entire life, I think she will try to follow through. She is loyal, at least she was at one time during our friendship. I know the reason for our estrangement is my fault, but it is also fair to blame my Mother Helen. She has been trying to divide us since we became teenagers, and her admonishments produced suspicion and fear:

You don't play with the hired help, Lydia. They're trash, and they can't provide you with the proper social connections that may lead to a good marriage. And besides, Natalie's mother is a whore. Do you know what that is, little girl? It's an evil woman who will use her body to take what is yours.

"Yes, Mother," I responded. There was no use in disagreeing with her, and besides, she might go into a violent rage, which was to be avoided at all costs. Despite her allegations, I still sought every opportunity to spend time with Natalie secretly, at least for a while. It wasn't all that difficult, because Mother was drunk most of the time, passed out in her bedroom, unaware and mostly unconcerned with anything I was doing.

A peaceful glow enveloped me like a warm hug, but soon I began to feel unusually drowsy. When I went to pour the forbidden fourth glass, against my better judgement, my arms and legs went weak, and my vision all but disappeared. Something was wrong. I don't usually react this way to two or three glasses of wine. It was then that I heard my locked door slowly open. In a stupor, I couldn't see the face of the intruder clearly, but abruptly a distinctive voice snarled. "Did you really think you could take what was mine?" I knew who was in my room. And then the screams began. The sound pierced the room as if in an echo chamber, and my ear drums reverberated with discomfort. When I finally realized that I was the one screaming, the darkness began to overtake me completely.

Before I disappeared into the gray spiral of whatever he had slipped into my wine, I heard my voice, weak and slurred, "How did you get in here, you bastard? What have you done to me?"

CHAPTER SIX

BEFORE DAWN

Natalie

I awoke at 4 a.m. feeling as though I had never slept. The request that my mother made of me before her death has been nagging for some time. It should have been taken care of long ago, but I didn't think it was that important -- until now.

As I drove though the Morgan Street neighborhood on Cobble Hill, past the dozen or so turn-of-the-century mansions still standing, I didn't need daylight to tell me that most of the once handsome homes are now quite seedy. For years, I have been watching them deteriorate and change into unpleasant hybrids. Abandonment, repairs, and tacky 20th century updates have turned Coventry's Gilded Age mansions into a hodge-podge of rundown apartment buildings, lawyer's offices, and restaurants. Abbott House has been the exception, but a family fortune has been spent to keep it as it was in the late 1800s.

The generations of family members who have lived within its walls have been an interesting lot, beginning with Daniel Abbott, an orphaned but ambitious New Englander. With no place to go but to a small Midwestern city, where old family money and social connections were not necessary for financial and social success, Daniel arrived in Coventry in 1875. The coming of the railroad a few years earlier had made the growing town a lucrative proposition. By 1890 he had amassed a fortune worthy of a New York entrepreneur.

His decision to marry Marguerite Evans, the daughter of the local hardware dealer, turned out to be wise. Although she was not a beauty, she was hard working and a quick learner. During the first five years of their marriage, they lived over her family's hardware store, where she rented out sleeping rooms to transient railroad workers. Marguerite wasn't afraid to get her hands dirty, but perhaps the stress and strain of hard work is what made child bearing so difficult for her. She and Daniel had two sons who grew into adulthood, but there have always been rumors of still-born babies. The mystery seems to be that none of them lie in the Abbott cemetery plot -- so maybe the rumors are false.

After five years of marriage and no sign of a child, Daniel and Marguerite adopted Ellsworth from the county poor farm and raised him as their own. Their only biological child, Thomas Abbott, was born after ten years of hoping for a baby, but Ellsworth was the one that Daniel Abbott counted on. Thomas was a ne'er-do-well, who was always a problem.

The hallmark of Daniel Abbott's success, the pride of his life, was his home on Morgan Street. It is the largest stone mansion in southern Minnesota and worthy of being on Summit Avenue in St. Paul. Now it appears that there is no saving it. The toll of time has been asleep, and the fortune has been spent, like most of the Abbott family members. Time always has a way of catching up to the present.

The silhouette of Abbott House came into view on the backdrop of a muted sunrise, and as always, I hear my Mother's words. "Turn a blind eye and a deaf ear, young lady. ... and when you don't, keep their secrets."

"Yes, Mama, I will. Don't worry."

CHAPTER SEVEN

INTERRUPTED

Natalie

The interior of Abbott House was bathed in darkness, except for silvery patches of light where the early dawn had found its way inside. I didn't want to attract any more attention by turning on the lights, so I made use of the small flashlight in my bag. My presence in the mansion at this hour would not be considered unusual, since all of Coventry knows that I manage the property; but, there was good reason to get in and out quickly with as little notice as possible. Scrutiny of any kind would be a problem, according to Lydia, although I'm not sure why.

Because of the scheduled demolition, I decided to take the time to photograph as many of the mansion's rooms as I could to preserve its history. The furniture and décor are the same now as one-hundred years ago, except for Lydia's childhood bedroom. Moving from room to room and snapping photographs from a variety of angles took more time than I had estimated. Finally, satisfied with my efforts and aware of the fact that I needed to be at work at 8 a.m., I headed toward the library, but stopped short at Lydia's room. Noticing that she had not removed the photograph of her father, I impulsively decided to put it into my bag, thinking I would give it to her at another time. The consignment company would have little use for a personal photograph. The library was my last stop, and time was running out.

When Mother became ill with a failing heart and high blood pressure, she seemed to be obsessed with some "books" and mentioned them every time we were together. The books, actually journals, had been placed in the false bottom of the window seat that sat under the stained-glass window of the library. After Daniel Abbott had died in 1919, its existence had been all but forgotten by his family but became well-used by the women of mine.

Following my mother's instructions, I lifted the heavy lid and looked inside. There was a black velvet cushion, which I removed. At that point, I changed my focus to the ornate front panel. Using my small flashlight to illuminate the carved replicas of ancient warriors lining the lower portion of the front of the window seat, I identified the critical figure. There were five of them, but Mother said the operating mechanism was within the second from the left. I turned the figure to the left until it stopped and then again toward the right. With increasing curiosity, I looked inside, and I could see that the false bottom had slid slightly forward into a position I could lift with my fingers. Pulling the panel upward, three leather bound books were revealed by my flashlight. ...and then, without warning, there was the sound of a door closing and heavy footsteps echoed from the entry hall. I panicked. It was too early for Hedda and Lyon. Quickly stuffing the books into the large black bag that was meant to transport cleaning supplies, I replaced the cushion and closed the lid just as the source of the noise was identified by the sound of his booming voice.

"Who's here? Show yourself!"

His voice preceded his six foot four-inch, 300-pound presence, and I knew right away who it was. It was Dale Forbes, a former classmate of mine and one of the police officers employed by the city. I timidly walked into the foyer and was met with his fleshy, red face and the strong odor of whiskey on his breath. I noticed that he had his hand on a revolver that balanced a bit off kilter at his ever-expanding waistline. Dale was a blustery sort with an overly friendly personality that couldn't be hidden behind his role as a police officer. I was greatly relieved when a gap-toothed smile suddenly filled his face. At that moment, I knew I could handle Deputy Dale.

"Oh, I am so glad to see you," I said with feigned trepidation. "This house gives me the creeps when it is empty and dark. I have been hearing noises, and I needed to pick up a few things."

Dale's eyes moved from my face to the working bag slung over my left shoulder. He took note of the feather dusters and cleaning rags emerging in bursts of color from the outside pockets. "It looks like you've been busy, Miss LaPierre." This visual evidence seemed to satisfy his curiosity.

Casually patting the bag, I commented in a cheerful voice, "No need to have things destroyed or taken by the consignment folks. Cleaning supplies are expensive, and although I don't really need them for myself, they can be used at the library."

"Good idea," he said, his booming voice echoing in the foyer. "Can I help you gather them?"

"That would be nice," I responded with an ingratiating smile.

I didn't want Dale to become suspicious, so I handed him the bag, and he followed me into the pantry. After I had loaded sponges, rubber gloves, and cleaners, he proudly carried all of it out of the house like a Boy Scout working toward a new badge. He never questioned what I had already placed in the bag before his arrival, despite its obvious weight. Dale, a seemingly uncomplicated man, showed no curiosity, but for a rather dreadful moment, I thought he was again going to ask me to go on a date.

Dale was a single, childless man in a town of mostly married people. He had been married for about a year to a girl named Roseanne, whom he had met in North Carolina during the end of his twenty-year stint in the Marines. He was proud of her buxom, blond looks and honeyed southern charm that was such a contrast to the no-nonsense style of most of the local women. Within days of their marriage, Dale had packed Roseanne and her numerous suitcases into his 1978 Horizon and headed north to Coventry. They moved into his mother's ramshackle house on the outskirts of town, and it wasn't a stretch to predict that Roseanne would quickly became disenchanted. She grew to dislike the brutal Minnesota winters, but most of all, she disliked his very critical mother, Blanche Forbes. Roseanne wasn't shy about sharing her thoughts and feelings with any other woman or man who would listen.

Roseanne's unhappiness culminated in a scandal when Mama Forbes came home early from her weekly bridge game and caught her in bed with the young, good looking man who drives the noisy, gear grinding dump truck for his family's construction business. Although their trysts only happened on Mrs. Forbes' ladies' aide and bridge days, it was difficult to keep them concealed from anyone who saw and heard the massive truck, as it parked in the alley behind the Forbes' home for hours at a time. The neighbors knew about it before Dale and his mother found out. Coventry, like other small towns, has always been a veritable bee hive of gossip. Within days of Mrs. Forbes discovery, Dale was sharing his woeful story in the bars, telling all who would listen that the unfaithful Roseanne had returned to her mother in North Carolina.

After the dust of the Roseanne scandal had settled, Dale began making romantic overtures toward me. I gently rebuffed his advances with the false claim of having been deeply wounded by a lost love during my college years and that I was unwilling to risk another painful experience. Of course, Dale carried my story to the bars, and now everyone in Coventry views me as a rejected, dried up old maid, but at least I am no longer bothered by unwanted suitors. As for Dale, it's common knowledge, thanks to his loose-lipped drinking episodes, that he frequents brothels in the Twin Cities, as well as web sites, looking for either an Asian or a Russian bride. The word in the bars and other gathering places in town is that he has found one from the Ukraine and is madly in love.

Dale finally spoke, shaking his large head from side to side, "Too bad about this old house. It was always a beauty and it's old Coventry history alright. Yup—too bad for sure. Well, you have a good day and drive safe now."

I turned toward my car, but I surprised myself with the boldness of my impulsive request. "Dale, would you be able to help me with that small writing desk in the library? I know that Lydia wouldn't mind me having it, and I'll pay her for it."

"Sure enough," Dale said, proud of his size and strength. We walked back into the mansion, but as he attempted to lift the desk, he groaned and said, "it's heavier than it looks." He looked around the room until he spied a moving cart in the corner, and we were quickly on our way to my car. The desk was easily loaded into the back of my small SUV, with little effort from Dale.

"We aim to please, Ma'am," he said jokingly, no questions asked.

I waved and said, "Thanks Dale," and I was on my way, feeling as though I had dodged a bullet. I had to restrain myself from pulling away too quickly and driving too fast, but I was relieved to get out of the driveway. Surprised at my own nerve in the face of a good deal of trepidation, my face suddenly felt warm with shame. I hadn't been truthful when I told Dale that Lydia wouldn't mind if I took the small writing desk. I don't really know what she would think. The truth might be that she would mind very much, given our difficult relationship, but it has some pleasant memories for me. My mother Grace had always admired its fine wood and graceful lines, and I would often sit there, when the Abbotts weren't around, doing my homework. I'll pay Lydia for the desk or else it will bring me no pleasure.

As I drove home, I began thinking about how I could get back into the house unseen, after midnight. Lydia insisted that this task was to be clandestine and completed in the middle of the night. I don't really know why, but she said only that it was a "family thing." As always, I didn't ask questions. It seems that everything in the house should now be hers, but Lydia had said, "I don't want anything, Natalie. I don't know what I would do with it. ... just the metal box in the cellar."

This was Thursday, and I knew I must complete this task before the weekend. There would be too many people out and about on Friday or Saturday night. Making sure I knew what Dale was doing, I adjusted my rear-view mirror and observed him going back into the house. I wondered how safe Lydia's secret really was.

Returning home, there was just enough time to unload the desk and the bag before taking Charlie to doggy day care where he will also spend the weekend. Knowing that I must return to the mansion after midnight gives me a spine-chilling feeling. Why do I feel that I must do something as unpleasant and frightening as this for Lydia? To that question I had no answers but to say to myself, "*because I always have.*"

CHAPTER EIGHT

IN A DARK PLACE

Lydia

The smell of blood penetrated my nostrils, and my brain is foggy, as though I had taken one too many of my sleeping pills. I soon understood that I was not in my bed but lying on a cold concrete floor in total darkness, clothed only in a satin nightgown. Shaking with fear and dampness, bound with tape and gagged, I thought it strange that there was no blindfold on my eyes. Perhaps he wanted me to strain my eyes in vain, as I searched for the faintest sliver of light – creating more desperation. The familiar odor of what I soon realized was the wine cellar in the basement of my own home was ironic. Being imprisoned in one's own home with no way out is the cruelest fate. I have few friends and rarely have visitors, so my isolation was complete, because no one would miss me. I was not getting out of here unless my captor issued me a reprieve, and that would be an unlikely development, given his motivation. All human beings have thoughts about their own death, and now I know the likely truth of my own, but it will not happen before he gets what he wants. He will make sure of that.

It seems as though I have been floating in and out of sleep. How long was I asleep – if I did indeed sleep? I can't be sure. Was it day or night? I didn't know the answers to my own questions. My sense of time has been lost, and I soon stopped thinking and began to listen very intently. In the black of a cellar with boarded up windows, I saw nothing and heard nothing that provided answers -- just the vague, muffled sounds of traffic on the street above. I didn't expect to hear much from inside the house, because he always moved like a cat and never watched television or played music. I don't know what he did in his room, but whatever it was, he did it in total silence.

I tried to escape the bindings by constantly moving my arms and legs. I even tried to loosen my tape gag with saliva. The result was only more exhaustion and panic. Finally, I stopped my futile efforts and let my mind take over. I have always heard that when human beings are near death, the life they have lived flashes before their eyes. I found there was truth in that old adage.

Memories that I had not thought of for years became intrusive, and ironically, I concluded that Natalie was the only person who ever loved me. Considering how I have treated her over the years, I would guess that she no longer does. I don't know if my father loved me, because he died in a fiery car crash when I was three-years old. And my mother was unable to love anyone.

And then there is Hunt, my ex-husband, who betrayed me with a rather unattractive French bitch who needed to wax her arms. I suppose I can't blame him once he learned that I had undergone a tubal ligation shortly after our marriage, but we had stuck it out for fifteen years – not always miserable, but never truly happy. We were good at the pretense of matrimonial bliss for the sake of his department store empire, but I was aware of his affairs. When his last girlfriend became pregnant, I knew that his affair wasn't a fling. He didn't care that she had no social graces or that she wasn't particularly pretty. Hunt wanted a divorce, and I gave it to him in exchange for what I thought was a solid financial settlement. He was soon remarried with a child on the way, and I was barren and alone. But the truth is, I have always been alone, and perhaps I wanted it that way. Getting rid of people from my life is something that I do well, and now I suppose I will die alone in this God forsaken place

Suddenly the door of the cellar burst open, and I heard him laugh. Rarely did this acrimonious man laugh, but my predicament seemed to be very humorous and gratifying to him.

The beam from his high-powered flashlight moved up and down my body and then I heard him say, "Good God, Lydia. You have soiled yourself. You are a disgusting woman! I will soon ask some questions, and you had better have the right answers if you want to live. I will be back, so prepare yourself." He abruptly left me in total darkness again, and I felt tears of hopelessness on my cheeks. I knew he had no intention of letting me live.

CHAPTER NINE

THE LIBRARY

Natalie

After the nerve wracking morning at the Abbott Mansion dealing with officer Dale, I resumed my normal daily routine in the library, feeling shaky and apprehensive. ...and then I heard the voice I had wanted to avoid -- Mary Jane Lupient, receptionist and extremely nosy friend. "Why are you late today, Natalie? You are almost never late. Have a hot date last night?" I wanted to tell her to mind her own business, but as always, M.J. thought she could intrude into my life in a way that most co-workers wouldn't consider. Since she is probably my best friend, I usually try to tolerate her remarks; but, today they just felt tactless and proprietary. Knowing her well enough to understand that she wasn't kidding around and would most likely continue her inquisition, I decided that playing along would be the best way to distract her.

"Oh, you know, M.J., I was out at the bars last night, and I had a hot date with Deputy Dale."

"Oh sure, Natalie. I know how hot you are for Dale." She cackled a bit and made a move to return to her desk in the lobby of City Hall -- until I stopped her.

"I need a favor, M.J. Will you see if you can get some of my volunteers in today? I have gotten behind in my work, given my time away from the library in recent days, and I could use some help."

"Sure thing, honey. Go at it easy today."

"Thank you so much, M.J. I owe you a dinner at the Bistro."

I hate it when she calls me "honey," but today I didn't want any discord. Within an hour, my best volunteer Betsy Anderson was sitting in the library going through invoices and preparing new books for shelving. This gave me time to plan the strategy for my nighttime mission to Abbott House -- the mission that Lydia had requested of me. I know this task will be much more difficult and risky than my early dawn trip this morning, but what I was barely acknowledging to myself is that I am deep-down terrified.

Sitting at my desk, the morning sunlight was somewhat calming and cheerful, but my heart had begun its unwelcome erratic cadence. After a few futile attempts to slow and steady its rate and rhythm, including pressure on my eyes, a glass of cold water—taking deep yoga breaths--I knew that it would go on for some time. The old familiar panic was already welling up inside. My body, always sensitive to adrenaline, had been flooded with it during my morn-ing adventure at Abbott House and with the anticipation of another trip after midnight. Needing to get myself on track, I reached into my purse for the beta blockers, long ago prescribed to slow my runaway heart. I quickly swallowed the pills, and within fifteen minutes, as if by magic, the beat had slowed, and the icy feeling in the pit of my stomach released its grip. I could think again, and I made a mental note to begin taking the medication on a regular basis, at least for a while.

I heard my volunteer call my name, "Miss LaPierre -- Miss LaPierre -- may I ask you a question?"

"Of course, Betsy. Thank you for coming in on such short notice. I must admit that I have gotten behind these past few days, and I am so grateful you came in today."

Betsy replied sincerely, "I know you have been helping Lydia Abbott with her mother's funeral, so getting behind is to be expected. I am happy to be of service to you, my dear."

Betsy Anderson, with her steel gray pageboy and serious, but kind demeanor, was a blessing to my understaffed library. I don't even mind that she always mispronounces my last name. She is a perfectionist, and her way is probably correct. My last name is French, a legacy from my grandfather Claude LaPierre who was a World War I casualty. But in Coventry, it's always been pronounced with two syllables, LAH-PIER... not LAH-PEE-AIR. We have never been sure why, but there are few people of French descent in Coventry and a lot of Norwegians, Germans, and Swedes. For new arrivals, just learning to speak English, it was probably easier to say LAH-PIER. My middle name was given to acknowledge Grandmother Beret who died in 1919 during the influenza epidemic, and my first name came from a child movie star my mother saw at the Hollywood theatre in Coventry.

Unable to concentrate, I fidgeted and yawned while forcing myself to get some work done. The happenings of the past few days have taken a toll, and needing some fresh spring air, I went out to pick up a sandwich for lunch and drop the film from my camera at the photo shop. Walking down the steps of City Hall, I noticed that Police Chief James Sullivan was staring at me from the entrance of the law enforcement wing. Uncomfortable with his scrutiny, I began to move faster toward my car, and in my haste to escape, I tripped on the curb, catching myself on the hood of the car with the palm of one hand. Although I was able to remain upright, I could feel my cheeks turning red with embarrassment, and I wondered if he had witnessed my clumsiness. Once behind the wheel, I took a sideways look to see if the Chief was still looking my way, and he wasn't. He was no longer there. I'm not sure if I was disappointed or relieved. We seem to have been avoiding each other since he arrived in Coventry to assume the job of Chief of Police nearly a year ago. Our high school romance was serious – too serious, and there was never closure for either of us.

Returning to the library after a quick lunch, I walked around to the back entrance to avoid both M.J. and the chief. Once I entered my office, I heard M.J.'s voice. "Hey girl, you still look mighty tired. You should go home."

Lying to avoid more of her interrogation tactics, I said, "I'm okay, M.J. I just need a good night's sleep," knowing full well that there would be no sleep for me tonight.

Grateful when 5 p.m. arrived, I walked out the door, but not before checking the hall and stairs again to make sure that Chief Sullivan wasn't lurking about. Maybe I was being ridiculous, acting like a childish teenager trying to avoid an old boyfriend, so I asked myself, *what would happen if we spoke? What am I afraid of?* Narrowing the answer down to *uncomfortable feelings* didn't clarify things, because I was unsure of what those feelings might be. Anxious to get home, I was fortunately able to slip out while M.J. was either on a bathroom break or talking to our handsome African American facilities administrator, Frank Gibbs. M.J. and Frank seem to have developed a friendship in recent weeks. They have both lost spouses in the last few years and are single. The two of them occasionally disappear during the day, and I sometimes find them laughing and talking in the alcoves of City Hall. All in all, I have decided that it is a good thing for both of them. The more time M.J. spends with Frank is less time she spends interrogating me, and they seem to enjoy each other's company.

CHAPTER TEN

JUST ANOTHER EVENING IN THE NEIGHBORHOOD

Natalie

Home from work, I'm keeping to my usual routine — changing clothes, stepping outside to get the mail, and waving at Mrs. Evans and her latest boyfriend who live across the street. I also made it a point to briefly speak to John, Mrs. Bergstrom's visiting nephew from Norway. "Hello, Natalie. How are you doing today? I haven't seen your little dog, and I have some food scraps that he might like."

"Thanks, John, but Charlie is staying at the boarding kennel for a couple of days. I'll be in and out over the weekend, and I don't want to have to worry about him. Besides – he likes going there once in a while. He gets to play with other dogs instead of being bored at home with me."

John laughed, and we had a casual conversation, as we stood on the sidewalk in front of his aunt's house. Our brief discussion ended with, "Have a nice evening, Natalie. I'll save the scraps for Charlie in the freezer."

"You have a nice evening too, John, and say 'hello' to your aunt Ragna."

The three leather bound journals I had retrieved from the window seat at Abbott House were placed randomly in my bedroom bookcase. I didn't want them to look as though they were a set, in the unlikely case that another person might somehow see them and become curious. The innermost thoughts of my mother and grandmothers must be protected out of respect for the decent lives they led. I am anxious to examine the journals myself, but that will be for another day.

Hunger was gnawing at my stomach, which was a surprise after having no appetite for breakfast and very little desire for lunch. Rifling through the freezer, I settled for a frozen dinner and decided that since fatigue and stress were gradually overwhelming me, I needed to sleep. Getting into my comfortable bed, I strapped the black sleep mask around my head, the one that had come with the set of expensive satin pajamas gifted by Lydia the previous Christmas. There are some perks for being her property manager, even though I rarely get the promised monetary compensation. I settled into bed and tried my best to drift off. I had set the alarm for 2 a.m., using the vibrate setting, but after lying awake in my dark bedroom for three hours, tossing and turning, I finally got up at 1:30.

Fumbling around in the darkness wasn't working, so I turned on my mini flashlight. I was able to see well enough to pull on dark pants and a dark sweatshirt, topped by the black baseball cap that I had retrieved yesterday from the lost and found at City Hall. That completes my anonymous, androgynous look. I'm not the type of woman who ordinarily wears baseball caps or gender-neutral clothing, and I didn't want to be seen making such a purchase at a store.

Grabbing the large black bag that I had also confiscated from the City Hall lost and found, I quietly slipped out the back door and into my backyard. The Abbott mansion is only about six blocks away, so I made the decision to walk to avoid parking my car on the street where it might be noticed. The sky was heavily overcast with no visible moon, and the darkness enveloped me like a black mist. As I turned toward the alley, an unfamiliar flash of light caught the retina of my eye. A flashlight? Maybe. Perhaps it was someone arriving home late and flipping on a porch light. A backward glance showed nothing but a muted slice of light that had settled on Mrs. Bergstrom's lilac bush. It seemed to come from her upstairs window in the hallway. I convinced myself that my nerves were playing tricks, but I am terrified of everything: the darkness — the inability to see the ground — my fear of falling -- and more. This task seems out of place for someone with a mild anxiety disorder and a heart condition, and Lydia is aware of both. It is outrageous that she would make such a risky, frightening request, but I hadn't said no. This is my own fault, and I must take responsibility for my predicament.

CHAPTER ELEVEN

MAY 10 – AFTER MIDNIGHT

Natalie

When I entered the alley, my imagined fears became real. In addition to the darkness in general, I heard barking dogs and fighting, screeching cats, but so far, I hadn't noticed any people prowling about. I began to be concerned about the possibility of a police patrol. If I encountered a patrol car at this hour, I would possibly be stopped and questioned, but since Dale is our only night police officer, there is probably no need to worry. Everyone in Coventry knows he is habitually drunk and sleeping in the park by 1 a.m., so Dale is probably the least of my concerns. He doesn't usually emerge until 4 a.m. to pick up speeders on their way to work at the local poultry processing plant. Nevertheless, there are nocturnal wild animals, dogs on the loose, and dangerous human beings who prowl by night. *Stop thinking,* I told myself. *Just put one foot in front of the other and move ahead.* After a couple of blocks, I glimpsed the lights of a patrol car on the next street taking a turn toward downtown. *That's odd. Dale is usually never patrolling at this hour.* I instinctively moved from the alley, where I was more visible, to the margins of backyards. I had thought that my long-time familiarity with the yards and alleys of River Flats would be helpful, but it didn't take long to realize that I was in uncharted territory. The familiarity I had as a child was long gone, rendered useless by new owners and modern renovations. There are home additions, new garages, children's playhouses, gazebos, patios and hot tubs. Only Mrs. Bergstrom's house, next door to mine, has remained exactly as it was when I was a lonely child making hollyhock dolls in her garden. The formerly open backyards are now obstacle courses, but I continued to move on.

In a short time, I arrived at my destination, the Abbott Mansion. I would have been more comfortable entering through the carved oak front door. It was well lit and familiar, but tonight, I must enter through the back door. The darkness of the Abbott gardens serves my purposes, although the winding paths and numerous flower beds, meticulously kept by Lyon, the hands-on caretaker for more than sixty years, disorient me.

Slipping the key into the lock was difficult, but I soon found myself in the kitchen. The basement door was at one end of the large pantry. Groping for the beaded brass handle, I finally found it, and in an instant I was on the threshold of the cellar stairs. I flipped the light switch and was dismayed when nothing happened. The light bulb must be burned out. *Now what?* I am unfamiliar with the basement of the house, having been down there only a few times with Mother. This was the territory of Lyon, not the maids. But I wanted to get this over with. The musty, dank smell was my guide, as I gingerly navigated the creaky wooden cellar steps, using the small flashlight in my pocket. The dampness and cold sent a chill from my feet to the top of my head, and in response, I zipped my black sweatshirt to my neck and pulled the hood over the baseball cap. The darkness was completely without reprieve, not just because it is in the middle of the night, but because the cellar windows had long ago been boarded up and barred. The light from my flashlight was barely adequate.

Once my feet touched the dirt floor, I surveilled the surroundings to get my bearings. The little that I could visualize looked somewhat familiar and yet changed. I was relieved that my flashlight performed well enough so that I could see the shovel and step stool where Lydia said they would be.

The stool had only five steps, and I committed that fact to memory, as I pulled myself into the targeted area of the crawl space. Bending at the waist to avoid hitting my head required that my face come close to the dirt floor. Old earth, unbleached by sunlight and unturned by wind and the industry of men, exuded the same odor that an occupied gravesite might release after one-hundred years of decay. A rustle coming from the top of the stairs caused a moment of panic until my flashlight discovered either a large mouse or a small rat scurrying down the stone steps. Turning my attention to the task at hand, I found the rotting wooden storage box sitting in the corner of the crawl space. What I need is underneath. Horrified as several dead mice, or maybe rats, fell off the top of the box when I pushed it aside, I had to stifle a scream. "Oh my God," I involuntarily exclaimed. Having a revulsion to dead animals that bordered on a phobia, I was nearly ready to back out of this misguided attempt to please Lydia.

"It's not deep," Lydia had said. "It won't be hard." How did she know that? I would bet my life that she had never been down here, but maybe I am wrong. What I didn't know about this mission is how much I didn't know. Such ignorance can make for a disastrous outcome.

I kept repeating her words to myself, "*It's not deep; it won't take long,*" but after shoveling for what seemed to be an eternity, I felt panic welling up along with tears, and I found myself trying to stifle a nearly irresistible urge to flee. …and then the shovel struck something with a loud clunk. Based on the sound, it was obviously metal, and after some exploration, I realized that the object of this search is larger than I had been led to believe. It took some time, but I was finally able to unearth it and squeeze it into the hockey bag. It was a tight fit, so my efforts were frustrating, and in my haste to close the zipper, the small flashlight also fell into the bag. I groped blindly until I found it, but those few minutes seemed like hours.

Relieved that I could finally be on my way, I again found the ladder. As I descended, I counted the unstable rungs, and then I heard the crack of splintering wood and found myself and the bag on the dirt floor. Loosened earth penetrated my nostrils, and the smell of decay and mildew were overwhelming. I landed on my right shoulder, but the adrenaline coursing through my body rendered me nearly oblivious to pain, at least for the moment, and made it possible for me to go on.

I finally reached the cellar steps and began to climb gradually, slowed down by the load I was carrying. Because my transport bag is meant for hockey equipment, it is longer in length than this task required, and one end trails along behind. Suddenly, I couldn't move. Pulling on the bag several times, I found that I was tethered to something. "Damn it, damn you Lydia Abbott!" My flashlight revealed that the bag had become hung up on a large, exposed screw that had been improperly drilled into the supports of the railing. And then, unthinkably, my frustration turned to terror when the flashlight exposed something that sent a shock wave through my body. Alongside the staircase, the beam caught a glimpse of what looked like a human hand, and further investigation revealed the sightless, staring eyes of Dale, the deputy police officer whom I had come across as I was picking up Mother's journals the previous morning. His face, neck, and torso were covered in blood, and the right side of his head was deeply cratered. The mixture of cranial fluid, blood, and brain tissue was crusting, as though his accident may have occurred several hours earlier.

Being trained in CPR, I felt for a pulse and checked the airway by sweeping my fingers into his slack, gaping mouth, while trying not vomit. I thought to myself, *Dale is dead*. I wondered if he had been lying here since our paths had crossed yesterday morning. My first instinct was to go upstairs and call 911, but given his condition and the questions that would be asked of me, I impulsively ran up the stairs, out of the house and into the back yards and alleys, almost dragging the bag containing Lydia's small, but rather heavy metal box. It was obvious that Dale was beyond help -- and then I remembered that the mansion's phone had been disconnected. *It's too late for 911 anyway – Dale is dead.* Panicked and barely aware of what I was doing, I instinctively pointed myself in the direction of home.

It was now about 4 o'clock in the morning, and there were a few houses with lights on in kitchens and bathrooms. At times, during my plodding flight through the alleys, I thought I heard footsteps behind me, so I stepped up my pace without looking back. After walking a short distance, there it was again – the definite sound of footsteps moving at the same pace as my own! In my haste, I tripped on something rock hard, slamming my shin into its rough surface. I didn't have to see my leg to know that it was swelling quickly, but I moved ahead without stopping to assess. My eyes caught a flash of light in Mrs. Bergstrom's house that quickly turned on and off twice. As odd as that was, I simply couldn't give it any thought, because I was already on overload. With relief, I entered my house through the back door but didn't turn on the lights. Moving quickly, my knee encountered an object on the middle of my kitchen floor. I turned on the flashlight and identified the desk that I had brought home from the Abbott House as the culprit. The impact to my knee surprised me, because I thought I had moved the desk into the corner of the kitchen until it could be cleaned, but evidentially my memory had failed me.

As I moved toward the living room to check the front door lock, I noticed that the entire neighborhood was dark except for a light muted by a drawn shade in Dewar Renward's living room. His lights were often on into the night, so this wasn't unusual. I chalked it up to what I have heard about the elderly sometimes having sleep difficulties—or perhaps I had seen nothing of the kind, and my eyes were playing tricks on me. A second look revealed a totally dark house. I did notice the silhouette of a person moving toward Mrs. Bergstrom's home. It was only 4:30 a.m., and I thought it strange to see an unknown person moving about at that hour.

My last observation was a police car driving through the neighborhood about 4:40 a.m. I had never seen a patrol officer moving through the neighborhood at that hour, but of course, Dale had not shown up for work and another more conscientious officer had taken his shift. Paranoia took over for a minute or two when I noticed that the patrol car moved slowly into the alley behind my house. It was a good thing that I had not turned on my lights. Despite the pain from my knee and shoulder injuries, I climbed the stairs and headed straight to the attic and the hiding place -- a false brick chimney in the center of the room. It looked like it went through the floor, as well as to the ceiling and through the roof, as any working chimney did. But that was an illusion. I have always called it "the chimney to nowhere," discovered by me when I was fifteen years old and helping my mother with spring cleaning.

"Clean the attic, Natalie. It's full of cobwebs and dust. Be sure you scrub the chimney too."

Following my mother's instructions, I was brushing the brick and mortar with soap and water, when a panel of bricks came loose in my hands. The displaced panel revealed an opening to the chimney that was the entrance to a hidden space. I was shocked, but also ecstatic, because I now had a secret place for my teenage treasures. Instead of closing the panel with mortar, I left it loose, but looking deceptively as though it was attached to the bricks surrounding it.

It was obvious that the previous occupant, who was a stone mason, had built this hidden space into the false chimney. There were rumors that he ran pro-German activities from this house during both wars. Perhaps he used it to hide his German propaganda and correspondence, but I had always thought the rumors were nothing more than small town gossip.

The throbbing in my lower leg didn't allow for sleep, and needing ice, I moved down the stairs and groped my way into the kitchen. The light in the freezer side of my refrigerator illuminated the room, and after grabbing the ice, I slammed it shut as quickly as I could. I was glad that Charlie was at the boarding kennel. He would have been nervous and most likely making a lot of noise with my unusual activity.

I hurried to my bedroom as fast as I could move and got into bed. By morning, the bag of ice will have melted onto my sheets, but I was too exhausted to care.

CHAPTER TWELVE

SAN FRANCISCO - DATE AND TIME UNKNOWN

Lydia

I thought I heard him return a few minutes ago, and my body stiffened from fear and dread. He's been gone for what seems like days, but perhaps that's my addled brain working overtime. I have had no food or water since he brought me here days ago, and I am aware that I can't last much longer. The darkness is oppressive, and I'm not thinking clearly. When he wants me to know that he is here, he leaves the door to the cellar open enough so that I can see the outline of his body and some of my dismal prison. Knowing that he has returned increases my fear. I don't know what he will do next.

It is almost a relief to remove myself from where I am, if only in my mind. I am so afraid and have been praying for the first time since my Sunday School days. I need my friend Natalie. She would help me, or she would die trying. Natalie was my best childhood friend -- almost a sister to me. I know that I ruined our relationship, but Mother didn't want me spending time with her. She said Natalie was as evil as her mother Grace. After years of Mother Helen's manipulations and my sneaking around to spend time with Natalie, she took an even more drastic action and sent me away to a girls' boarding school in the east.

I remember how frightened I was when I got on the train with Ellsworth and traveled to St. Margaret's in New Hampshire -- but I never showed it. I knew better than to show weakness when I was with Uncle Ellsworth – who is actually my adopted uncle. I simply wasn't prepared for the ostracism and loneliness of attending an upscale boarding school with strangers from wealthy, old guard families. The other girls didn't accept me, and I was harassed in a way that only very privileged teenage girls can harass another girl. In time, I learned that the only good money was old money, and ours wasn't old enough.

Rejected and shunned, there were no weekend visits to family mansions of the rich and beautiful for me. Alone in an alien place, only the geeky unattractive girls sought my friendship. At first, I rebuffed them, but then I wised up. I needed a clique, and the geeks were thrilled to have me and treated me like a princess. I have always had an aversion to unattractive people of all sorts, but inevitably, because of my despairing situation, I had to become one of them -- a mascot of sorts, a pretty girl amid the ugly. They were only too happy to do my homework and write my papers. I secretly hated those fat, pimply faced untouchables, but they were all that stood between me and total segregation. They were easily cowed into doing my bidding, and I knew I could work with that.

Mother wasn't happy with my situation and viewed my boarding school days as a complete failure. In her mind, St. Margaret's wasn't for college preparation. Time and money spent on school was solely to make connections that might provide a rich husband, preferably of the old money type with impeccable social standing.

After graduation, upon my arrival back in Coventry, Mother Helen summoned me to her room. She was lying in bed, not yet dressed at 4 p.m. I became overwhelmed with the stench of alcohol mingling with her expensive perfume. I often thought the familiar odor must have been similar to that of a saloon with a whorehouse upstairs. Her only words for me were, "Well, you have little to show from your four years at that expensive boarding school-- no marriage prospects, no decent social contacts…"

I finally managed to mumble, "I'm sorry, Mother."

"Oh well, Lydia," she slurred. "There's still college. That may be the charm. Ellsworth is thinking he can pull some strings at Wellesley. You would never be admitted on your own merit. You can leave me now. You must be tired, and if you're not —- I am. Remember, stay away from Natalie. She's a whore like her mother."

Mother's familiar words describing Natalie as a deceitful, immoral person had an incremental effect over the years, and I gradually sought her out less and less. As time went by, I began to avoid her altogether, especially after I noticed how pretty and petite she had become. Maybe Mother Helen was right -- Natalie was dangerous.

I wasn't too worried about my future. I had secretly made other plans. A scout from a modeling agency had visited school and asked if I would take part in a photo shoot and runway show for a magazine article. They were featuring girls going to Ivy League colleges in the fall. And that's where I met him -- a rich man and the heir to one of the well-known department store companies in the country. Mother could go fuck herself. There would be a wedding, but no more school. I made sure of that.

I was jolted back to the present and my situation in the cellar by what I thought were footsteps, but I must have imagined them. I listened, and there was only silence, along with the musty smell and the cold dampness of the concrete floor. I remained alone in my prison. Desperate tears were welling up, as terror was ricocheting through my brain. *Why hasn't he returned?* Not that I wanted him to, but I am holding out improbable hope that he will release me. Most likely, he wants me to be completely despairing and out of resources before he begins asking questions. I am already willing to give him anything he wants. Again, there were footsteps in the cellar, alternating with more silence. He's back, and he was taunting me, trying to create more fear, and it was working.

CHAPTER THIRTEEN

THE MORNING AFTER

Natalie

I had yet to sleep at 6 a.m., and my shoulder and knee continued to throb with pain. My right shin was also injured and had bled profusely under the skin, creating a large red and purple hematoma, visible beneath the dripping bag of ice. I won't be able to wear a dress or a skirt for some time, if I don't want to be questioned about my injury. Thoughts of Dale's cratered skull and staring eyes interrupted my attempts at sleep. Knowing that I would be thrust into the middle of a murder investigation if I reported finding his body, I was unable to take that step. There would be a myriad of questions – questions that begged answers, such as why I was there in the middle of the night and questions that could implicate Lydia in something that was still a mystery to me. I don't know why she wanted the box from the cellar, and I still don't know why my trip to Abbott House must be kept between the two of us. It would have been much easier to have completed this task during the light of day.

Stressed and sleep deprived, I attempted to normalize my day. On any other day, I would have taken my little Cairn Terrier for his morning walk; but, since Charlie wasn't here, I decided to go for a walk myself, with the goal of disposing of the hockey bag in the fast-moving river. I placed the elongated bag, tightly folded, inside my zippered jacket, and my plan was to throw it off the old railroad bridge that is now a bike trail and walking path. But the bikers, walkers, and runners were out in full force, enjoying this early spring morning. Although I desperately wanted to unburden myself of any evidence, sense overtook my anxiety, and I left the tightly folded bag in my jacket, vowing to deal with it later, when there was less traffic on the path. It was now time to get ready for work.

I showered and dressed in loose fitting black pants and a light blue linen blazer – a shade that has always been flattering to my skin color. Despite my attempts to camouflage the evidence of what I had recently been through, I still looked rather ghastly. My final attempt will be to brighten my lips and cheeks with pink lipstick and blush. The lipstick was especially helpful. I wear lipstick every day, and there is almost nothing about my appearance that it can't fix. Dark hair, along with pale lips and skin, make for a worn-out look.

I was walking to my car when I heard, "Good Morning, Natalie." It was John, Mrs. Bergstrom's nephew. He moved a bit too close to me, and I couldn't help but back away.

"Oh, hello, John," I responded, trying to be polite without really looking at him directly.

I reflexively made the decision not to give him too much attention. In my exhausted state, I didn't want to have to be social or answer any questions. But he was an imposing figure and difficult to ignore. I met his eyes briefly, and my overall impression was of a large man, well over six feet tall, with a mop of sandy brown hair and a golden tan face that one might see in a Norwegian travel magazine. He could have been Thor in the flesh, but as interesting as he was to look at, I nervously turned my head in a futile attempt to avoid his gaze. Although we had chatted a few times before, I am now getting a different vibe. Mr. Bergstrom was becoming a bit pushy, and I'm not sure why.

"I must leave for work now, Mr. Bergstrom. Have a nice day." Turning on my heels and heading toward my vehicle, I quickly opened the car door and slid behind the wheel. I kept the window closed, so there was no final word or smile, as I backed my car down the driveway and into the alley. In my haste, I clipped Mrs. Bergstrom's blooming lilacs, but dared not look back. I didn't want any further contact with this man -- at least right now.

When I pulled into the parking lot of the library, there were already familiar cars in the employee stalls, and I realized I was late enough that I may have to field some questions. As I nervously shut the door and locked it, my eye caught the stray lilac bloom sticking up from the motionless windshield wiper. I pulled it out with the intention of throwing it on the ground, but for some inexplicable reason, I brought it to my nose and inhaled its spring scent. As I walked through the heavy brass door of City Hall on my way to the Library, Frank Gibbs met me in the rotunda area. In his friendly voice he said, "Miss LaPierre, I have been worried about you. You're never late. Is everything okay?"

"Oh yes, Frank," I said in a slightly quivering voice. "I just had a bit of a situation with my little dog, but it's all okay now."

"Glad to hear it, Miss LaPierre. I know you're alone, so someone must watch out for you. This town isn't as safe as it used to be, you know. It's getting bigger all the time."

"Thanks for looking out for me, Frank," I said as calmly as possible. As much as I liked Mr. Gibbs, everyone's reaction seemed suspicious. I walked toward the double doors of the library with the hockey bag still stuffed inside my jacket. Its bulk reminded me that it belongs on the lost and found table, but I decided not to place it there. The newly installed security cameras would catch me in the act and might bring up some unwanted questions. Was I recorded when I picked up the bag and other items a few days ago? The answer to that is most likely "yes." I turned around to check out the angle of the camera hanging inconspicuously from the ceiling, and I noticed that Frank was still watching me as I walked down the hall. He's in charge of every aspect of the building, including security, and if something suspicious had appeared on a monitoring tape, he would know about it. I began to wonder if he was aware of something and had become suspicious. The best I could do was to hope for a very quiet day, but since it was a Friday, that wasn't likely to happen.

CHAPTER FOURTEEN

FRIDAY, MAY 10 – 8 A.M.

Natalie

M.J. didn't spare me from her daily inquisition. She clomped into my office, her coarse, straight hair tied in a low riding, steel gray pony tail and wearing her signature Birkenstocks. With M.J., what you see is what you get -- no makeup, no frills, and no false niceties. She is something of a loner with few friends and no family, and her much older husband died a few years ago. We forged a friendship created in part by our similarities in social status and underlying, but never acknowledged, loneliness. Neither of us were whiners about our situations in life—not even to each other. We appreciated our mutual company at work and enjoyed occasional dinners together. As we conversed, during our evenings out, we also sometimes shared our witty, irreverent observations about Coventry and the people who lived there. I knew that what passed between us was held in trust, and she understood, correctly, the same about me. "You look like shit," M.J. said with her usual aplomb.

Pulling myself together, because I knew that I must, I mumbled, "Oh I know, M.J. I had too much coffee last night, and I couldn't sleep because of the caffeine. You know what caffeine does to me." I was concerned that she would continue her questioning, as she had the previous day, but she quickly gave up and whirled her zaftig self through the door and into the reception area of City Hall when she heard the phone ring. I whispered to myself, *"Maybe she will leave me alone for a while."* Most people underestimate M.J.'s abilities, but I have always known that she is shrewdly observant. After answering the phone, M.J. returned and stood in front of my desk with her head cocked and one eye narrowed. I could tell that she was coming to all sorts of conclusions, so I understood that I must be careful not to give her any clues as to my recent activities.

"I'm going to leave you alone this morning, kiddo," said M.J. unexpectedly. "You have been through a lot with the funeral and all – especially dealing with that bitch Lydia for the short time she was here. She really dumped on you. I hope you get paid this time."

Offering no commentary on Lydia or anything else, I said, "Thanks, M.J. I am very tired today." By 4 p.m., I could barely function, and when 5 p.m. came, I was out the door.

CHAPTER FIFTEEN

SAN FRANCISCO - DATE AND TIME UNKNOWN

Lydia

I felt as though my body had been broken into a hundred pieces. It wasn't that I had held out for long. I am too weak-willed, and pain is really a foreign entity to me. His assault was as brutal as a trained interrogator, completed with the expertise of one who has done such things before. It was only a few minutes before I gave him what he wanted -- the name of the person who is helping me and exactly what I had hoped to get from Abbott house, along with its location. I was ashamed at my inability to withstand pain, but I only wanted to relieve myself of the brutality expertly portioned out by an evil man. I don't know of what horrors I had hoped to spare myself -- pain, fear, maiming, death? In the end, I was not spared of any of those things.

The cold damp floor of the basement had easily penetrated my satin gown, and the pain of his assault was unrelenting. At one point, he smiled and walked out the door of the wine cellar, and I thought that he would now leave me in my own misery. I was so foolish as to believe that he would spare my life – suddenly, his high-powered flashlight pierced the darkness.

"I just wanted to see your face once more Lydia, he rasped. You are supposed to be a beautiful woman, but right now, there is no beauty left -- just the remnants of your misguided humanity."

I felt the sharp pain of a needle in my neck, and I knew that most likely I would not regain consciousness. Surprisingly, the silent darkness came as a relief. The last thing I heard was his diabolical laughter.

CHAPTER SIXTEEN

THE INVITATION

Natalie

When I arrived home, I went straight to my bed and slept soundly -- until I was awakened by a knocking on my door about 6:30 p.m. My first thought was that it must be the police. I thought about going out the back door, getting into my car and driving somewhere—anywhere. But in the end, I decided the scrutiny would be justified if it was the police. I walked to the front door as if to the gallows -- slowly opened the door, and there stood Mrs. Bergstrom's nephew John. My hair was disheveled, my clothes were rumpled, and I felt the color drain from my face. As I began to apologize for my condition, he stopped me with an invitation in his rather charming Scandinavian accent.

"Hello, Natalie. My aunt was wondering if you would like to come over about 7:30 for some dessert and coffee. Her nurse brought us a lemon pie. I have also invited Mrs. Evans and her friend."

I was in a daze, but I accepted the invitation as though on autopilot, but after he left, I thought to myself, "Oh God what have I done?" Fearful of giving wrong answers that would cast suspicion my way or onto Lydia, I regretted my decision. I didn't want any questions, even in a social setting. I certainly wasn't thinking clearly about anything when I simply said, "Yes, John. I love lemon pie?"

I drew a hot bath, hoping that my frazzled nerves would quiet down after a quick soak. The guilt over Dale's death ate at me constantly. Did my presence at the Abbott mansion have anything to do with it, or was it a coincidence that we were there at the same time? There are so many unanswered questions, and I imagine that someone will soon be asking them of me.

Knowing that there will be a gruesome discovery on Monday morning when the workers walk through the mansion before the demolition begins, made me lose my appetite, even for my favorite pie. Trying to steady myself, I began reviewing the facts. The loose ends of my middle-of-the-night visit to the mansion's cellar have been taken care of. The hockey bag was now in the river, courtesy of a brief mid-afternoon walk on the brush-lined path under the bridge near City Hall. By now, any lingering evidence should have washed downstream in the fast-moving water. The metal box, having been removed from the damp earth of the crawlspace in the Abbott cellar, was now stored in a false chimney in my attic. It would not be found unless someone was actively looking for it. Access to its contents required a key or some specific tool, and I have neither. I don't know what is in the box, or what will happen next. Although my instructions from Lydia were sketchy, there was one thing I understood when she said, "Don't look inside the box, Natalie. Wait for some word from me that will make everything clear."

As time passed with no word from Lydia, I began to feel very much alone. Why doesn't she call? Where is she? The pit of uncertainty was growing in my stomach, but I could do no more than to get ready for an evening of lemon pie and neighborly conversation. Another thought crossed my mind as I walked to Mrs. Bergstrom's home. I had better start locking my house both day and night, and the outdated locks need to be replaced. First thing next week, I'll get Jim Hauer, my handy man, to take care of this.

When I entered Ragna Bergstrom's house, I put my concerns aside, because her appearance was troubling. Shocked at how thin and weak she had become, I could hardly take my eyes off her, as she picked at her dessert. Mrs.

Bergstrom seemed to be in something of a stupor, and I'm alarmed. I now understand how ill she really is.

Neighbor Bernetta Evans, a plump, curly-haired redhead, was another story. She giggled incessantly and fawned over her new boyfriend whom she called "Rocky." Rocky was dressed in tight black pants and a white sleeveless T-shirt. He didn't utter a word during the first half of the evening, but he did grunt at everyone else's comments, as he constantly massaged his bulging upper arms. When Rocky finally began to speak, he sounded like a mob hitman, as characterized in Hollywood B movies. I couldn't help but wonder where Mrs. Evans had found this one. His predecessors were often unusual or odd in some way, but Rocky seemed to be rather dangerous, and much to Bernetta's displeasure, he was also overly attentive toward me. He asked a lot of questions and made persistent eye contact, which provoked her to grip his tattooed arm so tightly that her fire engine red nails began to dig into his flesh. Finally, Rocky grew impatient and flung her arm aside. Angry at his reaction and lack of attention, Bernetta abruptly made some excuse and walked out the door. Rocky remained planted on Mrs. Bergstrom's couch. He ate two pieces of lemon pie and showed no sign of leaving, until John and I stood up and moved toward the door.

John walked me home and lingered on the porch, as though he was a bit smitten. Before I entered my house, he lightly touched my shoulder and placed his face somewhat too close to mine. Was he testing my feelings? I wasn't sure what his motives were, and under difference circumstances, I may have been more interested. It was undeniable that he is a handsome man, but exhaustion overruled any spark that may have been ignited between us. He turned to look at me as he walked the path toward the sidewalk and smiled with promise. I found myself smiling back but didn't really know why or if my smile was genuine.

How easily life goes on in its humdrum journey, despite euphoric happiness or the greatest of tragedies. Less than 24 hours prior, I had completed what in my mind was akin to a commando mission. I had also navigated a dark alley with stolen goods in the wee hours of the morning, and then less than twenty-four hours later, sat down in Mrs. Bergstrom's living room, warm and cozy, eating from her blue and white delft china. I was amazed at myself, and not necessarily in a good way.

All I wanted was to get into bed and sleep, but I was expecting the next call from Lydia and thought I should stay awake in case the phone rang. At one point, I picked up the leather-bound books I had taken from the library of the Abbott house, but realizing that I would be unable to concentrate, I returned them to the bookshelf. Tomorrow is Saturday, so I could stay up late tonight -- if I chose to do so, but my eyes were heavy and watery with fatigue and stress, and my legs were still shaky.

As I locked my doors, I noticed there were still a few lights on in the neighborhood. Dewar Renward, the rather frail, elderly man across the street, had all shades pulled, but I noticed his shadow as he walked past the window. Then his lights suddenly went out – and turned back on again. Mrs. Bergstrom's house was dark, apart from a soft light shining in her spare room upstairs where John was sleeping. And my neighbor across the street, Mrs. Evans, in the house next to Dewar's, seemed to be having a rip roaring argument with her boyfriend in her front yard. I was ready to pull my own blinds, when I saw a figure walking toward Dewar Renward's house. Life is happening all around me on this Friday night before midnight, an unusual state at such an hour in my neighborhood of mostly older people and young families with children. I chocked it up to spring fever and took an extra strength Tylenol.

As for my own house, it seems strangely out of sorts. I can't explain it, but there is something about it that seems off. There is an unfamiliar odor about it, and things don't seem to be quite in their usual places. Perhaps it is my high stress level and the strange hours that I have been keeping. I gave up on waiting for Lydia's call and mercifully succumbed to oblivious sleep.

CHAPTER SEVENTEEN

SATURDAY, MAY 11

Natalie

Saturday mornings are my time to lounge in bed, sip tea, and read. But this Saturday in May was, of course, not typical. Despite the smell of lilacs coming through the open French doors of my bedroom, I remained overwhelmed by the events of the previous few days. Although I missed Charlie, I had done the right thing by taking him to the boarding kennel before my trip to the Abbott Mansion. I am not in good enough shape to deal with him this weekend.

I love my small craftsman house, and over the years, I have turned it into a modern sort of English cottage – a soothing refuge for someone like me. I've kept it simple with light grey walls and dark floors. The walls are decorated with original art that tends to be more contemporary than one would expect in an English cottage. It suits my dislike of anything ornate or fussy in home décor, and the lack of clutter gives me the feeling of calm. It has been my home since Mother bought it in 1957, ignoring the local gossip that it served as a meeting place for a nest of German spies, during both world wars. It was too good a bargain and something she could afford. I never thought much about the spy stories. I was focused on the fake brick chimney, where I kept all my private possessions away from her scrutiny. Mother was never aware of its existence, because I never told her. I use it now for the metal box I confiscated from the Abbott cellar.

All hell will break loose on Monday morning when the demolition crew finds Dale Forbes dead in the basement. I regret not reporting my discovery of his body. If I did, I would have a lot of explaining to the police and to Lydia. The police would want to know what I was doing there at 2 a.m., especially once they saw that I had been digging in the crawl space, and Lydia would be angry if I break my promise to keep the mission to Abbott House a secret. I'm not sure why she wants it that way, but she said that it would place us both in danger if we were found out. It also terrifies me that I may be considered a suspect in Dale's death.

To distract myself, I pulled the leather-bound books from the bookcase in the corner of my bedroom. Each volume had been bound in a different shade of leather, which intrigued me, and upon inspection, I realized that they were personal diaries. Since they were written by my family of women, I was almost afraid to open them for fear of what I would learn. Was the identity of my father inside Mother's blue leather-bound diary? Is this the way she wanted me to find out who I was? Nothing made sense, and yet everything made sense in its own way. Mother was very secretive, and I suspected that I didn't really know why.

The excitement in the pit of my stomach grew, as I inspected the journals for a logical starting place. I noticed that one of them was written in Norwegian, a language that my mother spoke but hadn't shared with me. Disappointment washed over me, because it was obvious, due to the yellowing of the pages, that this was the oldest journal, and logic deemed that this was the place to begin. As I opened each page, searching for anything that might be written in English, the only thing that made any sense to me were the two letters written in small script at the bottom right of the inside back cover: AH...Anna Haugen...my great-grandmother. I hastily opened the other two journals in the hope that I could find a pattern that would provide a clue. And there it was -- written in the same place in each journal—two letters in different handwriting, but I understood each set. *AH, BH* and *GL*: Anna Haugen, Beret Haugen, and Grace LaPierre. My great-grandmother, grandmother, and my mother had left me a timeline without intending to. But, because of the language issue, I had to begin my reading out of sequence. I laid the black journal aside and picked up the one bound in burgundy leather – Beret's diary. The written pages of this journal were far fewer than the other journals, out of circumstance I guessed. My grandmother Beret had died young.

I opened the book and was struck by the perfect shape of her Palmer Method inspired letters. I was also pleasantly surprised when two old photographs fell from the yellowed linen pages. I immediately recognized my great-grandmother Anna, a small dark woman sitting in a chair. She had her arm around a blond child about the age of three or four. Anna was a striking beauty, with shining, dark eyes and a petite, but voluptuous body. She also had a serious look about her that came from her eyes – a look that remained with her for her entire life. The child was undoubtedly Beret, serious in demeanor like her mother. Perhaps their station in life didn't allow for much smiling, but it could also be the nature of photographs from that era. Too much expression may not have been seemly in those days.

The second photograph was of a young girl about the age of fourteen, also obviously Beret, taken a few years later. She was standing with her hand on a chair in front of her, diminutive in her button boots, sailor blouse, and wearing a large bow at the back of her fair head. Beret was not the striking beauty that her mother was, but based on later photographs, she grew into a very pretty young woman with soft, gentle looks.

My original plan was to read the journals in order of age, which meant that I would have to wait until Grandmother Anna's journal was translated. I decided that there had been enough waiting, as I opened Beret's diary.

CHAPTER EIGHTEEN

1913-1919 – EXCERPTS FROM BERET'S JOURNAL

April 1, 1913

The first thing I need to do is to find a good hiding place for this diary. I have noticed that my mother hides her diary so well that even I don't know where it is. I caught her writing in it a few times, but after that, it seemed to disappear, like magic.

I am Beret Haugen. Mama works at Abbott House, and we live on the top floor of the mansion in three rooms. None of the other servants live in the mansion, except for the head housemaid, Tillie. She has her own two rooms off the main kitchen.

Mama's diary is written in Norwegian because she is from Norway. In her country, she didn't learn how to write in English. She can write in English now, but maybe doesn't like it so much. It is also possible that she does not want others to read what she is writing. I am an American girl, so I will write in English.

I think I have found a hiding place in the closet between my room and Mama's room. There is a wood panel in the wall behind the old dresser. If I pull on the knob it opens, and if I reach to the right, there is just enough room for my diary to sit without being seen.

I want to write about many things, because I am not allowed to talk about some of the things that I am curious about. One of those things is my father. Everyone else has a father or knows who their father is. They know if he is dead or if he packed a bag and walked out the door. As for me, I don't know who my father is, and Mama won't tell me. Maybe she is too sad to talk about it, or maybe she is too angry. If I saw sadness or anger on her face, perhaps I could understand, but I see nothing at all. There are no signs on her blank face. Nothing. One thing is for sure, I am fatherless. I have no protector, and neither does my mother. We are truly alone, so it is fortunate that we have each other.

September 5, 1916

I am 16 years old and now in my last year of high school. After graduation, I'll work for the Abbott family as a housemaid. I already work in the mansion on weekends when they need an extra pair of hands. I'll miss school, because I like to learn. I especially like my English teacher, Mrs. Pell, who has always let me read from the "older" books section.

On Saturday morning, Mama and I will take a train to St. Paul, where we'll meet her brother Ola and his wife from Chicago. We will all stay in a nice hotel and do some sightseeing. I am excited to go to Como Zoo and also to the new Conservatory that opened just a year ago. I saw pictures of it in the newspaper. The statues and flowers look beautiful.

Mama is so happy to see Uncle Ola, because she misses her family. And I'm happy because they have a daughter named Sonja. She is about my age, and we always have such fun when we are together. She is my first cousin, the only one in America. I have many in Norway that I don't know.

This is a good time for us to be away from Abbott House, because we have to leave anyway. The mysterious man is coming. We can't be there when he comes. Mama has only said that he is a bad man and she doesn't want me to be around him. I also saw Mr. Abbott give Mama money for our travel expenses and the hotel. It seems strange. He always gives her money when the man comes to visit, but I don't know why.

December 15, 1916

Tonight I went to the Christmas dance in the high school gym. A boy named John was my date, and we went with my best friend Josie and her date Claude. He is a year older than the three of us and just got a job as a ticket agent for the railroad.

My green velvet dress looked nice with my strawberry blonde hair, and my new cream kid leather shoes are pretty, but expensive. Mama bought them for me anyway. I had a red and white corsage, and I felt beautiful. I don't have a serious boyfriend like some of the other girls, but I would like to have one. No matter what, any boyfriend of mine will have to be the right boy.

Josie and I switched dance partners a few times, and when I looked into Claude's dark eyes, I felt something special. There was a spark between us, but we had to let each other go, at least for tonight. As we danced our last dance together, Claude whispered in my ear. "Can I call on you tomorrow, Beret?" I didn't hesitate when I said "Oh, yes. Please do."

April 6, 1917

The past three months have been wonderful. Claude and I have spent most of our free time together and have been so happy. But as of today, our country is now in the war overseas, and Claude will most likely leave to fight in France. He said it was his duty. We have decided to get married next month after I graduate and before Claude ships out for his basic training. He is brave about this, but I'm not. I have to stop crying, because it is upsetting for Claude to see me so sad. We are so much in love.

July 4, 1917

We had a May wedding and two weeks of happiness as husband and wife, before Claude left Coventry on a train that is full of young men destined for war. All of them will soon be soldiers. They are bound for the south where they will train before they cross the ocean to fight in the war. I saw him off at the station, along with his parents. His mother and I cried, but Claude kept a brave face for all of us.

I was already pregnant when he left, but didn't know it. I have now shared the news of our child with Claude in a letter, but I don't know if he has received it yet. I wish we could have been together when I told him about our baby. It would have been nice to feel his arms around me and his sweet kiss when he learned the news.

I still live with Mama in our rooms at Abbott House. The Abbotts said that we could stay there when my baby arrives next February. They are good to me, and I'm so thankful. Now I must pray every day for Claude's safety.

October 3, 1917

Yesterday, Claude came home on leave. He has finished his training down south, and in two weeks, he will ship out for England and then will go to France to fight the Germans. The Abbotts gave me this time off to spend with my husband. We have had long walks together and our friends have invited us to parties, but most of all, we just like to be together alone.

October 15, 1917

Claude left today on a train that will take him to the east coast, where he will board a boat that will go to England. The past two weeks have been wonderful. Claude and I have had some dinners with his parents, and he was invited to have dinner at the Abbott mansion with Mr. Daniel, Mrs. Abbott, Mr. Ellsworth, Mama and me. We ate in the big dining room and were served by the other maids. I felt funny about that, but I know it was all for Claude before he shipped out. The Abbotts strongly support the soldiers, and they treat me so well, almost like I am family sometimes. That's why I have never looked for another job. No one else would be so good to me. Mrs. Abbott smiles at me often, and once, she took my hand in hers. I think she is worried about what will happen when Claude leaves to fight the Germans.

Claude and I are very much in love, and we are both so happy about our baby who will be born in February. We didn't want to let each other go. It's too hard to write about. All I can do is pray.

February 12, 1918

Today my baby girl was born, and I am happier than I ever thought I could be, even though the one I love is across the ocean fighting a war. She has curly dark hair, and her eyes look as though they will also be dark, like her French father. My baby is beautiful and healthy. If only Claude could be here with us. I miss my husband so much that it hurts. His letters come, but they are always quite delayed from when he wrote them. All I know is that Claude is now somewhere in France. I must write to him tomorrow morning to tell him all about our beautiful baby girl. I pray this war will be over soon and that he will come home safely

<u>*July 30, 1918*</u>

Today I received a yellow telegram brought to Abbott House by two soldiers. I knew what it would say before I read it. Claude will not be coming home alive. He died at a place called Chateau-Thierry in France. His body is to be sent home, but we don't know when, so his funeral is delayed. I am heartbroken, but still so full of love for my husband. He was the only one for me. He was my happiness and the light of my life, and now he is gone. I must live for my baby Grace now. My mother Anna will help me. My diary wasn't meant for sad things. I now have little reason to put my thoughts down on paper, so I will stop, at least for now.

<u>*September 25, 1919*</u>

This morning before sunrise, the new ambulance service in Coventry brought a very sick Mr. Daniel to Abbott House. Mother and I woke to pounding on our door by the newest housemaid, Clara. "Come quick, Anna! Mrs. Abbott needs you! The Mister is dying in the library. They brought him from The Woman. He is in great pain and his breathing is hard. His face and lips are blue!"

Mother told me that she might need me and shouted, "Get dressed, Beret! Hurry!" I did what she asked and readied my baby girl Grace. I took her to the kitchen to be looked after by the other housemaids and cooks. My husband Claude lost his life in France, but I am not alone, because I have a home here with my mother.

Old Doctor Bates was sitting by Mr. Daniel, who was lying on the leather sofa in the library. Only my mother Anna and I were allowed inside the dimly lit room with the family. We understood that we were there for Marguerite, as she had come to depend on Mother Anna since Tillie could no longer climb the great staircase. It was only a few minutes before The Mister took his last breath. I was surprised that his eyes were open after death, unseeing and blank, until Dr. Bates closed them. "Sorry, that I couldn't save him--massive heart attack--no chance." Everyone else was silent.

The staff was softly crying outside the door. Daniel Abbott, despite his wealth and power, was a kind and beloved man by the staff of Abbott House. The Abbott's adopted son Ellsworth was there attempting to comfort Daniel's wife, Marguerite. But really, there was no need -- she did not cry or make a sound, and when he stopped breathing, she simply left the room, followed by my mother.

I heard Mr. Ellsworth say, "Thank you, Doc. Please call the undertaker. I'll be at his funeral parlor this afternoon to make arrangements." In a few minutes, Mister Daniel Abbott was left alone in death, lying on his back in his underclothing. No one attempted to cover him, and The Mister, being a dignified man, would have been embarrassed at his state of undress.

Ellsworth visited the dead Mr. Abbott one more time before he walked through the sliding mahogany doors and into the hall. He said to my mother, "Anna, have food and beverages ready for the visitors we will likely have today once the news gets around Coventry. And Anna, please let our new chauffeur Lyon know that I will need the car brought around."

We all knew that Ellsworth was going to see Her -- the one whose name is never spoken in this house – Mr. Daniel's mistress. I wondered what his business could be with Her, and then my thoughts returned to the scene in the library. As my mother climbed the stairs behind Marguerite, I took a bronze satin comforter from the linen closet and covered the Mister. He deserves that.

September 30, 1919

Influenza! Abbott House has influenza. It had mostly run its course in other cities and countries, but the Spanish Flu arrived late to Coventry. The doctor has quarantined us. A visiting cousin from Wales has already died here, and Tillie, the head housemaid, has been taken to the hospital.

None of the Abbott family will go into the daughter-in-law's sick room, not even her husband, Mr. Ellsworth. Old Dr. Bates whispered to me that Ellsworth Abbott's young wife Isabel will not survive, so he won't admit her to the Coventry hospital, even though the family has tried to bribe him with money. I don't think they care about her so much, except that she is eight months with child -- the first Abbott grandchild. I have heard Ellsworth and his mother Marguerite talking in whispers. It is not that they want better care for young Mrs. Abbott, but they want the influenza contagion out of the house. Ellsworth asked me to care for his sick wife, and I said, "Yes." They have already resigned themselves to losing Ellsworth's child. Old Mrs. Abbott didn't want me in the sickroom, and I heard her arguing with Mr. Ellsworth. He said that he wanted me, not some strange nurse.

The young missus moaned and cried pathetically. "Where's my husband? Why is he not here? Is he sick? Is he dead?" Isabel Abbott is only nineteen-years-old and is burning hot with fever and weakened by a deep, rattling cough that forces the brown, red sputum from her lungs. She has so quickly lost weight to the disease that her pregnant belly has become a lump that looks like a small ball sitting on a skeleton.

I cleaned the waste and phlegm and when her time came, pulled the tiny, dead baby boy from her body. What a struggle he must have had, because I could see by his perfect face, caught in a fierce grimace, that he wanted to live. I washed the baby in the clean basin of water and dressed him in a tiny white gown and cap from the cedar chest that had been hand-made by his father, Ellsworth Abbott. I swaddled him in a crocheted white blanket, and for a moment, I thought his tiny hand clenched in protest. My eyes must have been playing tricks.

The undertaker, Mr. Chambers, was waiting outside the door, and when I tried to hand him the dead baby, he signaled me to put him in the small white coffin myself. I laid the Abbott child on the satin lining and returned to the sick room where I now lived. My heart longs for my own little girl Grace, downstairs in the kitchen. She is being cared for by my mother Anna and the other servants.

Young Mrs. Abbott seemed a bit better after the birth of her stillborn baby, but I feel much worse. I need to try to sleep tonight.

Natalie

That was my grandmother Beret's last journal entry. Beret died two weeks after she first entered young Mrs. Abbott's sick room. She had no way of knowing that she had only a short time to live when she wrote those final words in her journal. Beret was taken to an isolation room in the local hospital, because she seemed to have a lighter case of influenza; but appearances can be deceiving when it came to this unpredictable illness. After many days and symptoms that seemed to be waning, her condition suddenly and rapidly deteriorated into a decline that couldn't be stopped. After gasping for breath for the better part of a day, Beret lay dead in a white iron bed with only her mother Anna at her side.

Ironically, Isabel, the Abbott daughter-in-law, survived a lung hemorrhage and went on to live fifty more years. But she also paid a price. Her penance was a barren womb and a subsequent divorce filed by her husband, Ellsworth Abbott. The young Mrs. Abbott needed to produce an heir, and the influenza had taken that possibility from her. Isabel was well taken care of financially, ultimately finding solace with the Presbyterians as a sort of dowager queen of the Ladies Aide. Beret has been lying in the cemetery since 1919, and her child, my mother Grace, grew up without her.

CHAPTER NINETEEN

THE COMING STORM

Natalie

After finishing Beret's journal, I regretted delving into it on this Saturday morning. Finally forcing myself out of bed, I headed into the bathroom to take a shower. As I walked past the French doors, a rare glimpse of Dewar Renward, the elderly man who was now living across the street, took me by surprise. He is dressed in a long-sleeved shirt and baseball cap, which is out of character for him. I have never seen him without his Indiana Jones jacket and hat, no matter what the temperature or weather. In an unexpected move, Mr. Renward turned toward my house and seemed to bore a hole through the glass panes of my French door. Instinctively, I backed away into the darker recesses of my room, rattled by his unusual interest. Had he seen me? I wondered. I was a bit disturbed by his scrutiny, but it occurred to me that I haven't been very neighborly toward Mr. Renward since he moved in a few months ago. Nevertheless, it is also fair to say that he seems to avoid me, and his house often appears empty. Perhaps he has a second home somewhere else. I made a mental note to take him some fresh baked cookies next week.

Bernetta Evans is out working in her flower beds, and I was glad to see that her boyfriend's car is gone. Maybe she kicked him out after the way he behaved at Mrs. Bergstrom's last night. She is at least sixty years old and continues to have a parade of much younger boyfriends coming and going, but Rocky, the latest man in her life, seems to be quite rough around the edges, as does his entourage of men and their girlfriends. There are strange cars and motorcycles parked outside her house at all hours of the night, and the loud rock music keeps the neighbors awake. Bernetta's relationships don't seem to last long, so maybe Rocky will move on soon, if he hasn't already. Based on their frequent fights, it sounds like she is fed up with him and his dubious friends.

I have also decided to avoid Mrs. Bergstrom's nephew John. I can't be sure of my reactions right now, and he seems a bit too interested. He's handsome and charming, especially with his Norwegian accent, but there is just something – something a bit off about him, or maybe what is off is me.

I need to use the remaining weekend to prepare for the firestorm that is coming on Monday, with the inevitable discovery of Dale's body. Undoubtedly, I will be called by law enforcement to answer questions about the mansion and who has been there in recent days. Everyone in town assumes that I have all the answers about Abbott House, and unfortunately, in this case, they would be correct. I dread what is ahead of me, especially the very real possibility that my high school boyfriend, James Sullivan, Chief of Police, would be the one doing the questioning.

The weekend was a haze of unpleasant thoughts and feelings, and I was unable to do anything productive. I wandered through the house like a person lost in the past, thinking of things that had been buried for a long time -- and of course, thinking of Officer Dale and how he met his death. It was most likely an accident – at least that's what I have been telling myself.

CHAPTER TWENTY

MAY 13, MONDAY MORNING

Natalie

Monday mornings can sneak up on those reluctant to return to work after a weekend, but this is the calm before the storm for me. As I drove to work shortly before 8 a.m., I expected our small city of 40,000 citizens to be more alive than usual, because of the revelation of a dead body in the Abbott house -- contradictory as that sounds. Instead, the atmosphere of Coventry seems silent and heavy with an unnamed dread. I noticed that most of the law enforcement fleet is missing from both the parking garage beneath the new wing of City Hall, as well as the outdoor lot. It took some time for me to realize that the silence was speaking volumes. The stress has gotten to me, and my anxiety disorder has been getting worse. Physically, I continue to deal with injuries from my Friday, 2 a.m. trip to Abbott House.

The coolness of the marble lined entry hall was welcome, as I headed toward my office in the library to disappear from whatever was to come. The hematoma on my shin pulsed under my black slacks, and the range of motion of my right shoulder seems frozen by pain. I need to take another Tylenol, but I was suddenly headed off by a very animated M.J.

"Have you heard about Officer Dale?" asked M.J., in an excited whisper.

"What do you mean, M.J?" I said in a rather tremulous voice.

M.J. paused for a moment, as though she thought she shouldn't be the purveyor of such news. "Dale's dead at Abbott House, and the entire force has been called in. They've been there since 6 o'clock this morning. Dale's been unaccounted for since last week on Thursday just after midnight. He made a stop at his favorite bar and then disappeared. His patrol car is parked two blocks away from the mansion. The contractor and crew who were checking the house prior to demolition found his body in the basement with his head bashed in – most likely from a fall. But what is strange is that they discovered another body in the basement crawlspace -- a woman."

That revelation got my attention, and I was speechless for a minute before I exclaimed, "A dead woman?"

The usually cool and detached M.J. had succumbed to the common human trait of loving to be the bearer of news, and she had instantly turned into the neighborhood gossip. M.J. is so deep into being the one in the know that she didn't seem to notice my shock. My hands were shaking, and the blood had left my face. Before I could comment, she whirled her zaftig body with a speed that I had not suspected possible and on winged Birkenstocks headed toward the law enforcement side of City Hall. "I'll get the latest information from Sergeant Macken, and I'll be right back."

On the verge of panic and reeling with thoughts of another body in the Abbott basement, I hurried toward the safety of my office. How close had I come to the other body when I was in the crawlspace? Did I brush up again her or accidentally touch her? The thoughts going through my head horrified me. I went directly to my office and took two pills, as I waited for M.J.'s return. Good or bad —- incriminating or vindicating, I very much wanted to know what was happening up on Morgan Street.

Debating with myself about going to the Abbott mansion, I rationalized that no one would be suspicious if I just showed up. After all, my family had deep ties to the place, and as the property manager, I had a key. It was also common knowledge that I often opened and closed the house. It didn't take me long to make the decision to intrude on the police investigation. As I walked out the double brass doors of City Hall, I heard M.J.'s excited voice behind me, and I haltingly stopped. "I've got more news, and you won't believe this!"

I turned around and faced my usually dead-pan friend, expecting to hear something that would incriminate me. "Guess who the dead woman is," M.J. said in a voice that echoed in the high domed City Hall entrance. "It's Rose-anne -- Dale's wife, who disappeared a while back. They're pretty sure it's her, but they don't have an official ID yet. Chief Sullivan is getting the state crime lab in. Sounds like she's been dead for a while. And we all thought she went home to her mama. It seems her mama's been dead for a few years, but no one checked any of this out. I suppose there was no reason to investigate her disappearance. And by the way, Chief Sullivan wants you up at the mansion ASAP."

"I'll get going right away, M.J." I guess the decision to go to the mansion wasn't my call. The decision had already been made by Chief Sullivan.

I felt guilty when I made a volunteer request of M.J. for the second time in a week. "I'm sorry, M.J. I really hate to ask this of you again, but would you call a couple of library volunteers? Mitzi and June would be helpful, if they can come. I don't know how long I'll be gone, and I need someone to hold down the fort here. Can you help me?"

My calm, cool friend had suddenly returned. "Of course, I'll help. I'll get on it right away. I'll let the patrons know that you are out for a while and they must either wait or come back when the volunteers arrive. Are you okay?" she said with an earnest voice.

"Yes, M.J., but I need to go. You know I watch over the house for Lydia."

"Yes, I know," said M.J., trying to cover her excitement and piqued interest with sincerity. "And the Chief has demanded that you show up. You had better get going."

One thing about M.J… She can be rather cold and sarcastic, so I was surprised when she took my hands and looked into my eyes with the care of a true friend. "Don't worry about anything here--and Natalie, be careful. I know about your heart condition, and this may not be good for you."

"I'm okay, M.J.," I said, halfway through the door.

As I drove to the Abbott mansion, I began to understand Dale's presence in the house on my first visit when I retrieved the journals. No wonder he was so eager to help me carry the bag and desk to my car. In his desperation to protect his secret, he was anxious to get me out of there. I began to imagine a scenario in which Dale had gone to the house in the early morning hours, as I had, to remove something that must not be discovered by the demolition crew. The proof of my success was hidden in a false brick chimney in my attic, but Dale never made it. He died in the Abbott House cellar, probably in a drunken state before he reached what he was trying to retrieve -- his wife's corpse.

Abbott House would have been a perfect place to hide a body during the past year, especially in the cellar where no one goes. Dale knew that Wareham Lyon, the ninety-year-old chauffeur and caretaker, would not be physically able to climb the limestone wall to get into the crawl space. No one else besides Lyon, his wife Hedda, and I went into the house, and Dale knew we were unlikely to discover what was in the cellar. He felt very safe with his gruesome secret, at least until the wrecking ball arrived. Once the demolition had been scheduled, he had no choice but to move Roseanne's body. It's likely that I interrupted his plans to do just that the morning I picked up the journals. But lingering questions remain. Why is he dead? Was it a fall or foul play of some type? I'm the lucky one, because I walked out alive. The dead body of Roseanne must have been very close to me, as I completed my task. No wonder the place smelled like a grave – it was a grave. What if I would have discovered Dale removing the body? What would he have done with me? I was the unexpected interloper. I shuddered at the thought, but put aside the self-questioning. There would be time for that later.

CHAPTER TWENTY-ONE

MAY 13 – DEATH AT THE MANSION

Natalie

Abbott House is crawling with law enforcement, including City Police, the County Sheriff's Department, and the State Crime Lab. Yellow tape surrounds the property to distance the crowd, but they seem to keep coming. News travels fast in small communities such as Coventry. By the time I arrived at 9 a.m., dozens of curious townspeople had already encircled the premises. Personnel from the local television station, as well as the Twin Cities' stations, were aggressively forcing their way to the front of the barricade. I had to park two blocks away, and the walk to Abbott House seemed incessantly long and slow.

A strange thing happened once I reached the surrounding crowd of onlookers. They hushed and stepped aside, allowing me to move to the forefront. The locals are aware of my connection with the house and the Abbott family, but the out-of-town reporters weren't as respectful. A couple of them shoved microphones at my face as they shouted, "Are you a family member? Do you have a statement? What is your relationship to the Abbotts?"

Crowds greatly distress me. I always feel as though I am in a tall maze with no way out, claustrophobic and on the verge of panic; but, I kept my head down and my mouth shut, as I moved along the cobbled walkway to the mansion.

Police Chief James Sullivan is standing on the veranda looking out into the crowd, as though nervously searching for someone. Suddenly, he is at my side, with my hand firmly in his. I was glad to enter the protected area and to finally move into the house. Two gurneys with unzipped body bags stand side by side in the large foyer. A strong odor of something like a dead animal hit me in the nostrils, and I nearly gagged. It took a while to understand that the unpleasant smell most likely came from the decomposing body of Roseanne. Chief Sullivan handed me a paper mask and gown, as well as paper shoe covers, but overwhelmed with it all, the crowds, the media, law enforcement, and the bodies, I felt my knees buckling. Suddenly a strong arm encircled my waist and sat me in a chair. I could vaguely hear James say, "Natalie... Natalie, are you okay?" His voice sounded as though it were in a vacuum. "Somebody get her a glass of water – now!" I was grateful for the patience he demonstrated in allowing me to regain my composure, but I was also embarrassed at my inability to deal with stress. My tact has always been to run and hide from stress and all things that make me uncomfortable, and I have been okay with that; but now, for the first time in my life, I can't run and hide, so I got up and went toward the gurneys. I wanted to see the bodies for myself.

The state medical examiner and the local coroner were bent over, looking closely at the deceased. I assumed that they were making a cursory examination before the remains of Dale and Roseanne were taken to the county hospital where autopsies are performed. From their unguarded comments, I learned that Roseanne did not die of natural causes. She had a fractured hyoid bone, probably due to strangulation, along with a broken wrist, most likely a defense injury, according to the medical examiner. Catching a glimpse of her terribly decomposed face and blond, matted hair, I was in horrified awe of how much a living creature can change after death.

In the light of day, I also had a better look at Dale than I had in the cellar. His cratered head wound was more extensive than I had thought. There was no way he could have survived such an injury. His eyes were still open, and his mouth was gaping, as though he was suddenly terrified by the certainty of his impending death. Dale's light blue police shirt was completely soaked with darkened blood that had dried and crusted on the buttons and badge. I'm not familiar with death in its different stages, the blood, the odors, and all of the changes to the human body – and my knees buckled again. "I have you Natalie," said James, as he led me to the leather sofa in the library. "I have you."

Again, ashamed at my fainthearted reaction, I mumbled, "Thank you – I'm so sorry," as I grabbed the back of a chair for support. We made it to the sofa, and James helped me sit down, just before his chief detective Michael Dunivan pulled him aside. All I could think about was the possibility that evidence of my presence at Abbott House on the night of Dale's death had come to light. Fighting panic at the thought of some type of accusation, I had the urge to flee, but I was not naïve enough to think I could escape this scene and walk back into my normal life. I carefully watched the interaction between James Sullivan and Michael Dunivan for some indication that their attention would turn to me. The possibility that I will be arrested for trespass, theft, and suspicion of murder felt very real. But their conversation seemed to be about Dale's motivation for being at Abbott House. I began to realize that I had become quite paranoid. I got off the sofa and walked to the open window for a breath of fresh air.

As I watched James and Dunivan, I saw none of the rumored animosity between the chief and his detective. The scuttlebutt around City Hall is that Detective Dunivan was angry because James Sullivan had gotten the Chief of Police job he had hoped to have for himself. The rather disheveled Dunivan had lost his wife about three years before and had taken it very badly, finding solace in his beer and Irish whiskey. Deep in thought, I was startled to feel Chief James Sullivan's hand on my arm. "Can we sit down again and talk for a minute or two, Natalie?" The sound of his voice, which hasn't changed in twenty-five odd years, takes me back to our past relationship, and strangely enough I relaxed a bit. *Here it comes*, I thought to myself. I didn't have the strength to refuse anything, so I allowed him to lead me to the sofa. He again asked a deputy to get me some water, and in a few minutes, I was able to compose myself.

Adrenaline must have kicked in, because I clearly understood that I had to be very cognizant of how I would answer his questions. I may have to be evasive or even deceitful, and that part of it was killing me. I am not good at dishonesty. My life is somewhat secluded, so I don't interact much with others in a way that would require deception, but keeping quiet was part of the agreement with Lydia. No one was to know that she sent me on a mission to pick up the metal box, but I also didn't want to become a suspect in Dale's death. How far would I go to protect Lydia's secret? At that point, I wasn't sure.

As James began to ask questions, it was apparent that he had a difficult time looking me in the eye. Was it shyness with an old love? Maybe, but I found myself in the same situation. His sandy brown hair and blue eyes were still an attraction for me. He looked good – even better than he had when we parted -- and he exuded the same friendly, kind demeanor that he always had. It was disturbing to me that I would probably have to lie to him to keep Lydia's secret. How ironic that I was protecting her from something that was unknown to me, but it was what my family had done for four generations. I was also protecting myself from becoming a suspect in Dale's death.

The discomfort connected to our past relationship was evident in our conversation. James didn't seem to know where to start, and he treated me with kid gloves, so to speak. But when we both settled in, he wanted to know when I had last been in the mansion. Of course, I didn't tell him about my 2 a.m. visit to the mansion's cellar last Friday. I also didn't reveal that I had removed a metal box for Lydia and found Dale lying alongside the staircase with a fatal head wound. But I did tell two truths:

"Oh yes, I was there last Thursday morning when I picked up some unused cleaning supplies along with three of my mother's books. I had also photographed most of the rooms to preserve history and my own memories. Dale appeared in the entry a short time after I arrived. He yelled in his booming voice asking who was there. I identified myself and told him that I was picking up a few things that shouldn't be taken by the furniture dealer or destroyed by the demolition people. He helped me carry the items to my car, and after taking the desk and books to my home, I took the cleaning supplies to the maintenance crew at City Hall, hoping that they could be used."

"How did Dale act?" questioned James. "Did he seem nervous, angry, or frightened?"

"Well, he yelled loudly when he arrived, because he knew someone else was in the house. I guess I was frightened, until I saw who the ear-splitting voice belonged to. I didn't notice that he was any of the things you mentioned, and he seemed to be happy that the supposed intruder was me."

James seemed satisfied with my answers and finished our conversation with a question. "We have a problem. We need to contact Lydia but have been unable to locate her. May we get her contact information from you? And there is one more thing… You mentioned that you took photographs of much of the Abbott mansion. Once they're developed, it might be helpful if we could take a look at them. Perhaps there is something in the photographs that might provide evidence. "

"Of course, you may look at the photographs. Actually they are at the photoshop being developed right now. I can let them know that Coventry PD would also like a set of pictures."

Lydia lives in San Francisco now," I said, as I wrote her address and phone number on a pad from my purse. I handed it to him in the hope that I had answered all of his questions. Lydia's address was public information, and there was no betrayal in what I had done.

"Thank you, Natalie," said James. I'll contact the photo shop and ask them for some enlargements, which the department will, of course, pay for. … that is, if it's okay with you."

"That would be fine, James"

There seemed to be no overt curiosity on his part, just pretty regular questions. His last question was, "Would you like a deputy to drive you home, Natalie?"

"No, James. I'll be fine on my own. My car is parked down the street." …and then it was over.

As I walked down the steps and onto the cobblestone path, I felt James Sullivan's eyes boring a hole in my back, but I resisted the urge to turn and take one last look. He was my first boyfriend during high school, and now it appears we can't bear the sight of one another.

I couldn't get to my car fast enough, but after initially resisting the urge to turn and look back at James, I ultimately couldn't help myself. We found ourselves facing one another, and when our eyes met, I whispered, "*Oh God,*" embarrassed at showing my interest. What I saw was a man who was looking at me with unconcealed regret on his face and a thousand questions. I wasn't sure what that meant, but I guessed that perhaps my face had also betrayed me.

Not wanting to be suspected of a motive of any kind, I turned and moved quickly down the sidewalk, again trying to avoid the opportunistic media and the curious locals. I was unsure if James was interested because he thought I had deceived him, or because he was simply curious about me after all these years. It seemed to be more than curiosity. I felt the tears well up, as I thought of how deceitful and evasive I had to be with this man who had once loved me.

CHAPTER TWENTY-TWO

MURDER AT THE MANSION

Chief James Sullivan

The investigation at the Abbott Mansion is moving along and is now in its third day. Right now, much of what we know is conjecture, but it will all come together. In a small town such as Coventry, many people know a little or a lot, but there is almost no one who knows nothing. The truth usually trickles out, whether purposely or by accident. A lot of people are often eager for their fifteen minutes of fame, and they carelessly share information that would have ordinarily been kept quiet.

The bodies of Dale and Roseanne have been removed for autopsy, and the state crime lab is going over the place with a fine-tooth comb. It will take two to three weeks to finish the forensic investigation, so the planned demolition of Abbott House has been called off indefinitely by court order. That will give us time for the interviews and background checks that will need to be done. If we must revisit the crime scene, it will still be there.

Dale's death is a mystery. His wife's death is not. Under questioning, Dale's rattled mother, Blanche Forbes, was a fountain of information. It didn't take her long to crack and spew the facts as she saw them.

She started with, *"I came home from bridge group and found my son's wife Roseanne in bed with the man who drives the dump truck."*

"What happened next, Mrs. Forbes?"

"Roseanne jumped out of bed, naked as a jaybird, and slammed the door in my face. She got dressed and ran out of the house and jumped into Dale's car. I don't know what happened to the dump truck driver man. He must have gone out the window. Dale was working an extra shift that afternoon, but I called him right away. He made a mistake by bringing that slut home with him in the first place."

By this time, Mrs. Forbes was in tears, but we continued. "When did you next see Roseanne?"

"I never saw her again. When Dale came home that evening, he said she had gone back home to her mother in South Carolina and that she had taken his car. My son was devastated and embarrassed by what that horrible woman had done, but Dale is strong and has tried to move on. He even went to Vegas to get a quick divorce. Dale wants to get married again to a nice woman from Russia."

As I reviewed the entire transcript of my questioning, it became apparent that there are problems with Mrs. Forbes' story. For starters, Roseanne's mother has been dead for years, and Roseanne's clothes are still in the closet she shared with Dale. We are now searching for Dale's car in wooded areas and lakes. Dale is our number one suspect in her murder. However, the question of who murdered him remains unanswered and is a total mystery. The stumbling block is that we don't have a motive.

It's been determined that Dale didn't die in a fall down the stairs. His wound came from a metal mallet type of weapon with a round ball on the end. There is an antiquated croquet set in the corner of the Abbott basement, and it's missing one of the mallets. Someone was either waiting for him, or they were surprised and had to get rid of him. The most likely scenario is that Dale surprised the killer and the mallet was a convenient weapon. We probably won't find the mallet. With all of the lakes around here, it's very possibly buried in the sandy muck thirty or forty feet below. Although Dale was an obnoxious buffoon to many people living in Coventry, there is no one who would have a motive to kill him – at least not that we know.

Natalie was probably the last person to see Dale alive. I have a gut feeling she knows more than she's letting on, but then I no longer know her well.

When I saw her at the crime scene and took her hand, I realized that I still have feelings for her. She is very much unchanged in looks and there is something about Natalie that is – well – so appealing. She is unique in her mannerisms -- the way she lowers her eyes after she speaks – the way she tilts her head when she is listening to someone ... her smile… and there are her gentle, kind ways that everyone in Coventry is aware of. But I am concerned about her. During our conversation at Abbott House, she seemed troubled. I guess no one can blame her after what has happened in this normally quiet town. I couldn't avoid noticing that Natalie turned around when she was walking down the path from the Abbott House. She looked straight at me, and there was a certain feeling between us. But then, I am probably imagining things. I must be cautious and not allow my feelings for her to get in the way of this case.

CHAPTER TWENTY-THREE

1963 – THE LAST SUMMER

Natalie

Everything about my meeting with James Sullivan brought back a flood of memories – his voice, his hair, his smile, his touch. I remember after his high school graduation in 1963, the look on his face was one of hurt when I said that we should not expect to have a future together.

"James, The Abbotts have made arrangements for me to go to a state college after my senior year, and my Mother's retirement pension has already been set aside for my tuition. Because of me, she will have no pension, so I must make good for her sake. After college, I'll need to return to Coventry to support her when she is elderly and no longer working. I know you have different plans for yourself. Breaking it off now will avoid a lot of heartbreak down the road. That means we can't have a long-distance relationship, or any kind of relationship at all."

The Summer of 1963 was our last summer. Any spare minute we had was spent together, and the bittersweet certainty of losing each another heightened every feeling, whether happiness, sadness, or love. There was a special electrical sensation between Jimmy and me – perhaps physical or perhaps driven by unfulfilled sexual desire, but we could hardly keep our hands off each other. With hormones on overdrive, we had spent his last year of high school deeply involved but trying to avoid our sexual longing and any impulsive decision to consummate it. Our last moments together seem like yesterday in so many ways. I remember saying, "Please go now, Jimmy, please leave it alone. If it's meant to be, we'll find each other again, but right now, I'm not in love with you." There was simply nothing else to say after I told the boy I loved the biggest lie of my life.

He nodded and walked toward his car and his future and then I heard him call my name and say, "I love you Natalie." All I could give him was a pensive smile, and I hated myself for my lack of honesty and for inflicting hurt on the best person I had ever known.

I walked around for weeks with an odd empty gnawing in my stomach, finally losing myself in my senior year and subsequently in college life. But I never again had such feelings for any other man or boy, and I kept them all at arm's length. That way there were no demands made on me to move out of my small, secure life. Superficial was the key word, and it kept me safe -- or so I thought. What was strange is that during his school breaks neither of us made an attempt to see one another. For me, distance was the only safe option to save me from making an impulsive choice – one that might keep me from fulfilling my mother's expectations. I wasn't sure why he made the same choice, but I assumed that he probably had found a new love.

The loose ends of my life unraveled with unbearable haste after James left for West Point, but it wasn't just me unraveling. The times were changing in 1960s Coventry, as they were in the rest of the world. Rock and Roll, Vietnam, the Beetles, the pill, sexual freedom, and most importantly, the assassination of President Kennedy turned us upside down. Experimentation became the norm, as my generation was trying to figure it all out in a world that was moving too fast.

Although I was intrigued by what was going on, much of my after school time was spent working at the corner drug store, except for the evenings when a bored Lydia beckoned me to the mansion. She was looking to fill her time before she went off to her boarding school in late September. It had become apparent that Lydia's expensive education had exposed her to more than just literature and French. I listened, attracted and appalled at the same time. Between the sharing of new secrets about boys, sex, and make-up, we moved from the nooks and crannies of the Abbott house to Lydia's bedroom. There, with her childhood surrounding us, she held court, sitting in front of her vanity table, her alabaster beauty glowing like a pearl. Lydia defied the myth that all teenage girls need a suntan to enhance their looks. Her expensive Madame Alexander dolls stared at us from their shelves, morose and untouched for years, and her mother, Helen, was most likely drunk in her bedroom, so we were left to our own devices.

"Do you want to know something, Natalie? I have learned a lot about the things people do in bed since I have gone to boarding school. I have even done some of them myself." Lydia had become knowledgeable in the ways of the world, to put it gently, the ways of men with women, men with men, and women with women — and she shared her forbidden knowledge with me. While I was initially shocked at Lydia's openness, I was also intrigued, and secretly I couldn't wait for the next titillating morsel to come from her plump, rosy lips.

I could accept her use of birth control pills and her experimentation with different types of sex, but the most difficult thing for me to accept was something in her eyes that I could no longer penetrate. It was clear that we had drifted far apart and had lost one another. Lydia soon left Coventry for her eastern boarding school, and after that, we seemed to be strangers, but I was strangely relieved.

CHAPTER TWENTY-FOUR

BECOMING A REAL GIRL

Natalie

That fall, while mourning silently for the loss of the only friend I ever had and a boy that I loved, I desperately wanted to make a change to my life. I felt like running toward something unknown – something that would make everything better, but there was nowhere to go. It was then that I decided to catch up with other teenagers and become more worldly, although I didn't know for sure what that entailed. In Coventry, the operative term for a "worldly girl" was "wild," and I badly wanted to be just that.

I began to wear lipstick and mascara, as most seventeen-year-olds did in 1963, and had my hair cut into a Jackie Kennedy bouffant. I also started to sew my own clothes, which meant wrenching that job from my mother's practical hands. The result was definitely more fashionable -- shorter skirts, tighter fitting slacks and tops, and like magic, I was noticed by the "in" group of girls. They began to include me in their after-school smoking and gossip sessions in Ruthie Freetly's bedroom above her parents' restaurant, where the jukebox played 50s and 60s music all day and into the night.

Sitting on her pink floral bedspread, as girlish laughter permeated the blue, smoky haze, I learned that there was life without Lydia. With the help of Ruthie, Missy, Tove, Charmaine, and Dina, I had joined the mysterious world of small-town teenage girls. We watched American Bandstand and talked about the boys we liked and the upcoming dances in the school gym. In the process of becoming a teenager of my time, I suddenly found that I had become a real girl. Walking the streets with my group of adventurous friends became the weekend routine, and boys started noticing me. As frightened as I was of everything, I had a date for the first dance of the school year with a handsome, but rather out-of-control boy named Rick. He drove a motorcycle and wore a leather jacket with metal studs. I had to sneak out of the house on the pretext of going to the library or babysitting, so that I could jump on his motorcycle or get into his friend's 1957 Chevy. We would drive around town and kiss in the back seat while his friend was our chauffeur. But after President Kennedy was assassinated, I felt anxious, as though some type of disaster was looming, and I began to avoid Rick. Most of my time was spent at my part-time job and alone in my own bedroom.

Two of my group, Dina and Charmaine, had steady boyfriends, and the "wild, boy crazy" Tove and Missy had mostly out-of-town boys seeking their company. Older boys would come from other small towns in the area, often wearing jeans and a white T-shirt with a pack of cigarettes rolled into the short sleeves. Their Brylcreemed hair was slicked into a DA, and they would be driving what we considered to be fancy, customized cars.

All my friends were occupied with boys in some way, apart from the blunt Ruthie and me. Ruthie simply didn't seem interested, and I was the introverted bookworm of the group, back to hiding in my small life. But despite my tendency for spending time alone, I was also looking to escape from my sadness over the loss of James.

We were a diverse group in our rather provincial small city, but at that age, I was unaware of just how diverse. The foreshadowing was there, if one was knowledgeable enough to understand. At that time in my life, I didn't have any idea that Ruthie would be running her parents' restaurant until she was forty years old, when she finally left Coventry with her lover Tina, the local hairdresser, or that Missy would be dead two months after graduation, the passenger of a married, thirty-year-old, highly intoxicated driver, whom she was orally servicing at the time of the accident – at least that was the rumor going around. Gladys Stadsvold, who worked in the records department at the City Hall, leaked the accident report and autopsy, and it wasn't long before everyone in Coventry knew the details. I also didn't know that Tove would have been married four times before she was thirty-five, her three children being raised by her first and second husbands. I had always suspected that Tove was beyond the group sexually, but I didn't really know what that meant, until I witnessed her sexual precociousness for myself when James and I decided to explore the flood plain at Lake Crystal State Park.

We came across Tove and an older boy lying on a tree trunk that was bent nearly horizontal to the ground, because of the constant spring flooding. Her skirt had been pulled up, and his freckled, bare derriere was between her legs. He looked like Alfalfa in the "Our Gang" series. I was speechless, but couldn't stop looking. James finally put his hands on my shoulders and led me away. Embarrassed at my reaction, I said, "Jimmy, please take me home." We returned to his parked car but didn't go home. We came close to becoming lovers that day – but only close.

Tove seemed unconcerned by what James and I had witnessed and never mentioned it – nor did I. I was always good at keeping other people's secrets, but I had one secret of my own that I never shared with anyone. One rainy night, while I was working alone at the drug store, a man everyone called Peeker came in and exposed himself to me. At first, I thought he was holding a piece of pottery in front of his fly, but it didn't take me long to realize that it was part of his own anatomy. His eyes were fixated on me, and I panicked, running to the back room. After a few minutes, when I got up the courage to look into the store, he was gone. I remained silent about what had happened because I thought I might be the one blamed. The daughter of a housemaid needed to be cautious about attracting the wrong kind of attention, but some other girl must have talked. A few weeks later, Peeker was found dead, supposedly drowned, but his private parts had been cut off. There was no investigation. Back then, such things sometimes went without scrutiny in small towns, if the victim was notorious in some way.

CHAPTER TWENTY-FIVE

JUNE 7, 1991

Natalie

Memorial Day had come and gone in Coventry, with a parade featuring veterans from all branches of the service, along with the high school marching band and patriotic floats. The cemeteries had been decorated like a field of spring flowers, and flags marked the graves of those who had served and those who had made the ultimate sacrifice. I was pensive because my father could have been one of the soldiers who didn't return home.

Memorial Day always seemed to commemorate the true beginning of summer. The activities culminated with a concert in the park, and I was there with M.J. and Frank. As I looked around, I caught a glimpse of a familiar face in the crowd, standing along the sidelines --James Sullivan. He also noticed me, and we casually nodded to each other across the audience of local onlookers. Again, I was uncomfortable with too much eye contact, so I abruptly refocused in the direction of the music. But remembering that James had served in Vietnam as an officer after his West Point years, I looked toward him again and nodded and smiled – he did the same. With patriotic music flooding the park, I began to wonder what his Vietnam tour was like, and I imagined that at the very least it was not a good experience – as was the case for so many other young men fighting a hopeless war. The fact that so many of them lost their lives was a tragedy. Feeling a tear escape from my eye, I turned my thoughts to current events in Coventry.

The chatter about Dale and Roseanne was beginning to quiet down, and the demolition of Abbott House was put on hold indefinitely. The buyers of the mansion backed out because the timeline was unknown, and they were losing money.

I tried to get back to my normal life, which meant not looking at any more family journals and avoiding the metal box which now resides inside the false chimney located in my attic. I also decided to distance myself from what I did for Lydia, the Abbott Mansion, and the deaths of Dale Forbes and his wife Roseanne. And that is just what I did. I retreated into my old coping mechanisms of hiding and avoidance. But there has been an unresolved mystery. No one has heard from Lydia, and no one seems to know of her whereabouts. I am seriously troubled by that development, or lack of development.

Relieved that my trip to Abbott House had nothing to do with Dale's death was like a weight taken off my shoulders. He didn't fall and die because he was investigating an intruder, which would have been me, but the mystery of his murder remains to be solved. He was there to make sure no one discovered the murder of his wife, likely at his own hand. So far, there has been no clue that would point to his killer or a motive.

I continue to be troubled by my omissions and lies when I was questioned by James Sullivan. I still haven't told him that I was in the Abbott cellar in the middle of the night and had accidentally discovered Dale's body at that time -- days before the demolition crew. I have also been dreading the day that I would have to do something significant to contact Lydia. I hadn't heard from her since our hurried midnight telephone conversation that was interrupted before we had finished. The unusual raspy male voice that was barking orders at her during our call had to belong to the person who disconnected us.

My lack of success in retrieving the box on my first try, the morning that I was interrupted by Dale, would have angered Lydia greatly. I succeeded on my second trip to Abbott House, but she doesn't know it. And now there are no calls from her -- no appearance on my doorstep. However, Lydia coming to my home would have been highly unusual, because in the thirty-five years that

I have lived in the house on River Flats, first with mother and then alone, Lydia has never been inside the door. Those of her social class don't go to working class neighborhoods such as mine, and she would not have appreciated being seen entering my home. Nevertheless, I continued to try to reach her by phone and failed every time.

James has stopped by my house several times in the past three weeks to ask additional questions about Lydia and presumably to check on me personally. He also has not been able to reach her, and he needs Lydia's input as he investigates the case of the Abbott House deaths.

"How are you doing, Natalie? ...anything I can do for you?" I wasn't exactly sure of his motives. Perhaps he thought I was hiding something or maybe he just wanted to see me. There was a sexual tension between us that was growing, and I found myself looking forward to his visits, even though they also made me nervous. James is still very much the kind, serious boy I dated in high school, even now at the age of forty-five.

When we shook hands or accidentally touched, that strange electrical impulse I remember from our youth was every bit as strong now as it was then. We had come close to embracing a few times, but both of us stepped away at the last minute. Nevertheless, our sidelong glances revealed exactly what was going on between us, as we continued to meet under the guise of police business. We were courting, to use an antiquated word, but it was a secret – even from ourselves – although a poorly kept secret. I began to wonder where this would lead.

John Bergstrom continued to live next door with his aunt Ragna Bergstrom. He said he was writing a textbook for the Oslo university where he was a professor of American Studies. The tall Norwegian visited me occasionally, and once we went to a movie and out to dinner. He seemed more interested in learning about the Abbotts and Lydia than in me. I thought his incessant questioning to be a bit odd, but I also understood that writers have a great curiosity about people. I just assumed that he was gathering material for another book on the culture of small town America, so I found it somewhat natural when he asked prying questions about the Abbott family and their lives. Perhaps that topic would make a popular read in Norway.

John never shared much about his life in Norway and, in fact, seemed to avoid the topic. But he did tell me that his aunt's health was in decline and that she was now confined to her bed. He was extending his stay to help with her care. I hadn't seen Mrs. Bergstrom for weeks, so I was disturbed by that news, and I wasn't altogether sure that John was the person to be caring for Ragna. While John and I occasionally spent time together, romantic feelings never developed for either one of us.

I find it interesting that John has developed a friendship of sorts with our neighbor across the street, Dewar or "Dew," as he usually referred to him. He is also quite friendly with Bernetta Evans and Rocky, her boyfriend. When I asked him about his relationship with the neighbors after seeing him crossing the street at a rather late hours, John said that he was helping Mrs. Evans with an urgent plumbing problem. I had to stifle a laugh at that comment, because I imagined that Bernetta Evans had quite a few "plumbing emergencies." It was also interesting that in the middle of one sleepless night, I saw him coming from Dewar's house at 3 a.m. I knew that he didn't want it mentioned, so I didn't. Perhaps he has been interviewing Coventry citizens about life in the United States for the book he claimed to be writing, but some of his visits are much too late for that.

When I offered to visit Ragna Bergstrom and do some cooking for her, John said, "That's nice of you, but she can no longer eat regular food and is on liquid diet. Also, her fatigue doesn't allow for visitors. There is now a nurse who comes in three times a week to bathe her and check on her medications."

"Well, if there is anything I can do, John, please let me know. I have grown very fond of Ragna over the years."

I had noticed a woman, presumably a nurse, coming and going from the house carrying a black bag. She always dresses in the same thing -- a brightly colored nurse's smock, topped with a hooded sweatshirt. On a couple of occasions when I was walking Charlie, I tried to make small talk with her, but she rebuffed my attempts and walked quickly down the sidewalk. I managed a smile and moved on.

I had also been thinking about asking John to translate my great-grand-mother Anna's journal from Norwegian to English but then thought that might not be a good idea. I decided to take it to the Coventry Historical Society instead. There I met with Erik Nelson, second generation American, to discuss all the ramifications of what this project would entail.

"Mr. Nelson, this is a fairly large project, and it's full of family information. If you agree to take it on, I need to be assured that you will maintain the strict confidentiality of what you have read."

It was apparent that he was an ethical sort, and he agreed to my terms with an affirmation, "Of course, Miss LaPierre. I am proud of my work, and I know that translations can turn up some surprises for families. You can be assured that I won't share information with anyone but you."

I took Great-Grandmother Anna's black leather journal out of my book-case, wrapped it in a shawl, and hand-delivered it to the 80-year-old Erik. He seemed happy to put his skill to use.

CHAPTER TWENTY-SIX

WHERE IS LYDIA?

Natalie

My mother's journal and the photographs I had taken of the rooms at Abbott House have been waiting for my attention for weeks. On the Saturday I had set aside for those tasks, James came by looking quite nervous.

"I'm concerned about Lydia, Natalie. The Coventry PD hasn't been able to reach her, although, thanks to you, we have her address and phone number. There is also no trace of any significant other. Our investigation is stuck without input from Lydia Abbott, so I need to personally investigate her whereabouts. The San Francisco PD has been contacted, but they can't undertake an investigation unless there have been reports that she is in danger or missing. Up to now, there have been no missing person reports filed on Lydia -- nothing. Since we have an open investigation in Coventry, I need to travel there and check some things out in person. I could use your help, Natalie, since you have a long-standing relationship with her and first-hand information. You'll think of things that I won't. Also, do you have a key to her townhouse? I can't enter her home without a legal reason, unless you, as her property manager, ask me to accompany you out of concern for her well-being." James finally got to the question he wanted to ask. "I would like you to go with me to San Francisco, Natalie, if you're comfortable with the idea,"

"What?" ...thinking that I hadn't heard him correctly. "Did you just ask me to go to San Francisco with you?"

"Yes, I did, Natalie," James said with a rather sheepish smile. I know it sounds a bit unorthodox, but this is a business trip for me, and if you are her property manager, it would be a business trip for you, as well. If you don't want to, or if you're not able, please say so now, because I plan to leave on Wednesday of next week and return the following Monday night. The department will pay for your airplane ticket, hotel, and food, so it shouldn't cost you anything, except a few days away from work -- and we can reimburse for that. I plan to be in California through the weekend, and you should be aware that there could be a good deal of footwork and time required."

At first, I thought his request was odd, but then it began to make sense. I made no commitment as I responded. "Yes, James, I have a key, and I can legally enter any of her properties, if I feel the need. Once Lydia moved out of Coventry and her mother became unable to care for herself and her home, someone had to have access.'

When I thought further about the trip, my stomach knotted, and my heart did a flip flop. I had never traveled or flown before because of my anxiety, but there was another inhibiting factor -- the fear of what we might find in San Francisco. I opened my mouth to say "no," but I heard myself saying "yes," mostly because I wanted to see for myself that Lydia was okay. But secretly, I also wanted to spend some time with James, and I suspected he wanted to spend some time with me. He is seeking me out more frequently lately, and I have come to look forward to his attention and his presence.

"Yes, James," I said. "I'll go with you. I'm also worried about Lydia. It isn't like her to make no contact, especially with all that's going on with Abbott House." He smiled and looked relieved at my reaction. Since we would be traveling together, I thought it was only fair to tell him of my heart issues and chronic anxiety, as well as the fact that I had never flown before. James seemed rather surprised when I shared this with him, but he was reassuring, and as a result, I was reassured. As for me, I was rather embarrassed about what I perceived as my weaknesses. That's why I keep my anxiety and agoraphobic tendencies to myself, unless I have no choice. Most people don't understand, and they always seem to be surprised. As he left, he said, "Don't worry, Natalie. It'll be okay."

On Monday, I filed forms with human resources to take four personal days at the request of the Coventry Police Department. Of course, they were approved, and M.J. immediately set about arranging for a substitute to fill in for me. She also agreed to take Charlie for the time I was gone. Despite all of her assistance, I knew a negative response from her would be forthcoming, complete with advise and criticism. I waited patiently for the other shoe to drop, and I didn't have to wait long. M.J. made no eye contact when she said, "Are you sure you should do this, Natalie. I can think of a dozen reasons why you shouldn't. For one thing, you're an unmarried woman, and he is an unmarried man. Think of your reputation – and you are the librarian of Coventry. Also, wasn't he your high school boyfriend? Maybe Chief Sullivan has ideas about getting you in a compromising situation. And, of course, people will talk. I think this is a mistake."

I responded with a brief comment of my own. "Thanks for thinking about me, M.J. I know you have my best interest at heart, but I need to get in touch with Lydia. I have a feeling that something has happened to her. Don't worry about James. I'm not interested, and he is a gentleman."

With that, M.J. did her signature about face and clomped out of the room, but not before halting her exit and turning around to face me so she could have the last word.

"Natalie, I know you well, and I know that you're more interested in James than you will admit. You never really got over him after your high school romance. I also know about your affairs in the Cities over the years, and I witnessed how difficult it was to get rid of a couple of those men once you realized that you were not interested in continuing a relationship. Be careful, my friend. This one lives in your own back yard."

I wanted to blast M.J. for her intrusive and ill-mannered comments, but there was no purpose for such a showdown. She knew that my mind was made up, but I also knew she was right about one thing. I was more interested in James than I cared to admit. I walked out the door and past her desk, and found myself unable to resist commenting. "This is really none of your business, M.J, and I don't see why you care so much." The silence between us spoke volumes. I realized that my best friend and I had just had an argument, which is rare for M.J. and me. I usually let her have her way with words, but for some reason, this time, I couldn't.

The travel and hotel arrangements were made by James' secretary, and before I knew it, we were traveling to the Minneapolis airport in his black Suburban. Although our purpose was serious and valid, I couldn't help but feel as though we had gone A.W.O.L. I was also amused to notice the grin that James had on his face. It's unbelievable that we are traveling together twenty-seven years after our teenage love affair ended. Although it was only in a business capacity, happiness hung on our every look and gesture.

CHAPTER TWENTY-SEVEN

JUNE 13

James and Natalie in Cali

I woke at 7 a.m. California time, or Cali time, as Lydia would say, hungry and feeling well rested. We had arrived at the hotel after midnight and went straight to our respective rooms on the tenth floor. I had noticed the smell of the ocean and a hint of the fish that had washed in with the tide, so the wharf must be near the hotel. James' room adjoins mine, and the sound of his shower let me know he was already awake. We had agreed to meet at 8:30 a.m. in the hotel restaurant to plan our strategy for trying to locate Lydia. With the two hour time change, I was starving.

James looked a little tired when he entered the dining room, and I guessed that I did too. He had dressed in a blue shirt that matched his eyes and tan khaki pants. Out of uniform, he looked younger and very much like the boy I had dated in high school -- but there was one difference. He was even more handsome now at 45 years of age. His sandy brown hair was still damp, and a few stray pieces had fallen onto his forehead, giving him a youthful look. Old feelings kept resurfacing from those long-ago days, but I must remember the reason that we are here together.

Our eyes met frequently, but both of us hesitated to let them linger on one another's face. There's no doubt I was self-conscious about my appearance, and his brief flashes of scrutiny made me uncomfortable, although I was doing the same to him. Not being sure of how to style my hair, make-up, and clothing this morning, I decided on simplicity. My dark hair was tied in a low pony tail, and just out of the shower myself, I couldn't stop it from springing into tendrils in front of my ears and down the back of my neck. I normally like to blow it dry with a round brush to make it as smooth as possible, but this morning there was little time for anything but lip gloss, tinted moisturizer, and a hasty once over with the hair dryer. I had dressed in slim leg jeans, a grey knit tee shirt, and a blue blazer. I also didn't forget to put on my mother's Tiffany pearl earrings and necklace of graduated sized pearls -- a surprising, but well-earned gift from old Marguerite Abbott before she died. It seems like an unlikely combination, but somehow it looks okay.

James and I were a bit awkward with one another, as we ordered breakfast and attempted to make small talk. Unfamiliar with our new-found together-ness, I began to think that perhaps this wasn't such a good idea. We had a brief discussion about what we wanted to eat, and then there was a silence, until James said, "Natalie, you don't look any different than you did in high school. I always liked it when you wore your hair like that."

A bit taken aback, I lowered my eyes and simply said, "Thank you James."

Surprised, but flattered, that he remembered how I wore my hair more than twenty years ago, I was going to respond again, but decided not to comment any further. James seemed to be embarrassed about what he had said, so I let him off the hook and dropped it. At that point, becoming very structured and professional, James pulled out his note pad and began to talk about our sched-ule for the day. "I think our first stop should be Lydia's townhouse. We can do a preliminary search of the premises and go from there."

I nodded and said, "You know best, James. I plan to take my cues from you and your experience. I'm a librarian and know nothing about police inves-tigations."

We ate leisurely and made small talk. I was a bit amused that James ate oatmeal for breakfast, as I did, but he had eggs and bacon with his, and I had egg whites. He asked me about my life since high school, and I gave him a brief outline of my college days and subsequent quiet existence in Coventry. He talked about his daughter Paige with a smile on his face and a light in his eyes. I learned that she incessantly begged him for a dog and loved music. He didn't go into detail about his marriage and divorce from Laura, except to say that it was never quite right for either of them. And then he said quietly, "The best thing to come out of that marriage was Paige. She lives with me during the school year but spends most of her summers with her mother, except for a mid-summer trip to Coventry for two weeks. We also alternate Christmas and Thanksgiving, so I have her for one of those holidays each year. All three of us had input into the divorce and custody agreements, but this arrangement is what Paige wanted."

James went on to explain that Paige's mother lives in Los Angeles and New York City with her stockbroker husband Richard and spends summers at their home on the Cape. For some reason, he shared additional information about Richard's background. "His wealth not only comes from Wall Street, but also from a large family trust fund. He can give Laura the life she has always wanted. Paige has never been close to her mother and didn't want to leave Coventry this summer, but her recent emails indicate that she has met a boy, and she now seems contented to be there."

I was a bit embarrassed that I had so much less to say about my myself. "My life is not very exciting, James. I have no family left, but I spend time with a few friends who also work at City Hall. And you know about my anxiety disorder, which keeps me from traveling alone. I am thankful for a job that I enjoy, because it keeps me busy and interested in life."

It occurred to me that I was somewhat lonely, and I'm now a motherless child and had always been a fatherless child. My life is small in every way – smaller now than ever before, since Mother died.

His last words before we entered our rooms to get ready for a long day were, "Take a light jacket or a sweater. San Francisco can be damp and chilly in the mornings and evenings." He still liked to take care of me, a habit that I found endearing and irritating at the same time.

"Thank you, James, but I think my blazer will be warm enough."

"Sorry, Natalie. I guess I'm used to giving orders." I could only smile.

CHAPTER TWENTY-EIGHT

JUNE 13, PACIFIC HEIGHTS

Natalie

Lydia's townhouse is located between Chestnut and Union Streets in the Pacific Heights area of Francisco. According to what I had read in preparation for this trip, her address was in a very desirable location, but I am not the judge of this city's worthy neighborhoods nor those of any city, coming from the prairies of Minnesota. My first impression of San Francisco was mostly focused on the architecture of the Victorian homes. We have Victorian style homes in Coventry, but here in San Francisco, many are unique. Also, the view of the bay was amazing.

Once James and I found Lydia's three-story townhome, I was unexpectedly impressed. Perched on a whitewashed stone foundation, it had been painted in subtle blue and gray shades and accented with white trimmed gingerbread. All three colors seemed to meld effortlessly together in the morning light, creating a lovely effect. A garage entrance was to the right of the steps, along with an empty driveway. That is where James parked our rental car, hoping that he wasn't violating any San Francisco parking ordinances.

As we anticipated, no one answered when we rang the outside bell labeled "L. Abbott". Since I had a key in my pocket, I wasn't too concerned about entering the building, but I also knew that Lydia would have hidden a key somewhere outside, and I wanted to confiscate all keys while we were here.

Stepping back, I looked on either side of the center steps, and I found the key within a couple of minutes. Between some rocks, partially hidden by the shrubbery, there was a fake rock that stood out slightly from the others. I was sure that I would find the key inside, because I knew that Lydia often used this type of hiding place. I picked it up and pushed on the bottom, and like magic it opened. Two keys on a silver ring fell out onto the ground.

We let ourselves into the rather small, but elegant foyer, with the key I had in my pocket and quietly climbed the four marble steps to the entrance door of her home. Both of us felt uncomfortable – almost like trespassers with unsavory motives, but my concern for Lydia made me more bold that I would ordinarily be. James and I knocked several times on the glossy black door, and with no response, decided to use the key. We found ourselves unable to enter with the key I had brought along, and it was at that point that I produced the second key, shiny and new, from the fake rock. I guessed that Lydia had recently had a new key made for some reason – maybe she had changed the lock. Suddenly we were admitted to a part of Lydia's world that I had only been able to imagine. "Wow, James! I have always known that Lydia has good taste, but this is amazing."

Lydia had been a life-long inhabitant of Abbott House in Coventry, with its dark, brooding, Victorian elegance; but, after being inside her San Francisco home, I realized that what I saw and felt in these rooms was the essence of Lydia and the woman she had become -- and perhaps had always been. I understood that she had found a place where she could breathe, and I now knew why she was always so anxious to leave Coventry behind.

As we entered the hallway to her home, the muted light suddenly exploded into a surprisingly open floor plan with a view of the bay from tall windows that lined the walls. It was obvious that the townhouse had been recently updated, most likely by Lydia herself. The dark floors and subtle grey-blue walls, bordered by white trim, were striking . From the living room to the bedrooms and bathrooms, it was a tasteful, warm, but modern décor. Only the luminous Lydia could have designed such a place of subtle light — a place where she could meld with the colors of her surroundings.

James and I entered each room and examined every nook and cranny, including closets, drawers, and cupboards. We looked for clues in the bedrooms and essentially invaded Lydia's privacy, which gave me an uneasy feeling. Based on our scrutiny, it seemed to be apparent that Lydia didn't share a bedroom with Clark, her "significant other," as she had referred to him. Her clothes were in the closet of her ice blue bedroom that faced the ocean, and the very few items of clothing that Clark had in the apartment were in the other darkly decorated and shuttered bedroom that faced the back garden of the house. His chest of drawers was nearly empty, except for a few pairs of boxer shorts and one pair of pajamas. His closet contained five shirts, three pairs of pants, and a lightweight khaki jacket. Several hats of differing types lined the shelf above the clothing. There was nothing of Lydia in his room and nothing of Clark in Lydia's. I was not entirely surprised, because she never spoke of romantic love between them. I guess I had just assumed it was so, and perhaps that is what she wanted me to think. It also occurred to me that there could be different scenarios. Perhaps he was gay, but the arrangement benefitted both. It was also possible that they had a raging love for one another but shared separate rooms.

Suddenly I heard James say, in his police chief voice, "Natalie, I found something." I walked toward the bathroom, my head still full of speculation about her life, but my imagination quickly turned to reality. It was what was lying in the palm of his hand, so small and white, that grabbed my heart like a vise.

James

Natalie seemed to be a bit surprised when I turned into a detective the minute we entered Lydia's building. It was clear that she was thinking and observing from an emotional perspective, but I was thinking objectively, as I had to. I didn't want to frighten her, but then and there, I detached myself from any preconceived ideas about Lydia or her boyfriend and was looking for clues in the usual places, such as in crockery, the dishwasher and wine cooler, and finally in the bathtub drain. I didn't want to tear Lydia's townhouse apart completely; the San Francisco PD will do that if necessary.

I had pulled up the bathtub stopper until it was lying limp in the tub like an odd metal fish out of water. I called for Natalie but warned her that she might be disturbed by what I had found. Lying on my open, gloved hand was a small finger, complete with traces of very pale pink nail polish on a fingernail that was broken into the quick. There were also strands of nearly white matted hair wrapped on part of the finger, which had probably attached it to the tub stopper. "Natalie, can you look…are you able to…?"

She walked closer and looked at what she knew was part of her friend's body. "I think it belongs to Lydia, James. I think it's hers." And then she fell silent and collapsed on the toilet seat cover.

"I'm sorry, Natalie, but I have to call the San Francisco P.D. There needs to be a full investigation. We can't sit on this. Are you okay with this next step?"

It took her a while to answer my question, but it was only a formality. There was no question about what had to be done. "Yes, I think so, James. I'll be okay in a few minutes."

It didn't take long before the condo was teeming with uniformed officers and two detectives -- one in a dark suit and the other in a rather rumpled navy blue sport jacket.

CHAPTER TWENTY-NINE

LOVE AND TRAGEDY

Natalie

One of the detectives, a very slim, dark man with an aquiline nose, was obviously in charge. Professional and deadpan, I vaguely heard him grilling James about our presence in Lydia Abbott's condo. James was protecting both of us when he responded in a firm, no-nonsense voice:

"Natalie LaPierre is Lydia Abbott's lifelong friend and caretaker of her estate in Minnesota. She has legal permission to enter any of Ms. Abbott's properties at any time. Ms. LaPierre hasn't heard from Lydia Abbott for weeks, and she is very concerned. In addition, the Coventry, MN police department has been investigating two murders that took place in Ms. Abbott's family home about a month ago. We need to speak with Ms. Abbott, and we have exhausted all other possibilities to learn of her whereabouts."

The cool, in-charge detective J.D. Worthington seemed satisfied with James' explanation, and my stunned demeanor likely added credibility to what he was saying. And why shouldn't it? After all, my reaction to finding my long-time friend's detached finger in the drain of a bathtub was a shock. The second detective, known only as Dan, was a bit heavyset and rumpled, but appeared to have a softer, more human approach. He also asked some questions, but they were more in the line of statements, not so much of interrogation. We were surprised to discover later that Dan, the rather rumpled officer, was the lead detective and would oversee the investigation. We also found out that his last name was Battista.

After two hours of James' explanations and a phone call to the Coventry Police Department verifying our identities, we left the investigation to the SFPD. They were to call our hotel and leave a message if they learned anything significant.

We got into the rental car and drove around the city for a short time with the windows partially open. Although I wasn't focusing on the sights, the change of scene and fresh air seemed to clear my head. Lydia had been more than a friend, more like a sister, and even though our relationship hit some rough patches as adults, I had adored her for most of my life. I was distraught. I was sad. I was also horrified at how she died, if she was indeed dead. I needed to cry, and I did.

Our plan of going to the wharf for a seafood dinner that evening had become unappealing with the gruesome discovery, and we headed back to the hotel in silence. Dinner consisted of sandwiches from room service -- mine mostly uneaten. James decided to sit in my room, as I tried to sleep. He was sitting in the chair in my hotel room when sleep finally came.

I awoke just before midnight to find James sleeping beside me, fully clothed. Instinctively, I reached for the comfort of his hand, and without thought, only mutual desire, his warm embrace drew me softly and easily into his body. We fit together perfectly. Our lips met in the dark, and the passion that had been denied for so long exploded -- we became the lovers we were always meant to be. Full of desire and love that could no longer be denied, James and I dissolved into one another, until we came apart reluctantly to an early morning knock on the door. James pulled on his pants and greeted an elderly, perhaps forgetful, bellhop with a cart of breakfast food meant for another room. We stayed in my room until noon, when we finally ventured out for lunch on the wharf.

In the meantime, we stopped speaking of Lydia, not out of disrespect for her, but out of concern for my precarious state of being. I needed a break from thinking about what likely horrific fate she had met. But, there was another reason to leave Lydia behind for a while. New or reignited love is often fragile, and neither of us wanted to break the spell that was binding us closer. Both of us knew that this time together, as new lovers, would be brief. We would soon be deeply mired in questions and facts relating to Lydia's demise. I was grateful for this reprieve. James' touch, his kiss, his passionate lovemaking were all I needed right now, and I sensed that he felt the same. Wherever Lydia was, her presence in my life had finally taken its proper place – no longer the most important person, but a significant person that I had loved like a sister when we were children. I left the unhappy memories of our relationship behind and was at peace with James – at least for now.

CHAPTER THIRTY

FRIDAY EVENING, JUNE 14

Natalie

Today is my 45th birthday. Thinking about how things have changed from last year to this year, and during the past several weeks, has shown me the unpredictability of life. Last year, I remember spending my birthday with M.J. at our favorite restaurant, The Bistro. That's what we did whenever she or I had a birthday -- two unmarried women looking for friendship in a world full of couples. It was difficult to admit to myself that I was lonely, so I avoided thinking too much about the future, which I presumed would be more of the same. How quickly life can change– for good and bad.

After the discovery of the evidence in Lydia's townhouse, this didn't seem like an appropriate time to celebrate my birthday, so I didn't mention it to James. We walked to the wharf and decided to have dinner at a cozy restaurant with checkered tablecloths and candles burning romantically on each table. The food was upscale, and my scallops were delicious. This seemed to be a special occasion restaurant, with one course after another. We had finished and were relaxed with fine wine and comfortably satisfied with good food, when, surprisingly, the waiters brought a cake blazing with candles and began singing "Happy Birthday" in a lovely harmony. Tears came to my eyes, as I looked at the man sitting across the table from me. "Happy Birthday, Lydia." How did he know? I hadn't told him it was my birthday today. After my own interrogation of the police chief sitting across from an unexpected birthday cake, he finally told me.

"I've been reviewing the paperwork from the murder investigation at Abbott House, including your interview. Your birthdate is on the form you filled out when we met for the first time at the Abbott mansion, and it popped out at me." He smiled and said, "... just routine, ma'am. Not rocket science."

Overwhelmed and unable to eat more than a few bites, I suggested that we take the cake back to the hotel. James agreed, and we walked into the salty air carrying a cake box and stealing kisses in the dark.

Everything was moving fast for James and me – probably because of our previous, but unconsummated love affair when we were so young. Although our feelings at that age were fueled by youth and raging hormones, there is no denying that we were also in love, even back then - a fact that our minds and bodies had never forgotten. Right now, there was only the two of us -- which was more than enough. Again and again, our desire ignited with a touch, a kiss, or just a look, and our passion stole our desire to explore this enticing city. Our links to the outside world were quick trips to the wharf for seafood and the pizza place around the corner. Our only exploration was of one another.

Finally, on Saturday, our fourth day in San Francisco, we were ready to sightsee. Heading north, we drove to a lovely winery and inhaled the fresh country scent of fruity vines and sun-kissed earth. The wine tasted both mature and young at the same time, like us — a magnificent state of being. James and I toured the harbor in a boat that had seen too many trips around Alcatraz and later had an amazing seafood lunch in a restaurant on the wharf. Laughing at what typical tourists we had become, we finally took a bus tour of the city, holding hands and kissing when we thought no one was looking — like teen-agers again. When the bus stopped at the beautiful San Francisco City Hall, three couples were climbing the steps, their happiness written in every look and movement. The women, holding bouquets mostly made up of roses and baby's breath, were dressed in all styles of wedding attire. The men, in dark suits, had their arms around the women's waists -- a gesture of protectiveness and perhaps to signify that they belong to one another. Happiness was in the air, and we followed that trail. James and I looked at each other, and without a word, climbed the steps to the entrance of City Hall, holding hands and being cautious to keep a respectful distance from the bridal parties. It was a beautiful place for a wedding – soaring windows, graceful architecture, and an atmosphere of happy couples milling around and taking photographs.

CHAPTER THIRTY-ONE

SUNDAY, JUNE 16

Natalie

Things were going well -- probably too well -- but we shouldn't have been surprised when the phone in James' hotel room rang with some ominous news. A family walking along the bay had come across a severed head that had washed to shore. When the police arrived and a search ensued, they found almost enough body parts to complete a human corpse. The "body" was now at the morgue, and the head was intact and suitable for an identification by a family member or a friend. The medical examiner's office knew from the information we had given to the detectives that we would be going home tomorrow. That meant that I, the friend, was expected to go to the morgue to identify the unknown body yet today.

The first question I asked of James was, "Do I have to do this? It's Sunday. Is the morgue open for business?"

James replied, "Well, you can refuse, but they could get a court order, and the morgue is open whenever they need it to be."

The large gray building that housed the county morgue was formidable, and I was weak at the knees anticipating what lay ahead. James protectively placed his arm around my waist, and I put one foot in front of the other, as he had told me to do.

The medical examiner, matter of fact and rather dour, met with us in his office to explain what would take place during the viewing. He also told us that the autopsy of Lydia's body contained evidence of a powerful drug used to anesthetize patients during surgery. The implication was, due to the large amount of the drug in her body, that Lydia was dead before she was dismembered. While that fact was somewhat comforting, my body was shaking and hesitant, as I held James' arm. We silently took the elevator to the lower level morgue. It was a cold, hard place, lined with wall-to-wall gleaming silver drawers. The ceiling lights were white as they illuminated the room. My eyes involuntarily closed from the assault of the glare. … and then it was time, and the drawer opened.

I turned my head toward James' shoulder as the blanket was pulled from a round object that I assumed was a human head. I was grateful that draping had taken place, which hid the fact that the head had been severed from the body. But I still could not fully look.

"Ms. LaPierre…are you able to view the body?" -- the medical examiner asked several times, becoming more and more stern each time. I didn't respond for what seemed an eternity, and the M.E, with his bushy gray eyebrows knit to the center of his forehead, became unexpectedly willing to wait for my lead. But, I had to get this over with, so I turned my head from the safety of James' shoulder to the stark reality of what lay on the table.

Totally unprepared for what I saw, because there is no preparation for viewing the decapitated, dismembered body of one's childhood friend, I heard myself whispering softly, "Oh my God -- Oh, my God!" I began nodding and averted my eyes from the matted, white blond hair and one half-lidded icy blue eye. Even with the decomposition that had taken place, there was no doubt that this was Lydia. I didn't need a DNA test to know the truth. Seeing her in death, I understood what she had gone through. The M.E. didn't offer to expose the other body parts, but I asked to see her hand, and he complied with my request. He brought out a small gray box and laid the contents on the table. The thumb and three remaining fingers were as white as paper, but there were no cuts and bruises. Whomever this hand belonged didn't have the opportunity to fight for her life before she was dismembered. Most likely she was already dead, a thought that somewhat eased my pain for a second time. I looked more closely, and I recognized the hand that I had held so often as a child as we played at Abbott House. I knew the shape, size, and lines on the skin as well as I knew my own. I nodded my head and said, "Yes, this is Lydia Abbott." And then I could look no more, which James understood, because he hurried me out the door.

"Will there be anything else, sir?" James asked the M.E.

The M.E. responded in his monotone voice, as if by rote. "…just to sign the paperwork—that's all. Let's go into the next room to take care of that. It won't take long."

As I signed the paperwork, I couldn't help but think of how a life can come to an official end with a piece of paper and a few strokes of a pen. Two days ago, I had felt that my life had truly begun for the first time, and less than forty-eight hours later, another life that had been so important to me had ended. I didn't understand why this happened and why anyone would want to kill Lydia. There were so many unanswered questions. I suddenly wanted to escape the situation and couldn't wait to get on the plane back to Minnesota.

That night, as James and I lay holding one another in the hotel bed where we had found so much happiness, lovemaking was not on our minds. We were both strangely silent in the wake of today's happenings until James spoke. "I will never let you go again, Natalie. I love you. I have always loved you." I had hoped that he felt that way, and I was at once reassured. But there was a dark cloud that wouldn't dissipate. I couldn't help but think of how I had kept the truth from him, and because of my fear, I may have tainted his investigation of the Abbott House murders. Perhaps what I had removed from the basement of the mansion was evidence that he must have. What would he think of me when, or if, he learned the truth? I knew I had to decide very soon. I couldn't allow him to love me so well, until he knew what I had done.

CHAPTER THIRTY-TWO

MONDAY, JUNE 17 – JUST THE FACTS

James

Although we were scheduled to fly back to Minnesota today, we had to cancel our flights. Natalie and I were instead summoned to Lydia's townhouse for more questioning. Dan, the lead investigator, wanted to know Lydia's life story, including any person who may have been in her life at any time. After a preliminary investigation on the part of the SFPD, they discovered that Lydia was in dire financial straits. She had spent her money and owed more than three million dollars to creditors, which included the mortgage on her townhouse. It was set to go into foreclosure in the near future. We also learned that Lydia had started a new case against her ex-husband, charging that he didn't live up to their pre-nuptial agreement. She was trying to get a new settlement of ten million dollars.

Surprised by this development, I had nothing to add to what they had already discovered. As far as I knew, Lydia Abbott was a very wealthy woman, and that was what Natalie also believed. Detective Dan seemed to be particularly interested in her ex-husband as a person of interest. He was also interested in the mysterious Clark, Lydia's supposed boyfriend, but neither Natalie nor I had any knowledge of him. We didn't even know his last name.

The questioning lasted until early afternoon, and when they finally let us go, I could see that Natalie was drained. As we walked out the door, she said, "I couldn't have gotten through this without you, James, but that has to change. I simply have to toughen up and find some strength within myself. I have long avoided conflict and difficult things by hiding in my house and burying myself in work. That isn't working this time. I'm sorry, James. I need to make some changes."

I responded by reassuring her that she was doing alright, and then she spoke again, appearing to be surprised by what she was thinking. "James, I haven't had an anxiety attack since we have been together, despite the extreme stress that we have been under."

"If I have that effect on you, Natalie, that means you are no longer alone in this world – and I am no longer without the woman I love. Together we are both stronger."

CHAPTER THIRTY-THREE

TUESDAY JUNE 18 - THE CONFESSION

James

Natalie holds back, and I don't know why. We are very much in love, but there is something wrong. Maybe she's just tired and there are too many unknowns in her life right now, but for some reason she seems hesitant to let me in. We need to have a conversation about this, but not now. I also must take care of making arrangements for us to stay in San Francisco a few days longer. We have to be available to the SFPD, but I also must have access to all of their information that would impact the investigation in Coventry.

When I went to my room to shower and dress, I called the Mayor of Coventry to explain the situation to him.

"Mr. Mayor, I have a request. I need four more days in San Francisco and so does Natalie LaPierre. As you know, a body presumed to be Lydia Abbott has been discovered, and the investigation is in full swing. I need to be here for information gathering, and Ms. LaPierre needs some time to organize Ms. Abbott's affairs, as her executor and property manager. What we learn could very well impact our murder investigation involving Lydia Abbott's mansion in Coventry. We already missed our scheduled flight yesterday, because we were again summoned for questioning by the SFPD."

The mayor was very receptive to my request and gave us until Friday to tie up loose ends. He offered assistance and said matter-of-factly, "My secretary will take care of changing flights and extending reservations at your hotel. She can also coordinate with your secretary, James, if that meets your approval. I'll extend your reservations to a Friday departure. That will give you four extra days." And then he put on the pressure: "James, I understand how important this is, so I'll approve it, but we need to get this Abbott case closed as quickly as possible. The people of Coventry are nervous about Dale's killer being on the loose, and it's not good for the image of our community. Let's get it wrapped up."

The mayor's expectations bothered me, but I responded with all due respect. "I understand, sir, and I'll make every effort to get this wrapped up as soon as possible. Thank you for the extra time to make that happen."

I also called Dan Battista, the detective in charge of Lydia's case in San Francisco for an update on the forensic study of her townhouse, but they had not yet completed it. After that, I went to San Francisco City Hall and then did some shopping. Natalie was tired and rested in her room.

At 11 a.m., I returned and checked on Natalie who had showered and dressed for the day. I told her about the change of plans, and she seemed very agreeable. We decided to take a day trip to Muir Woods and have dinner at a winery.

We both enjoyed the drive, but after exploring Muir Woods, she turned to me and said, "James, don't start the car just yet. There is something you need to know about me before we go any further with our relationship. After you hear what I have to say, you can decide where you stand with our relationship. You may no longer respect me."

"What are you talking about, Natalie? What could be as bad as that?"

"Hear me out, James. This is important. I have not been honest with you about Dale's death and my trip to the mansion. As I told you, the morning I picked up my mother's journals at Abbott House, I saw Dale alive in the entry. That is the truth. But... that isn't the only time I was there and wasn't the only time I saw him. In the early morning hours of the next day – about 2 a.m., I went to the mansion again at Lydia's request. She had asked me to pick up a metal box in the crawl space of the Abbott basement. She was adamant that I do it in the middle of the night to avoid detection, but I'm not sure why. I wasn't supposed to tell anyone about what I had done for her, and I didn't, but on the way out of the basement, when my bag caught on a nail, I found Officer Forbes lying alongside the stairs, dead. I presumed that he had fallen, and I knew he was dead by the looks of his injury. Horrified, I ran as fast as I could back to my house. I thought it was my fault, because he was most likely looking for an intruder and fell accidentally. That intruder would have been me."

Natalie hesitated by avoiding direct eye contact with me. I finally said, "Please continue, Natalie. Don't make assumptions about this until we can discuss it together."

She spoke in a barely perceptible voice. "James, I did lie to you when you asked me if I had returned to the mansion after I picked up the journals. I withheld evidence from you and your investigation, because Lydia told me that I must keep this a secret, and I was also concerned about being implicated in Dale's death. Now that we know Lydia is dead, keeping this a secret no longer matters. Nevertheless, I am the one who needs to take responsibility for my actions. I am ashamed and sorry, James."

I was silent for several minutes, and then I got up and paced the room before I responded. "Natalie, thank you for telling me this, but I'm not going to report it right now, and we might not have to report it at all. It may not be that important, given the discovery of the body only a couple of days later. I love you, and nothing is going to change that. Now I have a couple of questions to ask you."

"Natalie, did you kill Dale Forbes?" She looked surprised and troubled at the question.

"No, of course not, James. I hope you don't think... I went to the cellar at Lydia's request to remove a metal box. Otherwise I wouldn't have set foot in the place at 2 a.m. I don't even know what is in the box. She was adamant that I wasn't seen and that no one else learned of what I had done. Why, I don't know."

"I have one more question, Natalie. Did you see or hear anyone else in the Abbott mansion or in the cellar?"

She was a bit more tentative, but then responded. "I don't think so, James. At one point, I did hear some noises toward the top of the cellar stairs, but I thought it was a rat. When I tried to switch on the lightbulb hanging from the ceiling, it was burned out, so I couldn't see much with only my small flashlight."

Taking her hands in mine, I said emphatically, "Natalie, I know that everything you have told me is the truth. Let this investigation play out, and if it doesn't go in the direction of the truth, we'll revisit our conversation. There is one other thing you should know. Today, I heard from Dunivan with an update of the Abbott mansion case. After examining the photographs you took, the experts think you may have inadvertently caught the image of another person standing behind the semi-sheer curtains in what looks to be a bedroom – maybe Lydia's bedroom. You will need to look at the picture when we return. It may be nothing, but it may be something that only you would be able to explain. Also, about the lightbulb in the cellar… It wasn't burned out. It had been turned in the socket until the bulb wouldn't light. Someone wanted the cellar to be completely dark." Natalie didn't speak or respond for a minute or so, and when she finally did, I saw fear in her eyes.

"That possibility is so frightening, James. Just thinking about someone else being in the mansion besides Dale and me sends a cold chill through my body. I could be the one dead, if Dale hadn't interrupted me in the library."

"Natalie, let's put the case behind us for a while. We need to move on and have a nice dinner at the winery down the road." I was happy to see a smile return to her face and a sense of relief in her body language.

As we traveled through the scenic countryside, I was thinking about Natalie's disclosure, and technically, it should be reported as part of the evidence. But aside from my concern about her, I didn't want to muddy the waters by throwing her into the suspect pool. Such a disclosure could actually bog down the investigation. Processing another suspect takes a good deal of time. I know she didn't kill Dale, and even though she was in the basement, there was a good chance that she would never have come across Dale's body, due to the darkness and the position of the corpse. Natalie didn't tell me anything I didn't already know, except that she had taken something from the house for Lydia Abbott, which is not illegal. Nevertheless, it is strange that Lydia wanted Natalie to go to the mansion in the middle of the night, unseen. Lydia must have had a reason for keeping it secret, but It's unfortunate that she can no longer tell us why. That might provide some answers as to why she and Dale were murdered.

CHAPTER THIRTY-FOUR

JUNE 18 – BLUE VELVET

Natalie

I felt relieved after I had finally told James the truth, but I don't want him protecting me. If he doesn't add my information to the report of Dale and Rose-anne's death, I have decided that I will. He just looked at me and said, "I don't think it's going to be that important, Natalie. Retrieving the metal box for Lydia wasn't illegal, but the circumstances of secrecy were somewhat strange. As for withholding evidence…we'll deal with that later, if necessary."

The vineyards at the winery looked surreal against the setting sun – like a painting from a time long past. It was serene, and I felt peaceful here with James. We were good together and happy together, and most of all, deeply in love.

After finishing our meal, we relaxed in the lovely setting. James looked a bit nervous, and I didn't understand why, until he pulled out a blue velvet box from his pants pocket and set it on the table. It was completely unexpected, and I began to shake, nervous that it was an engagement ring -- or that it wasn't.

With a smile, James said, "I've been busy today, Natalie, as he opened the lid. A beautiful diamond caught a glint of the sunset as he looked into my eyes and said, "Will you finally marry me? I have been in love with you for twenty-seven years."

I was speechless for a minute or so, and when I found my voice, I said simply, "Yes, my love. It's about time."

The smile never left James' face, as he took my hand and talked about planning a wedding and a future together.

"Well, all we have to decide is when. I have an idea – now don't be shocked, and you can say "no," if you don't like it. How about tomorrow at San Francisco City Hall? It's a famous place for weddings, and we may never get out here again – and the truth is, I have no intention of ever letting you go. This morning, I stopped to see the clerk, and there is no waiting period for a marriage license in California. We're not kids anymore, and we can do what we want—without worrying about what anyone else thinks. You can shop for a dress tomorrow after breakfast. If we delay until we get back to Coventry, we may have a long wait, given what we're dealing with."

James was silent for a minute -- and then continued. "I've done some checking, and there is an opening for a ceremony tomorrow at 3:30 p.m. The clerk said that he knows of a great photographer -- actually his 90-year-old Sicilian uncle -- who will take pictures for $100. He also knows of some witnesses who dress well and work cheap -- the clerk's words, not mine, -- his daughter and her boyfriend. They have been saving this special deal for two kids in love. I guess that would be us. How about it, my love?"

I finally found my voice and said softly, but with humor at our situation, "I thought you'd never ask. It's been twenty-seven years, James, and we're not getting any younger. Although we've now only been together for this short time, I can't imagine my life without you. Pick me up from my hotel room at 2:30 tomorrow, and we'll walk up the stairs of San Francisco City Hall together. ..and by the way, my love…you have been amazingly busy."

"Just a little busy, Natalie, but worth every minute of my time. I've been so worried that you would say 'no' and it would be over."

With a smile on my face, I said, "But there is another thing you may not like. Tomorrow is our wedding day. Until then, you must let your bride be a bride -- and there is another tradition that we must observe. You have to sleep by yourself tonight."

Driving back to the hotel, so light with happiness and love, that we seemed to fly as we followed the bright crescent moon to San Francisco.

CHAPTER THIRTY-FIVE

WEDNESDAY, JUNE 19 – SAN FRANCISCO CITY HALL

Natalie

Today, I bought my wedding dress at the bridal shop around the corner from the hotel. At forty-five years of age, I had given up on the idea that I would someday be married, but my day has come. My dress is a beautiful cream tulle, off-shoulder tea length style, and it suits me well. When I put it on, I feel like I'm twenty again, only better. I have loved James for twenty-seven years. We have waited long enough. This is the best day of my life –the day I will finally become the wife of the man I have always loved. This could have never happened with anyone else.

James

I took my blue sport jacket on this trip, but it's not good enough for our wedding. This morning, I walked down the street to a men's store and found a dark blue suit, a light blue shirt, and a medium blue tie. Although I've been married once before and have a daughter that I love very much, I've never stopped loving Natalie. Natalie and I lost each other when we were very young. We have a lot of time to make up for. This is our day and the beginning of our time together, and it won't be long enough if we live to be one-hundred.

Antonio, the friendly clerk at City Hall, has taken care of everything, including license, witnesses, and photographs. It's all falling into place. This is meant to be.

Natalie and James

Today is our wedding day. We were married under the rotunda, and the sunlight from the soaring windows created a magical setting. The witnesses were the clerk's daughter and her boyfriend, and they took their roles seriously, dressing well for the ceremony and being very helpful. The photographer, Lucca, is the clerk's ninety-year-old uncle from Sicily. I guess you could say it was something of a family affair.

We asked them to have dinner with us, and they accepted. Lucca said, "Thank you for the invitation." Looking at Maria and Gino, he said, "We will go to dinner, won't we?" Maria and Gino nodded with approval, and we were off to the popular Italian restaurant around the corner, where we found other newlyweds also celebrating. Lucca gave the first toast, "All newlyweds must toast to a happy future and have a wedding dinner with friends. …and we are all friends joined together by the love of this man and woman. Much happiness and love for both of you forever and ever."

At dinner, there were several more toasts with our new Sicilian friends and friendly strangers. The waiters joined in with songs and lots of joyful laughter. It was apparent that our happiness was contagious. Delicious food, romantic serenades, and a wedding cake shared with the other restaurant customers -- we felt as though the lights of San Francisco were twinkling just for us.

CHAPTER THIRTY-SIX

FRIDAY, JUNE 21 - HOME AGAIN

Natalie

We arrived back in Coventry on Friday afternoon. James drove me to my house, and immediately afterward he went to the police station to check in. After more than a week together, it seemed strange to be apart, but James and I had decided, for the time being, that we wouldn't let anyone know of our marriage. We didn't want to distract from the Abbott case. I was exhausted, so having a three-day weekend to recover was a gift, courtesy of the Mayor of Coventry. It would be business as usual come Monday morning.

As much as I was looking forward to being home and settling in for a cozy evening with James, something didn't seem right. The interior of my house looked a bit untidy, and it seemed to smell slightly different -- a smell that I recognized but couldn't place. Since my concerns about the intangible were something I couldn't deal with at the moment, I decided not to give too much thought to such vague mysteries. Dropping my bags on the floor in the entry hall, I drove to M.J.'s house to pick up Charlie. Being the rather poorly behaved little Cairn that he is, Charlie immediately began whining and dancing on his hind legs, begging to be picked up and taken home. Once in the car, he made it clear that he wanted to sit in the front seat and look out the window. When we drove near the Dairy Queen, he began to beg for his favorite treat. Against my better judgment, I pulled into the parking lot. I guess I was indulging the both of us. After attaching his leash, Charlie and I sat outside on the picnic table eating our ice cream cones. He made quick work of his favorite treat and ate half of mine. Satisfied, he began to pull me toward the car. Charlie wanted to go home. As we drove with his head on my lap, he let out a contented sigh and went to sleep. He was a happy dog, and I had missed my headstrong little guy more than I realized.

As soon as we pulled into my driveway, Charlie began wagging his tail and making excited whining noises, but when we entered the front door, his reaction became more aggressive. Charlie began to bark and run wildly from room to room, as though he was searching for something. My first thought was that I needed to get this dog into obedience school, because his behavior was worse than usual. Dissatisfied that he found nothing on the main level, he barked and climbed the stairs toward the attic door. I followed, but stopped short of entering when I noticed that the door was ajar. I never leave it open, because the attic is not insulated. The air inside is warm enough to heat up the house on a sunny day in late June and to drastically cool it down in January. There have been too many things out of place during the past month — the small writing desk I had tripped over in the dark; the pictures that were just a bit askew on the walls; the doors and drawers of the secretary that were not quite closed properly. And instinctively I knew -- someone has been coming into my house, despite the installation of the new locks. The idea that some-one could be in my house right at that moment sent me running blindly down the stairs, while calling for Charlie to follow. When I reached the front porch, I was relieved to run into Mrs. Bergstrom's tall, blond, nephew John, almost knocking us both over.

"Natalie, what is it?"

"John...I think someone is upstairs in my attic. Charlie won't stop barking!"

"I'll go up and check. You stay right here by the entrance door," John said nervously. Before I could stop him and suggest calling the police, he had bounded up, taking two steps at a time. He was gone for a few minutes. When he reappeared, it was with a squirming Charlie in his long arms. Charlie contin-ued growling, and when John put him down, he tried to go back upstairs.

"All Clear, Natalie -- no one is there, and I checked all of the rooms and closets. Maybe Charlie is just excited to be home, or maybe a nesting bird got into your attic. I thought I heard some bird sounds, but I couldn't see anything. In any case, Natalie, I want you to come over to my aunt's house for a while, because I think you have had a scare and need to calm down."

I protested and said, "But won't the commotion disturb your aunt?"

"Oh... I forgot to tell you. Aunt Ragna has gone to stay with her niece in Minneapolis — at least for a while. She needs more care and doesn't want to go to a nursing home. I'm taking care of the house for her until I have to go back to Norway in a month or two."

John looked embarrassed when we entered his aunt's house and said with a nervous laugh, "I must get this place cleaned up very soon. I guess I'm not much of a housekeeper. Maybe I need to hire one."

It was obvious that neither Mrs. Bergstrom nor John had been taking care of the place, but given my elderly neighbor's weakened condition, she didn't have the strength. There were piles of papers on nearly every surface and dirty plates and cups on the coffee table and end tables. John walked me back home after an hour of conversation, during which I caught up on the neighborhood news. It seems that Mrs. Evans, who lives across the street, had contacted the police on two occasions because she suspected nighttime prowlers. I said, "Maybe it's our night owl neighbor, Dewar." John just smiled and didn't respond. It also seems that her boyfriend Rocky is still there, but there are fewer visits from his unsavory friends. Most disturbing of all, however, I learned that John's great-aunt Ragna Bergstrom is not doing well in Minneapolis. I asked for the address of her daughter so that I could mail off a card and letter.

John looked around the disorderly house and said with a self-conscious smile, "Give me some time to find it, please."

"Of course, I will, John," responding nonchalantly, as I turned to go into my house. "I'll check with you tomorrow." And it was at that point he said something that surprised me.

"Oh, Natalie, how is your leg? All healed now?"

"Yes, it's fine, John," I said casually. But suddenly, I was taken aback -- I didn't think I had told anyone about my leg, I also began to wonder why John was on my front porch when I ran down my stairs. My trust in him was eroding.

My first instinct was to call James and express concern about the open attic door and the condition of my house, but I decided to wait. He needed to tend to business at work, and I must learn to deal with my fears and anxiety on my own, if at all possible.

At 6 p.m., James walked in with a bag of groceries and a smile. "Hi, I'm home!" We fell into each other's arms, sending the contents of the bag to the floor.

Feeling loved in his welcoming embrace, I said, "So, this is what marriage is like, my love -- impulsive, sometimes messy, and frequently wonderful." I had been missing too many of life's small pleasures without realizing it. I took his hand and we walked to my bedroom. Dinner could wait.

By the time we ate, we were so hungry that we settled for steaks, toast and a quickly thrown together salad. To starving lovers, the food was delicious, the atmosphere was cozy, and Charlie had quieted down. He sat next to James, his head resting on one of his shoes, dogpaddling and emitting small, occasional squeaks, as happy dogs sometimes do when they sleep. James was obviously amused with his new found canine friend, and I began to tell him about Charlie's alarmist reaction when we returned to my house after the trip. He listened intently with a knitted brow and a scowl that became darker as I chattered on. I also told him about the strange odor and the items in my house that I had found to be in disarray or moved about on a few occasions. I thought James might make light of my suspicions, but his reaction was quite the opposite. He suddenly turned serious. "Natalie, I want to see the attic -- now."

"Why, James? You're scaring me."

When James saw my reaction, he toned down his rhetoric and said, "I'm sorry, Natalie. I don't mean to alarm you, but what you are describing is concerning to me and needs to be checked out."

CHAPTER THIRTY-SEVEN

JUNE 21 – EVENING

James

Natalie was watching, as I looked in every corner of the attic. I had sent her downstairs for plastic bags, sticky notes, and a pair of tweezers. After cleaning the tweezers with alcohol, I went to work, and Natalie watched me with a serious face. I could tell that she was afraid of what I would find.

"Now I'd like to see the hidden compartment in the false chimney." Natalie nodded and opened the hidden panel. We found the metal box still inside. If someone had been here searching, they hadn't found it. I smiled and said, "Good for you, Natalie, for creating such a well-hidden compartment."

"I can't take the credit for the secret hiding place in the chimney. It's really a Nazi hiding place, and it was already here when Mother and I moved into this house in 1957." James look at me with a quizzical face and said, "Nazi?".

"I'll tell you about it when we have more time."

Since the box seemed to have survived intact, we decided to leave it in the chimney, at least for now. It was still light outside, and I didn't want to be seen carrying it to the car.

In the living room, I surveyed the secretary and the small writing desk from Abbott House but didn't touch them. Instead, I made a call to law enforcement for an investigative crew to check for fingerprints and other evidence.

"Pack a bag, Natalie," I said, sounding a bit too much like a police chief. "We're going to my apartment. You can't stay here until we have an idea of what has been going on and why. I'm concerned about your safety, given your close ties to Lydia and the Morgan Street mansion. We can't take any chances that someone might be after you for the same reason they came after her. There are simply too many unanswered questions."

Natalie

My house was swarming with law enforcement personnel within five minutes. Nevertheless, I said, "James, come sit with me in the swing. I have something important to discuss with you." I was going to mention the metal box in the false chimney. I wondered if it should be removed by either him or me so that it wasn't confiscated at this point.

"I'll be right with you Natalie," James said, as he walked over to his assistant chief, Michael Dunivan. Dunivan, as he was referred to by colleagues and friends alike, seemed to have information for him, and that made me nervous. I walked into the kitchen, where I waited for a half an hour, as I cleaned up the remains of our dinner.

James was most definitely in charge, and I was surprised that the officers referred to him as "Sully." I began to wonder when he was going to tell them that I had recently confessed to leaving the scene of a murder with something that could have been evidence. Perhaps he had already told Dunivan, and he was pushing James into taking action. They kept looking at me as they talked. I noticed that James' face had darkened, and his brow was knit into the scowl that I now know is a sure sign that something is troubling him. He walked to the porch and stood alone for several minutes. I wondered if I had become a suspect in Dale's murder, or at the least, a "person of interest."

I watched James walk slowly into my house from the porch where the investigation was wrapping up. Not only was he in charge, but he was well respected by his men. *I must never ruin that for him*, I thought to myself, but perhaps I had already done so or something close to it. I waited for him to tell the investigative team about the box that is supposed to be in my attic, but he never revealed my secret, so I didn't have to ask him about it right now. Once everyone was gone, and we were standing on the front porch alone — James, me, Charlie, and an overstuffed suitcase, unexpected tears began to flood my eyes. "It's okay Natalie," James said as he took my hand. "I'm still here -- I'm still here – and I'm not going anywhere. I know you're overwhelmed by everything that has happened."

"I'm sorry, James. It just got the best of me for a minute, but I'm okay now," I said, lying through my teeth. I was scared to death – for a lot of reasons.

After the house was locked and a tape that said, 'keep out' was on my front door, I noticed that there was a manila envelope, nearly invisible among the flowers in the white wicker planter. Evidentially, the forensic team hadn't looked there. I picked it up and tucked it in the bag on my shoulder. I knew it was from Mr. Nelson, the man I had paid to translate my great-grandmother Anna's journal. As we walked out the door, I remembered the journals in my bedroom bookcase. Impulsively, I said, "I need to pick up the other two journals from my bedroom. I'll be right back." I looked in the bookcase, expecting to find them, and my heart sunk. The two journals were gone – Beret's and my mother's. I had already read Beret's, but not Mother's. I was devastated at losing the information the leather-bound book might hold and angry at myself for not putting them in the chimney with the box.

CHAPTER THIRTY-EIGHT

JAMES' APARTMENT

Natalie

James' apartment was modern, neat and organized, just what I would have expected, and the simplicity of it all is what I need right now. It had floor to ceiling windows and a beautiful view of the river. The fact that it is a high security building is also something I can appreciate.

James noticed my interest and laughed when he said, "I'm not a decorator, Natalie." I just smiled and James, appearing to be a bit self-conscious, continued, "I rent this place, so the furniture and the decorating came with it. I wanted to make sure that the job worked out before I committed to a purchase. It's a little stark and sparse, but it makes upkeep easier for a busy man with a disorganized teenage daughter. I have never been good at dusting and cleaning, so I have a cleaning lady come in once a week."

I responded truthfully. "I think it's very stylish, in a big city way, and the lack of clutter is quite soothing to me."

James seemed pleased, as he slid my hand into his. "I'll show you around the place, so you know where everything is. I want you to be comfortable here, Natalie."

There were three bedrooms — his daughter's room and a guest room in one wing, and the master bedroom in another wing on the opposite end of the house. Before going down the hall to the master bedroom, he stopped in the foyer and picked up my suitcase and carried it down the hall to his room. Our eyes met when he laid my suitcase on his bed, and my smile of approval seemed to be what he was waiting for. This arrangement could be rather scandalous in the small city of Coventry — the police chief and the librarian cohabiting. But we are a married couple, so I said in a firm voice. "James, we need to talk about whether or not to announce our marriage. I think we are creating more of a distraction from the case by having people think we're not married. Remember, this is a small city, and there are definitely still attitudes about male/female relationships."

We both showered and got into comfortable clothes. James hadn't yet mentioned anything about announcing our wedding, but we were tired and went to bed. Before we went to sleep, while I was still in his arms, James broke his silence. "I don't blame you, Natalie, for not telling me right away about the night you went to Abbott House, he said quietly. I know you didn't want to be there, and I have come to understand the hold that the Abbott's have had on you and your family."

"But James, I have to take responsibility for withholding information from you."

He silenced me with a gentle finger to my lips and said softly, "Natalie, it was second nature for you and your mother to do the Abbott's bidding, and you had also been brought up to do what your mother expected. She was protecting her job and you. Lydia should never have put you in such a dangerous position and then asked for secrecy. There must be something in that box that she doesn't want anyone else to know about – and that includes you."

James was again quiet, seeming to weigh the pros and cons of his next concern. And then he continued:

"I have to decide whether or not to report your entry to Abbott House on the night of Dale's death. And by the way, Natalie, the medical examiner's report has listed Dale's cause of death as a homicide. His head injury wasn't from a fall. He was bludgeoned with a heavy object like a wooden mallet with a metal band around the end. The indentations are clearly visible on Dale's skull. This information hasn't been released to the media yet, so we must keep his cause of death quiet for a while. What we don't have is a motive."

This was the first time in my life that someone had made Lydia responsible for something I had done at her request. At that moment, I had more clarity about myself and my life than ever before, and I realized that Lydia wasn't the only one who took advantage of the power discrepancy between us. My mother also bore some responsibility for perpetuating the idea that I must obey the Abbotts. While I understood that she was operating on the premise that obedience and keeping secrets keep people like us safe, Mother didn't realize that she was also placing me in danger. She had plied me with enough fear to achieve a mentality of subservience that began in my childhood. I am also not without responsibility. I should have dealt with these issues long ago, but perhaps I felt safe in the vise of obedience, as had she.

Tonight, I felt very safe in James' arms, but I couldn't let him take a fall for me. I wouldn't enslave him as I had been enslaved, because in time, he would want to be free, and we both would lose.

CHAPTER THIRTY-NINE

MONDAY, JUNE 24

Natalie

After a quiet weekend with James, driving to the lake and eating at out-of-the-way quaint inns, it was time to go back to work. I entered Coventry City Hall on Monday morning, and a boisterous M.J. nearly bowled me over with a huge hug. "God, I missed you girl! It's been too long. This place can't run without you, and those volunteers are hopeless. I'm so glad you're back!" I was glad that M.J. wasn't holding a grudge because of the words we had before I left for San Francisco, but what she said about the volunteers wasn't true. My volunteers were very efficient, and I had only been gone for a little more than a week -- but that was quintessential M.J. – boisterous and proprietary toward me.

I could tell that M.J. was waiting for a response to her comments. I wanted to refute what she had said about my volunteers, but right now, it wasn't worth it. "It's good to be back, M.J., and I can't thank you enough for taking Charlie while I was gone. I would like to pay you, if that's okay."

"Good God, Girl," M.J. said in a brash voice. "You know I love that little troublemaker. Frank came over a few times and we took him for some long walks along the river. Thanks to Charlie, I finally got a little exercise. Don't even think about paying me for doing something for my best friend – something I enjoy."

I was grateful for what she did and for the peace of mind it gave me while I was away, but I said, "If you won't take money, I'll find something else for you

135

my friend." After giving her a hug, I walked through the library doors to what I knew would be a mountain of paperwork.

My bag, sitting alongside my desk, contained the translation of great-grandmother Anna's journal, and I was eager to read it, but I dared not start before I finished my work to a point that was at least acceptable. When James appeared in the doorway, looking for all the world like a young man in love, an exasperated M.J was right behind him. "Sorry, Natalie. I told him you were very busy, but he said he had to see you." James came to my desk and put his arms around my shoulders, much to M.J.'s surprise. "Oh... I see," she snipped. "It must have been a very productive trip." And with that proclamation, she whirled herself around and went out the door, but not before giving it a good, hard slam.

"Come here," James said, as he pulled me behind the stacks where we shared a passionate kiss.

"Is this what you came for, Chief Sullivan?"

James smiled and kissed me again, but he then turned serious. "I have something important to share with you, so let's sit down." We went to the far end of the library where there was a sitting area located behind a mahogany paneled divider.

"The forensics report on your house is in, and I found it to be very interesting, or I should say disturbing. We didn't find a full set of prints anywhere, except for a few of yours and mine in the kitchen and the bedroom. The rest of the house, including the attic, appears to have been wiped down. It seems that your home was invaded sometime between the time you left for San Francisco and the day you returned."

When I heard his news, I felt a cold chill from head to toe, and the hair on my head stood on end. "What should I do now, James?"

"Well," he said, "you can't go back to your house or even go inside under any circumstances, unless I am with you. We must figure this out, but I need to take a statement from you when we get to station. Natalie, I also have to ask you to disclose the fact that you entered Abbott House on the night Dale was killed."

My heart sank, but I knew it was the right thing to do. James continued, "You need to say that you were there at Lydia's request, to retrieve some of her property, which is true and not illegal. We will turn in the box, but not just yet. I also don't want you to say that you saw Dale at the bottom of the stairs because the body was difficult to see in the dark. At a later time, we may need to acknowledge that you found Dale lying alongside the cellar steps dead -- or maybe not. Remember, everything you did at the house was at Lydia's request, and of course, the journals were your property."

"Why, James? I would rather disclose what really happened right now."

"Natalie, there was another finding that we believe places you at imminent risk. The white dandruff-like particles that were throughout Lydia's San Francisco townhouse were also found in your house and the mansion. That leads us to believe that you are being stalked by the same person who killed Lydia. The state crime lab is in the process of comparing them, but based on preliminary findings, they are suspiciously similar. We don't want to place you in more danger. There will be time to give more information when we have to."

James continued, "Tonight you and I will go into your house to retrieve the box in the attic. We can't leave it there any longer, but I want to wait until dark. It wouldn't be smart to allow anyone to see us coming out of your house carrying it, especially if an unknown person might be trying to get it for himself. Someone may be watching. ...and one last thing, Natalie. Can you go down to Law Enforcement and take a look at the photos? Maybe you can answer some questions."

I said, "Sure, James. I'll go down on my lunch break."

James was going out on a limb for me, and while I would go along with him for the moment, I also knew that I wouldn't let him be discredited, if it comes to that. "I won't let you destroy your credibility and career because you are protecting me," I said in a firm voice that sounded like I meant what I said. ...and I did.

"We'll get through this Natalie. I promise. You haven't done anything to endanger anyone but yourself. As for obstructing a murder investigation, you did tell me, so I am taking responsibility when it comes to disclosing evidence. Oh, and Natalie – please walk down to law enforcement to take a look at the photographs of Abbot House – as soon as you can." His protective attitude towards me was both reassuring and disturbing. I feared for him more than myself.

After a kiss that made me wish we were somewhere else, James left for work, and I pulled Erik Nelson's work out of my bag. He was scrupulous and very neat, so I assumed that the reading would be easy and hopefully wouldn't take too long.

There were twenty-five pages of typed transcription, obviously done on an old manual typewriter with uneven type and a few keys that were damaged, but Mr. Nelson had also placed a handwritten note inside the manila envelope:

> Dear Ms. LaPierre,
>
> I thoroughly read your great-grandmother's journals, and as I did so, I developed an understanding of the private nature of her writings. Please be assured that this information will remain with me and will not be shared with anyone else.
> Sincerely,
> Erik Nelson

I hadn't yet read my great-grandmother's journal, and it was close to noon. I needed to keep my promise to James. I locked the journal in my desk and walked down the hall to Law Enforcement, where they were expecting me. The photographs were laid out on a table, alongside a magnifier that would enlarge them onto a screen. I looked at each one and found nothing suspicious, until I focused on the picture taken in Lydia's bedroom. I could see the shadow that James was talking about. It did look like the form of a man, but I would never have found it myself. I don't remember the Abbotts placing anything behind the drapes – ever. It would have been visible from the outside, and they would have considered that unacceptable.

I finally commented. " It looks suspiciously like a human form, but I can't be absolutely sure. I do know, however, that there has never been an object of any kind placed behind the drapes in Lydia's room. That's all I can say without going to the mansion myself and having another look."

The photography expert said, "That can probably be arranged, Ms. LaPierre."

I walked back to my office in the library with an uneasy feeling. I did think there was a person behind those drapes, and that I had most likely dodged another bullet. I lost my appetite for lunch, so I decided to read Anna's journal after some more catch-up work.

CHAPTER FORTY

ANNA'S JOURNAL

Monday, March 27, 1899

My brother Arne and I are starting our trip to America today. After leaving our home in Otta, Papa walked beside Arne and me for several miles to a place called Kringen where we took our leave of one another. His eyes glistened with tears when he hugged and kissed us good-bye. We spoke of a time when we will all be together again, but that is probably not true. We are just showing each other a brave face, hoping to keep the tears from coming.

Brother Arne cries all the time. I told him to leave me and return home, but he will not. He is too ashamed after father and mother scrimped, saved, and went without to save for our passage. And there are no jobs in Norway for either of us. Mama and Papa can't support all nine of us forever. Our older brother Ola is already in America, in a place called Green River, Minnesota. He will help us get settled when we get there.

Saturday, April 1, 1899

Arne and I are now in Liverpool after our boat trip to Hull and a noisy, dirty train ride. Papa paid for us to have a hotel room after we arrived, and when the time came, also arranged transportation to the boat. Two meals were included in the price of the room. We are lucky, thanks to Papa and Mama. Many immigrants cannot pay for lodging, so they sit on trunks and boxes on the wharf, sleeping upright in place, waiting for the big boats to take them to America. Some were there for days. The children and babies were crying with boredom and hunger.

The hotel is crowded and not clean. As I walk through the halls, I have seen large families sitting and sleeping on the floors of hotel rooms, waiting for their ships to arrive. They look sad and hungry. The mothers of crying children are gaunt with nerves and hunger, as they nurse infants and comfort their older children. Unwashed hands dip into nearly empty knapsacks looking for morsels to stop the hunger pangs. I am grateful that Mama and Papa took care to make sure we were fed when they booked our trip, even though the food is not what we are used to. All of the meat that we are given to eat seems to be mutton. The smell of mutton is foreign to us, and I have to force myself to eat it. The breakfasts have porridge that is runny, but there is herring. Surely there is better food than this in England, but if there is, it is not for immigrants like us. I am ashamed that I am complaining.

Arne continues to cry most of the time, and last night, he kept me awake. We sleep together in the small bed, with a rolled up blanket between us. I don't know what will help him. I hope being in a new country with more opportunity will lift his liquor. Last night I prayed to be spared from the bedbugs and the lice we have heard about. So far, I think my prayers have been answered. I awoke without the red bites on my ankles. I brushed my long hair carefully before knotting it on top of my head, as I do each day.

Monday, April 3, 1899

Arne and I boarded the Ultonia today, finally on our way to America. We signed on as a married couple so that we could stay together. Otherwise, the rules say that we must be separated ... me with the single ladies and Arne with the unmarried gents. We have separate bunks. Arne sleeps on the top bunk, and I sleep on the bottom. A family of four shares the compartment with us. We will keep to ourselves, because we don't want any questions, and we have been warned about pickpockets, thieves, and men who may try to take liberties with the girls. We are safer together, but I wish Arne would stop crying.

We have been on the big ship Ultonia for three days, and my brother Arne is very sick. He continues to lose his food. He has had nothing to eat and very little to drink, and with each day, his eyes grow larger as his face grows smaller. I was sick for one day, but now I am better. I force myself to eat, for I must keep up my strength. The food is good, and we have milk, fruit, and meat that is not mutton. Steerage is crowded and smells of unwashed bodies and vomit, but that is to be expected on a long ocean voyage, when a lot of people are living between decks. The stewards try to keep it clean by mopping the floors twice a day, but I know it is hard for them to keep up with so many people.

I don't like the man who is in the compartment with Arne and me. His face is beefy and red, and he is so tall that he cannot stand fully upright. His breath is foul with the smell of decay and ale. I think he must have brought liquor on board, which is against the rules. He is with his wife and two small pale children, but he pays little attention to them. He doesn't respect the situation that we are in, and at night I hear him taking his marital rights with his wife. I hear her crying softly, until the sounds of his pleasure stop. He looks at me often during the light of day. Twice he pretended he was falling and grabbed onto my breasts to steady himself. I am disgusted, and I try to avoid him. He complains about Arne's crying, and belittles him by saying to me in jest, "What is wrong with your wife?" He frightens me, but my anger overcame my fear, and I said, "I'm going to one of the ship's officers if you do that again." He did not touch me again, for there are strict rules about molesting women, especially young girls. If caught, any man who molested a woman would have been deported back to his home country. Arne looked ashamed that he did not help me, and I did not want any more shame added to his already heavy burden. "It's alright, Arne; it is best that I confront the beast."

Excitement! Today we arrived in Boston, USA. There was a bustle on the ship as the passengers gathered themselves and their belonging for the walk down the gangplank. The sun was shining in a bright blue early spring sky, and everything seemed larger and more colorful than in Liverpool. There were not so many people sitting around and looking hungry and sad, waiting to get on a boat.

We gathered our belongings, including the large wooden trunk with my name painted on the front. My father made it for me, so my hand lingered a bit longer than necessary, as though I could bring Papa to life in this strange country. After walking up and down the carriage stop, I finally found a wagon that would take us to the train station -- one that we could afford. The finer carriages were not for us, but I could not stop watching the ladies and gentlemen, beautiful in their colorful fabrics and fine hats, get into the velvet lined coaches. What is life like for such people, I thought to myself?

I counted my money carefully and found that while there was not a lot of it, we would not be hungry, if we continued to be frugal. Arne finally stopped crying, and as he looked at the purse that had been entrusted to me by our father, he had a sad look on his face. I think he felt ashamed that he has been unable to care for me, and more ashamed yet that Papa knew he was not the one to carry the burden of responsibility to America.

We must get past the medical examination that will allow us to remain in America. I have never had a doctor examine me before, and I was afraid that Arne would not pass inspection, due to his long illness on board the ship. I was not sure it was all from the seasickness. I thought it could have been from the liquor that he might have bought when I was in the toilets or at the dining hall. I discovered this when I asked Arne to count the money in his clip. Arne tearfully admitted that he had bought liquor on the ship from a man who was selling it the men's toilets. I was angry, but I kept my silence. Anger serves no purpose when we are in a strange country and must count on one another.

Arne stood in one line and I in another, and we waited our turn for two hours, according to the big clock in the waiting area. Finally, they called my name and then Arne's. It was over quickly, and the doctor signed our forms. We had made it to America, and soon we would board the train for the long journey to Green River and my brother Ola.

CHAPTER FORTY-ONE

Natalie

James came into the library at 5 p.m., and I put Anna's journal aside. I was able to spend an hour or so delving into it, but there will be more of the journal waiting for me when I am able to find the time.

"It's time to leave, Natalie, and I want you to come back to my apartment tonight. I don't want you to be alone right now"

"I would be fine, James. I don't want to impose on you, and I have to go to my house anyway to pick up a few things. Our marriage hasn't been announced, so it's probably better that I don't stay at your place quite yet."

"No Natalie. It's better that we don't go back to your house. You have your suitcases from our trip to San Francisco. They still have clothes in them, and you can use my laundry facilities, if you need to. We must figure out our living arrangements soon, Remember, we're a happily married couple, and I like having my wife around the house," he said, as a smile that crinkled his blue eyes lit up his face.

"Well, I guess you're a determined man, and I won't argue with you, I said rather coyly, as he drew me into his strong, warm embrace. People may start talking about the police chief and the librarian cohabiting, since they don't know we're married." That comment was a reminder that we soon need to make a decision about announcing our marriage.

During a candlelight dinner at James' apartment, he asked if I would be willing to go back to my house to pick up the box from the chimney later this evening. "There is a possibility that it could be found by our unknown stalker or his accomplices at any time, and I think it contains evidence and clues to what is really going on. Is 10:30 too late? I am concerned about being seen."

"Of course, I'll go with you, James, but we also need to have a discussion about announcing our marriage. People are talking, according to M.J., about the police chief and the librarian spending a week together in San Francisco. And it appears that we were seen going in and out of your apartment last weekend."

He laughed and said, "I think you mean that M.J. is talking, as usual. I also think she's more than a little jealous. She has a strong sense of ownership over you, Natalie. Well, she's just going to have to get used to the fact that you're now a married woman with a husband who can't take his hands off you."

"And vice versa," I said with a smile. "This is all so new to me –living, loving, and laughing with my husband -- I think I like it." And then we became quiet, just savoring this moment together.

James broke his silence and said, "I've been thinking about announcing our marriage too. Speculation can be much worse than the truth. We don't want to make this a source of gossip or a distraction from the Abbott House case. Natalie, what do you think about putting the news of our marriage in the Coventry Post? We can deliver a written paragraph tomorrow, and it will make the social pages of the Wednesday paper. I have already told my assistant, Michael Dunivan, and maybe you had better tell M.J. ahead of the announcement in the paper." James winked as he said, We can't have people talking, can we? We know how she worries about you."

"Okay, James. I'll write something and deliver it to the newspaper office tomorrow. What about Paige? Shouldn't you at least call her and break the news before she hears from someone else? I'm sure she has friends in Coventry who may mention it to her if they are corresponding this summer."

A pensive James responded. "I've been thinking about Paige myself, and I'll call her tomorrow morning. This will be a big surprise, but once she meets you, Natalie, she will love you."

I was more concerned than he was, probably because I had once been a fifteen-year-old girl myself. At that age, their emotions are all over the place. I wasn't at all sure that Paige would "love me."

CHAPTER FORTY-TWO

JUNE 24 -- NIGHT

Natalie

After dinner, James went back to the station for a couple of hours to catch up on more paperwork that had accumulated while we were in San Francisco. Because his apartment is in a security building, I felt safe being alone. Eager to continue reading my great-grandmother's journal, I settled into the sofa with Charlie at my side, but before I opened the yellowed pages, I made a decision. The loss of my other two journals had been devastating, and I needed to make one last effort to get them back, so I decided to make another search of my house. I was desperate to determine if my father's identity was within the pages of my mother's journal. I decided not to tell James, because he would disapprove and stop me before I left his apartment.

I parked the car two blocks from my house and walked in the alley before entering through the locked back door. My home seemed so eerie – so empty and abandoned, despite my furniture and other belongings still being inside. I wasn't sure where to start, but for some reason I went upstairs to the attic. This time the door was closed, so I pushed it open, knowing that it would make a squeaking noise from an unoiled hinge. Using my flashlight to examine the inside of the chimney and to look in every drawer and on every shelf of the furniture that was stored in this room -- I found nothing but the metal box.

The upstairs guest bedroom was my next stop, and finding nothing there, I moved down the stairs, but abruptly stopped midway, when I heard muffled voices. I thought to myself, *why didn't I listen to James? This was a mistake.* Terrified, I crept back upstairs and hid under the bed in the guest bedroom, which was a very tight squeeze. Sliding as best I could, I moved to where the headboard attached to the frame. The end of a sheet had slipped down into the crevice, and I was able to hide between it and the wall. There was definitely someone in my house besides me – likely more than one person. The footsteps and voices came from downstairs at first, and then I heard footsteps walking up the stairs, down the hall and into the attic. Judging from the sound of drawers being opened and rather noisily slammed, as well as the scraping of furniture on the old wood floor, it was clear that intruders were rifling around – until the squeaking sound of the unoiled hinge told me that they were out of the attic and had closed the door. When I heard them enter the guest room where I was hiding, I clasped my hand over my mouth to prevent any involuntary sounds of panic while they went through everything. It seemed as though I was hiding under the bed for hours, shivering with nerves, afraid I would give myself away. I couldn't see or hear anything that would identify them. They were silent as they searched everywhere, even looking under the bed where I was hiding. Finally, one of them spoke in an unidentifiable whisper. "There's nothing under there. Nothing would fit."

Finally, I heard footsteps go down the stairs and then heard a door shut, which I assumed was the back door. I waited at least twenty minutes before making my own exit the same way I entered, also through the back door, but not before checking the hiding place in the chimney to make sure the metal chest was still there. It was, and I thought, *thank you Mr. Klinghofer!*

I was amazed that I was able to put my fears and anxiety aside. This isn't something I would have considered undertaking, even a few weeks ago. My actions beg the question: Have I become more daring and brave or more stupid? *Probably a bit of both,* I thought.

CHAPTER FORTY-THREE

Natalie

When James burst into the front door of his apartment two hours later, he called out, "I'm home Natalie!" I had decided not to tell him of my adventure or misadventure just three hours before, but I will most likely have to eventually report that someone was trespassing and searching my home while I was on the premises -- just not now -- not tonight. There were other things to discuss.

I had resumed reading my great-grandmother's journal and was stunned and speechless at the revelations I encountered. James hugged me and planted kisses on my face, but he noticed something different about my demeanor. Even though I threw my arms around his neck, I was not myself. "What is it, Natalie?"

"James... I've just finished reading Anna's journal. I would like you to read parts of it -- just the important parts." I knew he was exhausted, and I was tempted to let him off the hook, but I also understood that this was important, maybe even significant to his investigation. James seemed to understand, as he scrutinized my face, that something was wrong. I had bookmarked the pages I wanted him to read, and as our eyes met, I handed the black leather book to my husband.

James read long enough to understand my state of mind. When he had finished, he handed it back to me and said, "Do you know what this means?"

In a voice that was hesitant, I said, "I think so. I think I know what it says, but that doesn't mean I fully understand what it means."

After a period of silence between us, James said with a weary smile, "Come to bed, my love. You must be very tired. We'll talk about this tomorrow and pick up the box in the chimney tomorrow night." It was certainly okay with me that he didn't want to go back to my house tonight. I had no desire to return – at least for a while.

Since James and I parted in 1963, I have always regretted not speaking to him of my feelings. Something inside me understood, even then, that this was a special man, and what we had known together was also special, but I couldn't see how making a life together could work out for us. I thought it was better to say nothing. Things are different now, and it's just the two of us. I didn't fail him this time.

Calling to my husband, I said, "I'm coming, James. And by the way, I love you, I always have – even on the day we parted so long ago." And then he surprised me with his response.

"I always knew that you loved me, Natalie. Even then. You were in a tough spot, and I decided not to push you any more than other people in your life already had. I just said a little prayer that it would all work out eventually. It took a while, but here we are. Maybe this is how it was meant to be." He smiled and took my hand. We walked to the bedroom together as though we had been doing it for twenty years.

CHAPTER FORTY-FOUR

Natalie

James fell asleep quickly, but I couldn't drift off, despite my exhaustion. There were matters to be resolved before I could rest. Resigned to what I must do, I placed my bare feet on the thick, beige carpet and got out of bed. The candle on the dresser still burned, allowing me to move about and find James' undershirt and my cardigan, which had been hastily removed the moment we walked into the bedroom. We were careless and had neglected to blow out the lingering flame. I extinguished the candle and quietly closed the door before turning on the hall light. Tired, but unable to sleep, I walked to the living room where Grandmother Anna's journal waited.

Nighttime didn't feel safe anymore, and a prickly, cold sensation of fear rippled through my body. I closed all of the window blinds in the living room before sitting on the sleek, modern couch. Getting back to my great-grandmother Anna's journal is weighing heavily on my mind. I must be sure of what she wrote and the implications.

Erik did a good job of translation from Norwegian to English – at least I hope he did it without embellishing and changing the meaning of my great-grandmother's words. Anna's words spoke volumes as I read of her journey to America and what she found when she arrived.

Today I leave Green River, and my brother Ola's cabin for Coventry. It is only about 15 miles from here, so the train trip will be short. Arne will stay with Ola for a while, but he must find work, because Ola is leaving Green River on August 15, and will not return. Ola has a rich widow with two children and a fine house waiting for him in Illinois. Ola has never met the rich widow, but he has seen her picture. She is rather stout, but not bad looking, as he told Arne and me.

Ola was approached by a relative of the woman's who lives in Green River. It seems that her dead husband had a hardware store, and the widow needs someone she can trust to take over the management. My brother Ola is a very hard-working, honest man, so I understand why the woman's relative thought he might make a good husband. After some thought about his own prospects, which seemed to be a long, uphill struggle, despite hard work, Ola agreed to marry the woman and move to a place near the big city of Chicago. I had counted on him being in Minnesota, so I feel nervous about being left with only Arne. He has taken to drinking liquor more often than he did in Norway.

Ola hasn't left us without a way of supporting ourselves. He has helped me find a housemaid position in Coventry, and Arne has found work with a farm family in Johnson's Prairie, where there are many Norwegians. They have a spare room in their big home where Arne can sleep. I pray that Arne will work hard and keep this job. If he doesn't, I don't know what will happen to him here in America. He will be more than 150 miles from me, and I have no place to take him in if he doesn't make good.

I was met at the Coventry train station by a grizzled man named John Jones, who appeared to be the Abbott's livery man and driver. "Get in, Miss," he said.

John Jones had an accent that sounded much like the people in Liverpool, and he spoke brusquely, seeming to be annoyed that he had to bother with me. I was surprised when he picked up my trunk and

threw it in the back of the carriage, as though it were a hatbox. After
he spit out his plug of tobacco, we were on our way.

I can tell that Coventry is more prosperous than Green River, because
most of the buildings are made of brick, and brick costs more than
wood, but there are also other signs. The train depot has a big, round
building, and the houses we saw on our way to the Abbott home
became larger and more fancy as we moved up the hill onto a street
called Morgan. Most of the ladies were dressed in rich looking clothing,
and they all wore beautiful hats. I looked down at my good dress and
felt ashamed and worried that the Abbotts wouldn't want such a plain,
poor little girl working in their fine house.

When I arrived at the home of the Abbott family, which Jones called
"Abbott House," I was amazed by how large and elegant it was. We
entered through the back door, and my heart was pounding with
fear. I can cook and clean, but maybe it isn't the kind of cooking
and cleaning they need. The main housekeeper, Tillie Johnson, was a
little gruff, and when she showed me to my small sleeping room, she
shook her head, sighed, and said, "Girlie, you're going to need a lot
of training." She gave me a black shift, and a white apron and cap,
and I worked until after the evening meal that they call dinner. The
family was dressed in fine clothes, like they were going to a party, but
there was no party – just the four of them and a cousin from Wales. I
have never seen such in my life.

Sunday, June 11, 1899

I have been working beside Tillie from dawn until bedtime. I'm still
afraid of her, but she seems to be warming up to me a little. The other
hired girls laugh behind her back and say that she is fat. She is large,
but she moves well, and when she hears Mrs. Abbott's bell, she moves
up the stairs as swiftly as a slim young girl.

Tillie doesn't use my God given name. She calls me "Girlie." I have
learned a good deal from her this week, and yesterday I found out what
my assigned duties will be. Starting Monday, I will set the tables for
all their meals and stand by in case they need something. The other
hired girl, Bridget, serves the meal. She is tall, slim and very pretty,

153

but so pale of skin and hair. I feel a bit self-conscious with my short, sturdy darkness

Old Mr. Daniel Abbott never speaks or looks at me, but he is kind, and I am not afraid of him. He is more interested in being in his library where he works for hours every day. He has many business associates visiting him. I have also heard the maids say that he owns some of the railroad that crosses the country from east to west. I know nothing of that either, except if there is truth to it, he is a very rich man.

According to the kitchen gossip, Mr. Abbott is supposed to have a young mistress downtown, which is where he goes when he leaves for his evening walk. She lives above his hardware store in an apartment and acts like a fine lady. They say she is beautiful, with hair the color of a chestnut mare and skin like the Chinese figurines in the curio cabinet. Perhaps that is why Mrs. Abbott does not talk with Mr. Abbott very much. I have heard that Mr. Abbott's mistress came to town with a traveling acting troupe. He saw her, and she never left Coventry. I wondered why such a lovely young woman would want to be with an old man like Daniel Abbott. All I know is that he sometimes doesn't come home until dawn breaks, and then goes to his small bedroom at the end of the upper hall.

The younger son Thomas doesn't seem to work very much. He is mostly in the carriage house smoking and talking to the livery man Jones. I have also noticed that the hired girl Bridget seems to have eyes for Thomas. I once saw her go into the carriage house a few minutes after he entered. While they were inside, the doors were closed, and when they opened again, she came out and her pale hair was undone, and her blouse was coming out of her skirt.

Thomas looks at me often, and once he brushed up against my backside when he entered the kitchen. Another time he was bolder, and as he walked by me, he pretended to stumble and put his hands on my breasts. He is a large man and has heavy features, but there is also a handsome countenance to him. But any handsome features are lost on me, because when he looks at me, it makes me feel naked and scared. It also makes the other hired girl, Bridget, angry. I have heard Tillie *tell her that she had better get her mind off Mr. Thomas if she knows what's good for her, and that he's not for the likes of her.*

Mrs. Marguerite Abbott, the lady of Abbott House, is from Wales. She has white hair and looks very old and tired. One of the hired girls told me that she is much younger than her husband, Daniel Abbott, but looks older, with large, craggy features, like her son Thomas. Mrs. Abbott wears black every day. According to kitchen gossip, she has had many pregnancies, but only Thomas survived, and the other son, Ellsworth, is adopted. Perhaps she is sad with loss. Mrs. Abbott pays no attention to me. Only Tillie is allowed into her room to clean or to help her with her bath and dressing. Mr. and Mrs. Abbott do not share a room. The Abbotts seem to see each other only at meals, and then they do not talk much. Most of the talking is between Old Mr. Abbott and his older adopted son Ellsworth. I must go to sleep now. I have written enough about this family.

CHAPTER FORTY-FIVE

JUNE 25, 1991 - 2 A.M.

Natalie

I took a break from reading and had a cup of tea and some toast, hoping to settle my queasy stomach, but my mind was still on my great-grandmother's diary. At one point, I thought I heard the sound of footsteps in the hallway, but then there was no sound at all – only silence. I blamed my overactive imagination on all that has happened in such a short time. Feeling better, I reached for Anna's journal and once again began to read her story:

Tuesday, July 4, 1899

> *The excitement of today's parade and fireworks at the lake set the Abbott house buzzing. This morning, Tillie and I made up the food for the big Fourth of July picnic. I put fried chicken, beans, cabbage salad, potato salad, and chocolate cake inside each of the brown woven baskets and lined them up neatly on the kitchen table. They were ready to be picked up and placed in the wagon that would take us to the celebration on Lake Crystal. The Abbotts are going to the pavilion, where there would be a concert and some fireworks after dark. Once all the daily duties and food preparations were completed, the housemaids were told that we could go to the parade in downtown Coventry, and then Jones would drive us in the open wagon to sit on the shores of the lake with many of the other townspeople. The beautiful white pavilion was not for us. It's only for the most important citizens of Coventry,*

but that didn't matter. We were all happy and looking forward to a special day of fun at the lake. This would be my first time of celebrating American Independence Day, and I almost feel like a real American. And then, Tillie asked me to go to the carriage house to tell Jones how many of us would be going. If only I had asked Tillie to choose someone else to take my place, but how was I to know what was in store for me.

I walked quickly to the carriage house and went inside the open door. I called for Jones, but no one answered, and I heard the door close behind me. It was but a few seconds later that I felt a strong arm wrap around my breast and pull me into the pile of straw in the corner. I didn't know what to say, so I said nothing, until my dress was raised. "No, please," I said in a small, scared voice. The carriage house was lit low from the small north facing windows, but I knew who it was before I saw a face. I could smell the familiar scent of the shaving cologne he brought home from the barber shop downtown. Thomas Abbott was on top of me more quickly than I could speak, mumbling about how he found me so beautiful that he couldn't take his eyes off me.

"I have tired of that ghost Bridget, his voice growing louder. Her skin is like the white belly of a fish. Lay still girl! You have no rights in this house."

I began to cry and beg and say, "no, no, please no." But that didn't stop him. The pain was sharp and sudden, and he seemed to go on forever in his pleasure. Suddenly it was over, and he was breathing hard, as he quickly fastened his belt.

"Don't you tell anyone, Missy! No one will believe a housemaid's tale, anyway."

Hurt and bleeding, I limped to the back door where I was met by Tillie. She was angry at my tardiness and raised her voice, asking me what I had been doing, and then I fainted. When I regained consciousness, she asked me if Mr. Thomas hurt me. I nodded and said, "But don't tell anyone. I'll lose my job."

She undressed me and washed me with warm water and soap and put me in my small bed. "I will keep your secret, as long as your body doesn't betray you, Girlie. I hope there is no baby to give you away." I hadn't thought of that until she mentioned it, and a sickening shame weighed heavily on my entire body. I could hardly breathe.

I stayed in bed all day and night, full of pain and fear. I wanted my mother, but I also knew that she is too far away, and even if she were here, I would be too ashamed to tell her what happened to me in the carriage house and to ask for her comfort.

Friday, September 1, 1899

Today I had to go to Tillie and tell her that I have not had my time of the month since Thomas had his way with me in the carriage house. I asked her what to do.

She said, "Girlie, you're going to have an Abbott baby, but no one can know about that part. We have to say that it belongs to someone else. I will figure out something to say to Mr. and Mrs. Abbott."

I am so filled with shame and fear, but Tillie said that she was going to arrange something. I am to wait to hear from her. By the next day, I had her answer to my problems when she knocked on my door with a solution that involved Mr. Jones and his drunken son, Evan.

"Girlie, Evan Jones has agreed to marry you. His father will take you to the county seat tomorrow and the judge will marry you in his chambers. No one knows who the father of your child really is—not even Jones and his son, Evan."

I am wondering why Evan Jones would agree to this arrangement. Is there something in it for him? My thoughts were interrupted by Tillie, "By the way, Evan is going to start working as a yard man here at Abbott House. It was then that I knew my secret was not so much of a secret. The Abbott's had to be involved in this arrangement, because Evan had asked for work many times before. Why hire him now, unless it was a payoff that protected their son Thomas and the Abbott family reputation?

I am repulsed by Evan Jones. He is as large and sloppy as his father is taut and wiry. He lives with his father in a house no better than a shack, and I have no intention of living there. For the time being, we have agreed that I would sleep in my maid's room at Abbott House, until he could find another place for us. I was grateful that I didn't have to live with this unclean, beastly man for a while. Tomorrow will be my wedding day, and I knew in my heart that it would be the second worst day of my life.

Tuesday, September 5, 1899

Today I was married in the county courthouse, but I made no special effort to be pretty for this stranger who stood beside me in the judge's chambers. Tillie has helped in many ways and tells me that no one knows anything about what happened in the carriage house or that Thomas Abbott is the father of my baby. I think that Mr. and Mrs. Abbott know something by the way they look at me when they think I am not watching them. They also seem to avoid me when I come into a room. Yesterday, Thomas Abbott smirked and winked at me when he walked through the kitchen and said, "Congratulations, Miss Anna."

I have also heard shouting coming from the closed door of Mr. Abbott's library. It was Mr. Abbott and Thomas.. I heard Thomas say, "It wasn't me. She's just a cheap whore of a housemaid, and it could be anyone's." Soon the door slammed, and Mr. Abbott came out of the library with a great scowl on his reddened face. I know that Mrs. Abbott has been in bed for a few days, because Tillie has been carrying her chamber pot up and down the stairs, day and night, and she is taking her meals on a tray. This trouble is because of me. I am afraid and ashamed.

I think I am a problem for the Abbotts, but they must go through with this lie for the sake of their reputations. I will play my role, for I have begun to think that I caused the attack in some way. I don't want this poor child I will bring into the world, but I must not do anything to make life more difficult for the baby than it will be. But at least, the wee thing won't be a bastard, thank to Evan. I wish I had loved him and had passion for him, and within that love we created the child who is still very quiet within my belly. Soon will come the quickening, and then the swelling. What will Ola and Arne think of their dear sister then? My shame grows with every day.

This is a terrible day. This morning I got a letter from my brother Ola in Illinois. He had received the news that our brother Arne had fallen out of a hayloft and is now dead. He was drunk. Oh, my poor parents in Norway. How sad they must be about their son. Arne never should have come to America where he was alone without family to care for him and to stop his drinking. He was not strong enough to know what he needed to do for himself. I am heartbroken.

Just after midnight, I received a visit from Mrs. Abbott. She knocked on my door and told me to meet her in the library after I dressed. I was frightened. I imagined that they knew about me and had decided to put me out of the house. I began to think of where I would go. They hadn't even waited until the light of day to send me on my way. I had a little money in my drawstring bag, hidden in the false compartment of my steamer trunk. I was paralyzed with fear, but I knew I had to do what I was told. When I walked into the library, I came face to face with Mr. Daniel Abbott, Mrs. Marguerite Abbott, Jones the livery man, and the Presbyterian minister. After I was asked to sit down in the green velvet chair, I was told that my husband Evan was dead. He had too much to drink at the local saloon, and when another man accused him of cheating at cards, Evan Jones tried to hit him. Too drunk to fight, Evan took a blow to his temple, and died instantly. I am ashamed to admit that momentarily, my heart leapt with unrepentant joy! I have been saved from a life with this drunken man. I rose from the green velvet chair and turned around to take my silent leave, when Mr. Jones handed me a black leather bag that jingled with coin. "This is what Evan died for tonight. He was trying to win enough money to buy a house for you -- one that you would like."

I looked him in the eye and through my tears and shame, I said, "Thank you, Jones. I am grateful for Evan's kindness, but we are all unfortunates."

I could hear John Jones' sobs as I walked through the kitchen to my room, and shame for my lack of compassion followed my every footstep. I needed to sleep. Tomorrow is a work day, but it is also Sunday. I need to go to church and pray for forgiveness, because I rejoiced in my husband's death. I felt sleep upon me for the first time since Thomas Abbott had his way with me in the carriage house. Before I fell asleep, I thought of Jones' grief, but for the first time, I wondered where he was when Thomas raped me. John Jones is almost always in the carriage house, often with Thomas Abbott. And then I understood...Jones knew what Thomas did to me. Maybe Thomas told him before it happened. Maybe Jones was in the carriage house with us, hiding in one of the dark corners behind a pile of straw. My sympathy for him ended at that moment.

Friday, March 30, 1900-Evening

Today, in the cold, dark, early spring morning, I became a mother. I labored only two hours by myself in my room before my little baby girl was born. Because I had seen my older sister's babies born, I knew how to tie off and cut the cord. I wrapped the afterbirth in old newspapers and put it in the chamber pot. She is beautiful and looks like my sister Beret. The only feature of her father is her light brown hair, but the dead Evan also had light brown hair. I lay with her at my breast during the night, warming her tiny body, and I already felt great love for this girl of mine. I was grateful that she was so quiet in this house of slumbering trouble, and because of that I named her Beret, for my quiet little sister who died too soon.

When Tillie arrived in the kitchen at 5 a.m., she knocked on my door and then entered. "Oh my, Girlie…what have you done now?" Tillie looked my baby over from top to bottom, and relief seemed to replace her worried expression. She picked her up in plump arms, and moved from my small room, muttering, "She's as normal as normal can be. A normal size… just a little on the small side, but a normal size and perfectly made."

I weakly protested being separated from my baby until Tillie said, "Don't fret, Girlie. I just want to put her on the kitchen scale. She's a mite scrawny."

Beret weighed only 5 pounds, 12 ounces when she was born, but she was hungry, and her wide, dark eyes showed me that she was eager to live. Soon she was nestled in my arm and at my breast. I didn't know what to do or where I would go, but because the Abbott's didn't want scandal, I thought they would put me out. If we were lucky, they might be very quiet about my situation, and they were.

April 15, 1900

Thomas Abbott has disappeared from Abbott House – forced out by his father and brother Ellsworth. Tillie whispered that he had gone to the Dakotas to homestead, and he took with him the pale housemaid, Bridget. It seems that the Abbotts know how to fix things real good.

My baby girl is beautiful. I don't think about how she came to be. My love for her has made her completely mine in every way.

After the workday was done, Tillie took me into the panty and said, "Girlie, you are the lucky one. The Abbotts want to help you and your baby. You are going to move upstairs to the small apartment over the kitchen. It has everything you will need, three rooms, including a kitchen and sitting room combination and two bedrooms. There is a crib in the attic that you may take for the baby.

I lost my voice for a moment. "But – why, Tillie? Why would they want to help me and my baby girl"?

"Girlie, think, and you will figure it out. You have an Abbott baby."

This will be the last time I write in my diary about anything but Beret. My life will never have a story that is just for me and a man that I love. It is set on a path that I can't change. But, I am thankful for my girl and my job. My love story is my baby Beret.

CHAPTER FORTY-SIX

Natalie

I finally fell into a fitful sleep on the sofa in James' living room. My brain, filled with new and shocking information, was actively trying to piece it all together and put it into proper compartments. I slept with fitful dreams in my head until I heard my name, "Natalie. Natalie, wake up." When I opened my eyes, I met the blue eyes of my husband who had his arms around me and was calling my name. I put my arms around him, and our bodies fit together perfectly when we embraced.

"Let's talk now, Natalie." His words sounded more like a question than a statement. I nodded, as he pulled out a notepad and two pens, one black and one red. He began making a chart on the yellow pad that I recognized as a simple genealogy chart. The yellow pad was soon full of red and black scrawl, and when he spoke of my ancestry, it was in a whisper and with a knitted brow. Deep in thought, James was trying to make sense of this during a murder investigation. Fragmented sentences, such as "great-great granddaughter" of the patriarch Daniel Abbott through your grandmother's birth… He had also written "cousin to Lydia" in glaring red ink on the yellow pages.

I am well versed in genealogy research, but the shock of what I had discovered left me without the ability to think clearly. And then it hit me: Not only am I an Abbott, but the only surviving Abbott -- whatever that meant. At that point, James said, "The Abbott property and inheritance are likely yours. I think we may just have discovered a motive."

"Natalie, We need to go to your house very soon – just you and me -- to pick up the box, but I want to wait until tonight after dark."

At that point, I knew I had to tell him of my solo trip to my house the night before and the trespassers I encountered. He reacted as I expected him to. His voice was raised, but full of concern and some exasperation. "Natalie, I told you not to go there alone. What were you thinking? Do you know how close you came to being discovered and possibly hurt or worse?" And then he hugged me, and I made a promise that I would try to keep.

"Yes, James, you're right. I won't do anything like that again. I should have listened to you." And then I thought to myself what I couldn't say out loud. *The truth is that I am almost desperate to find the two missing journals. Having access to my mother Grace's journal is the only way that I am likely to discover who my father is. I need to get them somehow. I'll have to find a way.*

CHAPTER FORTY-SEVEN

JUNE 25 – 9:00 P.M.

Natalie

When we pulled up to my house, as the last light of day was fading, it looked the same as it always had. The front porch was cheerful with flower boxes, wicker chairs and a table. The swing hung from the strip paneled wooden ceiling, ever so slightly swaying with the gentle breeze. It warmed my heart in a comfortable, familiar way, but when I put my key into the lock, it met no resistance. I was able to push the door open with just the turn of the brass, beaded knob. "James, it's not locked!"

As the door opened and swung into the house, James immediately drew his gun and stepped inside. "Wait on the porch, Natalie, and if you see anyone inside, or if you hear a gun discharge, run to a neighbor's house and call for help."

My heart was pounding at the realization that James was placing himself in danger. My home had again been violated. Since the night I returned here alone, I had foolishly brushed aside the illegal entry of at least two men. I keep asking myself why anyone would want to break in and rifle through my belongings. But I had to get over the idea of who I thought I was – the simple daughter of a housemaid. Because of my new-found connections to the Abbott family, I had to start thinking of myself in different terms. The break-ins, the stalking, and Lydia's death more than likely had something to do with the Abbott family

– and the small metal box. I breathed a sigh of relief when James appeared in the doorway with his gun holstered.

"What did you find -- anything?"

"Nothing that was noticeable. If the intruders were looking for something, they put the place back together well. But maybe you will notice something out of place or missing. Let me know right away if you do."

I walked across the threshold and into the dim light, and I began to survey the place that I have called home since I was ten-years-old. I moved to turn on the lamps, but then thought better of it. James said, "No lights, Natalie. We don't want to attract attention. I'll use my flashlight"

At first glance, it looked like it always did, but I am a person who has specific places for the decorative objects that sit on surfaces such as tables and in bookcases. Not only does everything have to be in its place, but I am a bit compulsive about how they sit. Helter skelter placement won't do. That's why I cancelled the cleaning service I had used for a couple of months last year. When they were finished with their cleaning, the floors always gleamed, and everything was wiped clean, but I had to straighten pictures and reposition almost everything that sits on a surface.

After the crime lab left, when we were last here, I had placed all items in their proper positions, so it didn't take long for me to figure out that someone had been here again, even though they took great pains to make it appear as though the house was untouched. And then I thought that perhaps the house was disturbed from the night before when I was hiding under the bed. Thinking back, I hadn't checked the lock on the front door. I had gone directly out the back. Maybe it was left open then.

Again, my mind strayed to the two missing journals, the ones belonging to Beret and Mother. Who would want them? – It had to be someone who had a stake in something having to do with the Abbott family. Another question bothered me, so I asked James, "How do you think this mystery person or persons entered my house? I've changed keys, and there is no sign of forced entry in the doors or windows."

"We'll figure it out," Natalie. The answer is here. We just haven't found it yet."

We next walked up the stairs to the attic, and I was pleased that my old hiding place again had not failed me. If this is what the trespassers are looking for, they must be frustrated by now. They had free run of my house while I was in San Francisco and have been here at least twice since. I couldn't help but feeling a bit triumphant when I removed the brick and wooden panel and found the metal box where I had left it. Mr. Klinghoffer was a master mason in my opinion.

James put the box in a duffel bag and carried it downstairs, placing it by the front door. I quickly repositioned several items in my living room and dining room so that I would know if another uninvited search had taken place.

James, with his serious police chief expression, whispered discreetly, "Just one more place to search," as he walked toward the basement stairs in my dark house.

"James, there's no access down there anymore. It was sealed when Mother and I moved here in 1957, because she was afraid of intruders. There is only a front door and a back door, and both are upstairs on the main level."

"Just humor me, Natalie," he said.

I responded reluctantly, "Okay, James. I'll go down with you, but I think it might be a waste of time."

I have always disliked and avoided dank, dark basements, including my own, but I grudgingly followed James down the wooden steps in slow motion. I knew he was right. I also knew it would have reminded me too much of the Abbott cellar and my nighttime trip into the clinging dampness that is only found in a very old house. I switched on the fluorescent light fixtures above the stairs and in the main basement room and surveyed the surroundings. I watched as James deftly climbed into the crawl space that was under the living room.

The basement was empty of storage items. If I ever stored anything, it was in the attic, not the damp basement, and besides, it gave me a creepy feeling to spend time down there for any reason.

James commented on how the walls were expertly cut and laid with quarry stone, again a nod to Klinghofer. According to local lore, he was considered to have been the best stone mason in town and the surrounding area. Coventry homeowners still boast of solid basements constructed by Klinghofer. The unsolved mystery of the Klinghofer family's disappearance at the beginning of World War II only sweetened their boasts and added mystery and value to their homes. According to gossip, strange men were frequently seen walking through yards and alleys late at night in 1917 and 1918, before disappearing into a cellar or an unlighted back door. There were also stories of meetings held in the Klinghofer home, my home, during that time period, and the rumors have been repeated over the years. I have always attributed such tales to the war hysteria that was prevalent during World War One. My neighborhood was known as German Flats at one time, but after World War II, the name was changed to River Flats, in an attempt to stop any discrimination against citizens of German heritage.

The main room of my basement had four limestone walls, one side-lined with a wooden stairway, and one half-wall with the dirt crawl space at the top. There was also one small, high window that opened to the side yard. No one could get through that window, especially since it was encased by metal bars. To the right of the window was a boarded up coal chute that I had never bothered to remove, and on the opposite side of the basement was a wooden door that led to a small root cellar, a common thing in 1914, when people had large vegetable gardens and only ice for refrigeration. James was still investigating, but feeling empowered by his proximity, I opened the creaking, wooden door to the root cellar and pulled the chain switch of the bare light bulb in the ceiling. I saw nothing but old wooden shelves lined with a few empty blue tinted mason jars. There were no windows inside this cool, damp room, and I had never liked to be in it any longer than I had to. Returning to the main cellar room, I saw that James was surveying the boarded up coal chute. It seemed to be secure, without access from either inside or outside.

"What's that room, Natalie?" said James as he pointed toward the root cellar.

"That's just a root cellar. There are only old fruit jars in there and a few ancient garden tools. Since neither my mother nor I gardened or canned anything, they must have been stored there by the previous owners, the Klinghofers."

James tilted his head and said, "Turn off all of the basement lights, Natalie." I started to protest, but James was into the root cellar before I could finish my protest. I don't like darkness, but I complied. He turned his flashlight on low beam, providing the smallest sliver of light. I cautiously followed him into the root cellar... and then James said in a whisper, "Be very quiet. I thought I heard something."

His words sounded so ominous that I wanted to get out of this place as soon as possible. The silence between us was deafening, and then I heard what he heard. ...so soft that it was hardly audible. It sounded like a television or radio, with muffled voices and bursts of canned laughter. James had turned off his flashlight, and I was surprised to notice that the root cellar was not completely dark. Behind the shelving, there were tiny rays of light, distorted by the prism of the glass jars. I felt a prickly cold, as I could see that there was a well-lit space of some sort behind these shelves -- unknown to both my mother and me. I became momentarily immobilized with fear until James spoke. "Natalie, look at this." He was moving about near the wooden shelves, and abruptly, a burst of light entered the room when he pulled on a section of unoccupied shelves. The shelving had swung inward, hitting James on the forehead, and he suddenly fell to the floor, momentarily dazed.

"Are you okay, James?" The light from the inner room revealed that James was bleeding from a gash on his forehead. "Let's go upstairs, James. We need to look at this and make sure you're okay."

"No Natalie, we have to go into this room. We may not get another chance." I tied his handkerchief around his head, and he rose to his feet, appearing a bit unsteady.

James and I squeezed through the narrow opening in the shelving, and we found ourselves in an underground room that seemed to be between Mrs. Bergstrom's house and mine. It was well lit and sparsely furnished. A scarred, rectangular, wooden table sat in the center of the room, strewn with books and black and white photos. Unmatched chairs that would have ordinarily been pushed under the table had been placed against the wall in a random fashion. There was also an old grime incrusted chest freezer on one end of the room and a maroon velvet couch on the other end. The sound of the television or radio was muffled and obviously coming from elsewhere in the Bergstrom house. I opened my mouth to speak, but before a sound could emerge, I saw James looking at the walls with an incredulous look on his face. My eyes followed his lead, and I saw a sight that I found to be terribly out of place and quite shocking in Coventry, Minnesota in 1991. Above the box freezer was a tattered, moldy picture of Kaiser Wilhelm, alongside a rotting German flag of the era. Above the sofa on the other side of the room, a Nazi flag had been hung, along with a framed poster of Adolph Hitler. "What is this, James? I think Mr. Klinghofer may have been a Nazi for real." I was a bit unhinged by what I saw, and my voice was barely audible.

"I'm not sure, Natalie, but we need to get out of here. I hear footsteps -- I think more than one person's."

As I swung around, my eye caught a glimpse of a blue, leather bound book among the clutter on the table. I instinctively grabbed for it when I identified it as Mother's journal. On my way out, I turned for a last look at the room, and I could see a door on the opposite wall swing open. The door must be the entrance to Ragna Bergstrom's home. We quickly retreated through the opening within the shelving and closed it just in time. As James pulled me into the root cellar, I nearly lost Mother's journal, but I instinctually tightened my grip, determined not to lose it again. I felt pain, as my nail broke and a rivulet of blood ran onto the leather cover.

The root cellar in my basement was dark, except for the small cracks within the shelving that were still emitting light. Neither of us could resist looking through the openings to see who had entered the concealed middle room. The first person to come through the small doorway on Ragna Bergstrom's side was John Bergstrom. He was not alone, and I soon caught a glimpse of a shriveled hand followed by a very thin wrinkled forearm in a short-sleeved shirt. I couldn't confirm the identity until I saw his face full-on -- and then there was no doubt. It was old Dewar Renward who limped to the freezer, lifted the door, and stared inside. John Bergstrom stayed on the other side of the room, with his eyes downcast to the wall and his arms folded, like a petulant child.

"Oh, for God's sake, John, get a grip," croaked Dewar's voice. "It seems to fit okay. You did a good job. Don't turn tail and run now." John Bergstrom remained silent and pivoted toward Dewar, but continued to avoid eye contact with him. That was the first time I had heard Dewar Renward's voice, and although I seemed to recognize it, I had to think about where I had heard it before.

Suddenly, the silence was broken by an excited John Bergstrom. "Dew, did you pick up your old housemaid's diary? It's not on the table!"

"No, said Dewar emphatically. It was here a half hour ago. I thought old lady Bergstrom said that she was the only person who knew about this room. My friend and I found it when we were kids playing in the abandoned Klinghofer house next door. We were looking for evidence of Nazis because of all the rumors. I never told anyone and neither did Cully, because he's been dead for nearly 30 years." With that comment, a loose lid from one of the mason jars fell onto the concrete floor, and both Dewar and John looked toward my root cellar.

James broke our silence and whispered, "We have to get upstairs and get out of the house. They have been found out, and so have we."

CHAPTER FORTY-EIGHT

ON THE RUN

Natalie

We moved quickly and as quietly as we could, up the old wooden steps and through the house, as we headed for the front door. James grabbed the blanket wrapped box, and we were outside and into the darkness in a second. "We should have taken my squad car," James said. "At least I could use the radio contact." As we pulled away, I saw the front door of Mrs. Bergstrom's house open a crack. The moonlight had lit up the front porch, but the inside of the house had remained dark. One thing is for certain, we knew that it was most definitely not empty.

My house had been repeatedly entered despite new locks, and I now understood why. They were coming through the cellar. They, meaning Dewar and John Bergstrom, and I wasn't entirely sure that they were acting alone. As the door to the Bergstrom house closed, a multitude of questions flooded my brain.

We rode to the police station in silence, and riveting thoughts of what I had unknowingly been living with left me with nothing to say. I was in shock, but also angry at the fact that I had been violated time and time again.

James asked with urgency in his voice, "Are you okay? A penny for your thoughts, Natalie." I most definitely was not okay and was desperately trying to make sense of what we had just witnessed in my basement, but I didn't want him to know that I was stunned and shaken by our discovery.

"I'm okay, James. I'm more worried about that injury to your head. It looks like it needs medical attention – maybe a few stitches."

Deep in thought, I remained silent as James nervously kept glancing into the rear view mirror, like we were prey on the run. I finally spoke when my composure returned. "Who is John Bergstrom, and who is Dewar? Why…"

James, trying to answer my rhetorical question, said, "Once we have the answers to your questions, Natalie, I suspect that we'll know the truth of what has been going on."

As we drove, James must have been developing a strategy and made sense when he next spoke of his plans.

"The department needs to conduct a search on your house and Mrs. Bergstrom's house as soon as possible, but there are a lot of unknown factors. We aren't sure about John Bergstrom's true relationship with Mrs. Bergstrom, but it seems that she has disappeared and hasn't been seen for some time, while he has been living there. That should be reason enough to issue a search warrant. I'm also going to ask for a warrant to search Dewar's place, since he was seen in the cellar of the Bergstrom home, and the owner is missing. I think Judge Rogers will approve my requests. If the department is able to conduct a search, we could learn a lot about who Dewar and Bergstrom really are. You'll be safe at the station, but we need to plan how we are going to keep you that way. Dewar Renward and John Bergstrom have been exposed, and they're now more dangerous than ever. I won't sugar coat this situation. You're in danger, Natalie, and getting you out of town, as soon as possible, is critical."

After thinking about the possibilities, I said, "I'm concerned, James – for both of us, but I'm also worried about Mrs. Bergstrom. I doubt that she is in the Twin Cities with her niece."

James responded, "I think you're right Natalie. You need to be prepared for the worst when it comes to Mrs. Bergstrom. As for what happens when the Coventry PD enters the houses… If I am worth my salt as an investigator, I can say unequivocally that they, meaning the old man and John Bergstrom, will be gone. In fact, they may have already split."

My anger was growing. I normally kept my emotions in check because of my issues with anxiety. Never able to deal with too many negative feelings at once, I always retreated into the safety of my home when things started to explode in my life. But this time, it was my house that was the site of trouble, and there was no safety there.

CHAPTER FORTY-NINE

MICHAEL DUNIVAN -- RIGHT-HAND MAN

James

Once at the station, I called my investigative group into work, even though it was past midnight. As always, Michael Dunivan was the first to arrive, and I sent another one of my men to Judge Rodgers' house to get search warrants signed for all three houses: Dewar Renward's, Mrs. Bergstrom's, and Natalie's house. The judge agreed with the whys and wherefores, and the signed warrants were expedited. Although we could now move quickly with this investigation, I knew that we will no longer find Dewar and John in either of their homes or Natalie's.

I can always count on Dunivan. He is the best, the most dedicated, and probably the smartest detective I know. His intuition is almost always right on. We have become great friends during the past year, even though I got the job that he had always wanted. He would have probably been the Coventry Police Chief if he hadn't had difficulties with alcohol. Some city officials also don't like the fact that he is a little "rough around the edges, but Coventry could have done much worse than Michael Dunivan as their police chief.

The team was at the targeted homes in minutes. Natalie and I followed, because there was nowhere else that I thought she would be safe. There are too many unknowns right now. I am also worried about Natalie. I know more about her anxiety issues than she thinks I do. In fact, I sensed her anxiety and fears when we were dating in high school. Natalie's life has been so tightly confined by her mother's need for secrecy and the Abbott family's demands that she is hypervigilant in most situations, so she draws back. The fact that she is being stalked by a killer, who is persistent and won't allow her a respite of any kind, is creating all kinds of stress for her. For some reason, she is his remaining prey, and he is relentless. Natalie can't fall back on her old defense mechanisms and is feeling trapped. She hasn't developed the coping skills to deal with adversity, because she has always retreated into the safety of her own world. This time she can't. Natalie must learn to fight her own demons, because I might not always be there to save her.

CHAPTER FIFTY

JUNE 26 - NOWHERE TO HIDE

Natalie

We knew that Dewar wouldn't return to the crime scene tonight, so I tagged along with James to my house where it was teeming with Coventry police. The state crime lab was also there by 2 a.m. All transportation authorities have been notified, and neither of the men will be allowed on buses, trains, ships, or flights -- domestic or international. They will be arrested upon approach.

James was in the kitchen when I heard his assistant Michael Dunivan approach from the basement spewing anger at what he had found:

"What a fucking sight... all that German war crap on the walls... And we found something else that will blow your mind! I've never seen anything like this, Chief. The basement room is like a time capsule, but that isn't what I came to tell you. We found Ragna Bergstrom at the bottom of the box freezer under at least 100 pounds of packaged beef and more than fifty bags of vegetables. They also must have poured gallons of some type of colored liquid over all of it and let it freeze, just in case someone opened the freezer. It sure slowed us down, which is what they intended. First of all, we couldn't see the body, and then we had to chip her out – very carefully -- so that any relevant evidence would be preserved. It took two fucking hours. She's as skinny as a rail, folded like an accordion, and probably starved to death."

I walked out of the room in an effort to regain my composure, after hearing Dunivan describe what was found in the freezer. Images of the frail Mrs. Bergstrom were running through my head until James said, "Put it aside for now, Natalie. We have to get through this investigation before we can allow ourselves to think too much."

James listened to Dunivan but didn't register surprise or shock. He calmly asked a question. "Does the Medical Examiner have any idea of the cause of death?"

Dunivan, in his animated way, responded, "How do you tell when a corpse has turned purple after being marinated in Kool-Aid. There are no signs of trauma on her body at this point. Maybe something will show up when they get her on the slab. It's possible that she could have been suffocated or killed with a drug overdose. Anyway, you should see the expression on that poor old lady's face – pure fucking terror. We have to get these fucking assholes!"

James fell silent and was surprised to see me standing in the door. Dunivan looked embarrassed and said, "Sorry, Miss LaPierre. I get a little excited on cases like this." With that comment, he disappeared into the cellar again.

James embraced me in an effort to mitigate the raw truth. "I'm sorry about Mrs. Bergstrom, Natalie, but right now my priority is to get you to a safe place. I have been thinking about options, and we seem to be pretty limited in our choices. For all I know, Dewar could be watching as we speak. He seems to be quite intelligent and possibly is used to disguising himself, based on our preliminary findings at his house across the street. John Bergstrom seems to be more of a simple man who is a follower."

At that moment, Dunivan returned even more flustered than before and said, "Holy shit! We found the Bergstrom guy floating in the old cistern in the back yard. His aunt Ragna Bergstrom didn't have it filled in and properly covered. It was an accident waiting to happen, but this death is not an accident and has Dewar Renward written all over it. Bergstrom has a bullet hole in the back of his head -- most likely because he knew too much."

After a few moments of thoughtful silence, James said, "I will also bet that Bergstrom is not Ragna's nephew. I want to contact officials in Norway as soon as possible and get some information on him, including photographs. I don't mean to frighten you, Natalie, but it's possible that Dewar and John have been in Coventry, living in your neighborhood because of you, and we have to find out why. We also need to examine the metal box from the attic and your mother's journal from the basement as soon as possible. They are evidence. And speaking of evidence, another journal has been found in the Bergstrom house. It's burgundy and was in an upstairs bedroom."

I thought for a moment and then spoke. "James, I know you need the box and the journals, but I ask that you allow me to at least read my mother's journal before turning it over to the department. The other journal is my grandmother Beret's diary, and I have read it, so the department may keep it as evidence."

"I think we can arrange for you to keep your mother's journal for a few days. In fact, I want to take both items with us – the metal box and the journal. I want to try to open it when we get to Dunivan's cabin. I'll turn it in to the department the next day."

Grateful for his voice of reason, I said, "That sounds like a great idea, James. Thank you, my love." He smiled and kissed me.

CHAPTER FIFTY-ONE

WEDNESDAY, JUNE 26 – UP NORTH

Natalie

The announcement of our marriage was in the Wednesday newspaper, and the word on the street is that James and I are honeymooning somewhere on the North Shore of Lake Superior. The truth is we have made plans to hide out almost in plain sight. There is a rental villa near Grand Marais in the names of James and Natalie Sullivan, but it will stand empty for most of the duration of our "two week honeymoon." We'll only be twenty miles from Coventry in Michael Dunivan's cabin.

We got into my car and headed north on I-35, the road to Duluth. After checking in at our condo rental, we stayed for twenty-four hours, making sure we were seen in the restaurant, the pool, and on our deck, watching the rolling waves of Lake Superior below. Arrangements had previously been made to secretly switch to a rental car late on the second night and leave my car at the resort. That went very smoothly, and we were again on the road to Minneapolis. After a night in a hotel, we will be on our way, via backroads, to Michael Dunivan's cabin on Lake Crystal, which will allow James to go back and forth between his work and our hideout. Since the cabin belongs to Michael Dunivan, he'll drive James to Lake Crystal each night and pick him up in the morning. James will hide in the back seat and keep a very low profile at work, to escape detection. We want it known that we are on our honeymoon and out of town.

Dewar is most likely not too far away and if he can find us, being followed is a certainty. He seems to be desperate for either the metal box or the journals – or both. James also believes that he was stalking us in San Francisco; in fact, he suspects that Dewar was disguised as the elderly bellhop who interrupted us at the San Francisco hotel with a breakfast we didn't order. He most likely was hoping to find me alone. Also, he may have been masquerading as Ragna Bergstrom's nurse. The lemon pie dessert gathering at the Bergstrom's was a ruse, designed to get me out of my house long enough to search it.

We are aware that M.J. will have difficulty accepting our marriage, but perhaps it'll be good for her to separate from me, at least for a while. I haven't communicated with her, because I am now on a leave of absence from the library. She also can't contact me by phone, because I am not at home to take phone calls. Right now, M.J. is most likely full of jealousy and resentment. They are both dangerous states of mind, so it is better that she knows nothing. I am glad that she is spending so much time with Frank.

CHAPTER FIFTY-TWO

LOVE IN TIMES OF PERIL

Natalie

After an hour and a half of driving, James and I checked into a hotel near the Minneapolis airport – one that gets a lot of transient traffic. We placed the tote bag containing the metal box onto a hotel cart and covered it with a Minnesota Vikings car blanket. The investigative team in Coventry doesn't know that I took the metal box from the Abbott house cellar, so no one will miss it. Once at the cabin, we can discuss what should be done, and with any luck, we'll be able to open it. I also carried my mother's journal under my arm, wrapped in my jacket.

When we checked in, James asked if we could use cash to pay, saying his card had been lost and he was waiting for a new one. There was no problem, and check-in was swift and uncomplicated.

As James and I walked through the attractive lobby and halls, we heard a couple of different languages and noticed several guests dressed in Middle East garb. The men were in long, white robes, with turban-like head gear, and the women were in long, black dresses and hijabs with attached veils that exposed only their eyes. I couldn't help but notice that the eyes peering from the opening between the headdress and the veil were stunningly dark and beautiful. Middle Eastern people were never seen in Coventry, so I was rather interested. I had also noticed, as we walked through the lobby, that one of the hotel shops sold this type of clothing. The airport hotel was most likely a stopover for them on their way to Rochester and the Mayo Clinic, where they are known to be frequent patients. James must have thought that I was taking too much time and was too exposed, because when I felt his strong arm around my waist and a quickening of his step, I knew that was a cue for me to move along.

By the time we entered our room, exhaustion was hitting us hard, and I couldn't wait to climb into bed -- but first we needed to eat something. I picked up the phone and ordered hamburgers and French fries, an indulgence for me, but standard fare for James. "Yes, we'll eat in our room," I told the kitchen.

I hung up the phone and stood in front of the mirror, thinking I needed a change of clothes and some fresh makeup, especially lipstick. I reached for my purse and pulled out the gold tube of lipstick when James said, "not yet, Natalie." Suddenly he was behind me, encircling my breasts with strong arms. He lifted my hair, kissed the nape of my neck, and whispered my name over and over. I turned around and met his lips, silencing his murmurs, as he held me. Lost in the moment, I didn't notice how easily he was able to undress me, until like magic, our clothes were on the floor in a pile. Buttons and zippers had been undone with no effort. I was mesmerized at how beautiful our image appeared in the gold leaf bordered mirror -- an image of lovers as old as time. We could have been the subjects of an erotic painting from the 14th or 15th century.

"Look at you, Natalie," James said softly, as his hands caressed my breasts. Your skin feels like satin and smells like spring, and your breasts are tipped with pink pearls. I love the darkness and the light of you -- the contrast of your skin and hair -- the silk between your legs." I was speechless and amazed at the lover's poetry coming from this man who had seen unspeakable evil in so many forms.

We surrendered completely to the passion that overtook us. His hands moved from my breasts, caressing my body and unleashing my longing for him. A moan escaped, as an involuntary intake of breath proclaimed my desire. Suddenly, James picked me up and carried me to the shower. We kissed and embraced, lost in the throes of our need for each other, while the pulsating water drowned out our pleasure. Perhaps it was the excitement and fear we had experienced earlier in the day that had ignited such longing for one another –

or more likely, it was our love, which was too long denied. Our lovemaking was evolving from a middle-aged man and woman in the throes of rekindled teenage love to a couple who were experienced adults. We were learning to please each other, as lovers do, if they're fortunate enough to have the spark and the passion.

"Between kisses, I heard him say, "Natalie, I love you more than I can say. Never have I known anything like this."

"Nor me, James, Nor me, my love."

CHAPTER FIFTY-THREE

WEDNESDAY, JUNE 26 - EVENING

James

After drying each other's bodies with plush white towels, we got into comfortable clothes. Natalie looked beautiful in a blue lounging outfit, her dark hair framing her face with curls, and her dark eyes luminous and shining. "Like an old married couple," I said, as she microwaved the uneaten food. Natalie smiled back at my words and said, "I think that's what we are -- but only 'sort of old' – and definitely married.'"

The metal box sat unopened on the dresser as we ate, waiting for us to violate its long reprieve from prying human eyes and hands. Frequent touches and kisses came between us and our dinner, although we were famished -- and then, there was a knock on the door.

I put my index finger to Natalie's lips, as I unholstered my gun and held it behind my back. After looking through the peep hole, I cautiously opened it. Standing in the hallway was a heavily pregnant Middle Eastern woman in the traditional garb, complete with black dress and hijab. She stared at me with piercing eyes that I found to be a bit unsettling, and in a heavy accent said, "Sorry…Sorry." …and then she was gone. We embraced and shared a kiss before preparing to take on our waiting tasks. Handing Natalie her mother's journal, I sat down and began the effort to open the metal box with a pocket knife.

"I wish I had some tools with me, Natalie. The lock is very old and unusual. This may not work."

I struggled for nearly a half an hour while Natalie was deep into reading her mother's journal.

CHAPTER FIFTY-FOUR

GRACE'S DIARY

April 6, 1941

I am twenty-three years old, but an orphan just the same. I was a baby when the influenza epidemic took my mother, and my father died in 1918 in France during the Great War. There was only my grandmother Anna to raise me. I work as a housemaid at the Abbott mansion, just like my mother and grandmother before me.

I decided to write in this diary, because two weeks ago, I met a man. I knew instantly that he was the one I have been waiting for. He is handsome with black hair and blue eyes and such a nice smile. He is a soldier. His eyes met mine in the mirror hanging on the wall over the soda fountain at the Sweet Shop, and we stared at each other for what seemed to be a long time. But then I felt embarrassed and looked down at my cherry coke. He turned around and walked over to a booth where another boy in uniform was sitting. They were with some very pretty girls who wore fancy clothes and bright red lipstick. The soldier and I kept glancing at each other, and I hoped he would talk to me, but he just smiled and walked out with a blond girl. I thought I heard him say that he and his friend were headed for camp Ripley in a few days for more training. They were both in the National Guard. His friends called him Ted.

Afternoon, May 1, 1941

I have been thinking too much about Ted, the handsome soldier that I saw a few weeks ago in the Sweet Shop. Grandmother Anna caught me daydreaming on the window seat when I was supposed to be polishing the oak railing. She surprised me when she said in that soft voice that means business, "Tonight I want to talk to you about some important things that you should know. You will need to write them down -- maybe in your diary." The truth was that I didn't want to spend time writing tonight. My friend Millie and I were going to a movie, but I cancelled out of duty and love for my Granny.

I said, "Yes, Granny, I will be home tonight, and we can write down everything you want."

Evening, May 1, 1941

Grandmother Anna sat in the rocking chair wrapped in her crocheted shawl, when she said, "I love you, Grace. You are all I have in the world. I'm not going to drag my feet with the words that are in my head and heart. They need to be said as soon as possible before I am no longer here to share them with you. You may be shocked and surprised, but that will pass in time."

I never expected to hear what Grandmother Anna told me. She spoke of the day that she was raped by Thomas Abbott and how she soon found herself pregnant with his child. That child was my mother Beret.

Thomas couldn't keep his hands off the young girls, and by the next year, he was sent to South Dakota to homestead, along with one of the other housemaids – his new wife Bridget. He was causing too much scandal for the family to bear. Thomas was very angry, but he caused it himself with his bad behavior toward women. Anna said that Beret never knew who her father was, or how she came to be born. Beret assumed that her father was Evan Jones, even though her last name was Haugen, like Anna's. When Thomas came to Minnesota for his yearly visit, Anna and Beret were asked to leave the mansion until he returned to South Dakota.

Thomas' last trip to Coventry was three years ago, 1939, lying in a shiny black casket. When they loaded him into the waiting hearse, a white coffin containing the body of his wife was placed alongside his. A short distance down the track, their only child, fifteen-year-old Helen, stepped off the coach car on the arm of her Uncle Ellsworth Abbott. He had gone to their South Dakota homestead to get her and bring her back to Coventry. The exile of Thomas Abbott had finally come to an end, and he died as he had lived, in the midst of some kind of scandal.

Months later, old Marguerite Abbott told Anna that Thomas Abbott was murdered by his daughter Helen. The family was shunned in their South Dakota farm community because of him and his chasing of very young girls. It had become impossible for Helen to go to school or church, because some cruel boys tormented her about her father. Helen finally put a pick axe in his back out of anger and shame for his behavior. Helen lost her mind and never fully recovered, and her mother Bridget hanged herself. That explains a lot about Helen Abbott. Marguerite Abbott told Anna to stay away from Helen, because she is a dangerous person. Helen is only eighteen years old, but she has already killed another human being. Granny thinks she could kill again if someone makes her jealous, angry, or gets in her way of having something she wants. "Stay away from Helen, Grace. If she knows you have Abbott blood, she may find that a good enough reason to kill you."

June 4, 1941

The Abbott family may have been upper class citizens of Coventry, but they also have a dark history that I would rather not be connected with. I guess it's good that Granny told me about this terrible thing that happened to her, but I must try to forget and move on. I won't tell anyone that I am part of the Abbott family because of the shame, but also because I am afraid of Helen. She and my mother Beret were half-sisters, so even though she is younger than I am, Helen is my aunt, although she may not like it or admit to our relationship. I think Helen tries to get rid of what she doesn't like.

August 4, 1941

I keep going to the Sweet Shop with my friends whenever I can, hoping to see the handsome, dark haired soldier again. One day I thought I saw him get in a car with an older couple, but they drove away, and I was left standing on the curb. In my heart, I knew that I would see him again, and then it happened. He walked into the Sweet Shop with his soldier friend and sat in a booth. They weren't with girls this time. He was in uniform, and I heard him say that they were leaving the next day for a camp in the south. He ate a burger and had a malt. We kept looking at each other, and finally, he came to me and asked me to dance. It was a slow dance, and he pulled me close to him. The song was "I'll be seeing you." I heard his friend say, "Come on, Ted. We have to go. We're going to be late." He just kept dancing with me until the music stopped.

And then he said, "I have to go. Please tell me your name." I told him and looked into his eyes and smiled. He moved closer and said, "I'll be seeing you, Grace. Will you be here when I get back?"

I said, "Yes, Ted. I'll be here." He gave me a kiss on the cheek before he walked out the door.

December 7, 1941

I was in the kitchen making breakfast for the Abbotts when the news came over the radio sitting on top of the new Frigidaire. Everyone gathered around in the kitchen and stopped their chores. This is a very bad day for Americans, because today Pearl Harbor was attacked by the Japanese. Lyon went to tell Mr. Ellsworth, who came down to the library in his robe, so that he could hear the news for himself. They say that many men have been killed and several ships sunk. I can tell that Mr. Ellsworth is worried. This news is frightening, especially because everyone says that Germany will now declare war on us. War! That is what claimed the father I never knew. What will happen now? What about my handsome soldier? What will happen to him?

Grandmother Anna is very ill. Her small body is swollen from the fluid that her kidneys can't get rid of. She is the only real family I have. Doc Ballantine said he will put her into the hospital this afternoon. I love her so much.

Marguerite Abbott is very ill, and her body is also swollen like my Granny's. Her legs are the size of an elephant, and she has a private nurse in her room all day and all night. The younger doctor in town, Doc Berkmann, says that it is her heart and there's very little that he can do but make her comfortable. I guess she's going to die soon. We are in the midst of illness and war.

December 7, 1941 - Evening

Tonight at 8 p.m., my beloved Grandmother Anna passed on. My world won't be the same. I am now completely alone.

Tonight at 10:30 p.m., Marguerite Abbott, Mistress of Abbott House died. Helen will now be the woman of the house at the age of eighteen.

How strange that they both died on the same day.

CHAPTER FIFTY-FIVE

MORNING, JUNE 27, 1991

Natalie

The revelations in Mother's journal were still on my mind. The fact that Thomas had been murdered, as well as the identity of his murderer, was unknown to me until now. I found it to be quite shocking. Also, it seemed that I was coming closer to the identity of my father. Was he the soldier named, Ted? I decided not to tell James what I had learned thus far. It was simply not the time, and I had more reading to do.

Responding to James' comment about returning to Coventry, I said, "I would really prefer not to go back to Coventry, James. I'm worried about our safety. Do you think that Dewar is still there?"

"I don't know," James said, reaching for my hand. "But we'll have to go back very soon. We need to know what's in that box, for your sake and for the investigation -- and I have to turn it into the evidence room within a few days. Would you like to go down for breakfast, and we can talk about it?"

"Okay," I said tentatively. After showering and dressing, we walked out the door, leaving Mother's journal and the metal box in the room safe. We felt secure enough in this hotel, because no one knows we're here. But there is something that seems strange. and I can't pinpoint it.

Anxious to be on the road to the lake, we walked briskly down the hall and with a sense of urgency. When I remembered that I had forgotten my heart medication in the hotel room, I said, "James, I'm sorry, but my medication -- I need to go back to the room." As I abruptly turned around, I sighted the Arab woman who had knocked on our door the night before. She was standing in front of our hotel room with her hand outstretched toward the door knob. Her blue eyes met mine for just a second, and it was then that I recognized her. The woman suddenly pivoted when she saw me turn towards her, and the sudden movement lifted the hem of her dress, just a bit, but enough to expose one leg. I was confused when I saw something completely unexpected. Her leg was clothed in khaki pants, and she was wearing men's tennis shoes. I was amazed at how quickly she disappeared down the stairwell.

Although the woman was exposed for just a couple of seconds, it was the eyes that gave her away. I felt as though I had been hit in the gut by a sucker punch. "James, that woman has blue eyes and is wearing khaki pants under her dress." In those revealing moments, I recognized that the pregnant woman who knocked on our door last night also had blue eyes -- not the lovely, dark eyes of the other Arab women we have seen.

"Dewar, it's Dewar, James!" James grabbed my arm, and we quickly entered our room. Understanding that we had been followed and were in danger, we surmised that Dewar is after the box and is waiting for an opportunity to seize it when James and I are elsewhere. He called security and alerted them to an attempted robbery in our room.

"Dewar must have been waiting, somewhere close outside our room, unseen, waiting for us to leave," said, James. "He may even have a room across the hall, spying on our every movement while lying in wait for his chance. I'd guess that he wants the journal, but even more likely, the metal box is the big payload for him. We have to plan how to get out of here, and we need some help."

James immediately called Coventry PD. "Put Dunivan on the phone," he said with urgency in his voice. His eyes had turned to a steely blue, but he reached for my shaking hand as though to reassure me.

"Dunivan, we had planned to drive to your cabin on our own after our decoy trip to the Cities, but we may be in a bit of trouble here. Our plans have changed, and we we'll be returning to Coventry, but under cover. We'll have to change our plans for a hide-out location. Anyway, I don't want anyone to know that we're back in Coventry, except for the escort. Dewar was, or maybe still is, in our hotel, and we need two cars and four officers as an escort." He went on to briefly share what had happened and then asked Dunivan if there was anything new in the investigation. James had pressed the "speaker" button of the phone so that I could also be updated.

Dunivan spoke in his fast-paced Irish brogue. "We're investigating in all three houses, and the state crime lab is still here. Dewar Renward had to go on the run quickly, so he left a lot of shit behind. We have found some interesting stuff in the belongings of Mr. Renward. There were passports for three countries, all with different names. We also found wigs and a variety of clothing, including women's, and a suitcase with an assortment of knives, guns, and some bottles of liquid that looks like it could be drugs. And speaking of drugs, we also found the powdered variety, and I bet it's cocaine."

Dunivan paused briefly, as if thinking, and then continued.

"And guess what – that white dandruff stuff is in all three houses. Who in the hell is this guy anyway, and what is that stuff he leaves in his wake?"

"We don't know, Dunivan -- just get two cars up here as soon as possible. We'll be at the hotel drop-off point in one hour with a new rental car. I don't want to involve the Minneapolis PD. There's too much we don't know yet, and talking to another department would just complicate things. In fact, there's no need for them to be involved at all, but if we ask for their help, it will open a can of worms. Just send some guys and keep it casual. I don't want this to look official, so they should wear plainclothes and arrive in unmarked cars. And by the way, Dunivan, this is off the record, so keep it quiet."

CHAPTER FIFTY-SIX

BACK HOME

Natalie

I thought James had overreacted by asking for an escort, but realizing that he knows more about such things that I do, I said nothing. The ride back to Coventry was without incident. There was an unmarked police car in front of us and one trailing close behind. I could tell that James was deep in thought, because he was mostly quiet, but every now and then he would reach for me just to give me a reassuring touch. The box was in the trunk, still waiting to be opened. I was frightened, but happy that James was with me. If the happenings of the past few weeks were about me, in some strange way, I wondered what I would have done if I had been alone. It occurred to me that without James and the protection he has given me, it is very possible that I might not have survived. I think Dewar might have killed me.

By the time we pulled into town, James had made the decision not to go back to either of our homes. Once in his office, he also contacted his ex-wife and told her that he was involved in a serious case and can't take Paige for her mid-summer two weeks. I could tell that she began to argue with him, but he was firm, and when he said, "I'm very concerned about her safety, Laura. I can't even go back to my own house right now." I could tell that she had become silent on the other end of the line, and her protests had stopped. He next asked to speak to Paige, and when he told her the she needed to stay with her mother for a longer period of time, she offered no resistance. Paige's boyfriend must still be in the picture.

Once James was off the phone, he pulled me close and said, "Natalie, if you don't mind, I want you to stay at my parents' condo in the Twin Cities until this is resolved. I'm not sure how long that will be. It could be weeks or even months. No one knows about the place, because they just bought it two months ago. Mom and Dad are visiting my sister in California for a few months, so we will have it to ourselves; and besides, it's a high security building, so it is the safest place I know."

The Twin Cities is eighty miles from Coventry, so I would most likely not see James on a daily basis. "Where will you stay, James?"

"I'll stay at the station, but I'll drive to see you as often as I can."

"Well, James, I guess there aren't many other choices for us, but I have to pick up Charlie from the kennel, and he'll need to come with me. I don't want to leave him again, if I can help it."

"That'll be fine, Natalie, said James. Residents can have dogs in their condos if they weigh less than fifteen pounds."

Laughing, I said, "Charlie shouldn't weigh any more than that, but my chubby little Cairn likes to eat…too many ice cream cones. Let's hope they don't put him on a scale."

James laughed and said, "You are bad, feeding that poor dog ice cream."

"Poor dog nothing… he is the happiest little guy around." And then I changed the subject and said, "By the way, I will also need some more clothes, if I can't return to my house. How do I manage that?"

"We'll do some quick shopping at Target again, on our way to my parents' condo. We can get everything you need in one stop -- toiletries, groceries, and clothes. I don't want to risk being seen at your house or shopping in Coventry,"

"Yes, Boss," I said facetiously, with a smile on my face.

James looked a bit wounded as he put his arm around my shoulders and said, "I'm so sorry, Natalie, but I just don't know how else to keep you safe."

"Oh, James, I was just kidding. I wouldn't know what to do in this situation without you. Thank you for keeping me on track and keeping me safe." With that, I took his hand in mine and brought it to my lips. I was surprised as hell at the happiness I felt in the midst of a nightmare. "I love you, James Sullivan," I whispered softly.

There was much to do before we got out of town again. M.J. had to be told that I would be taking some time off until this case was settled, and I again had to ask for a substitute and additional volunteers for an indefinite period of time. It was with dread that I approached her, remembering her anger the last time we talked. Our friendship may be broken, because of all that has taken place between James and me.

"Hello, M.J., I said rather nervously. I hate to ask you again, but we need to get a paid person with the proper credentials to sub for me for a while – someone who can actually function as the librarian. I'll be gone for an undetermined period of time, so that will complicate things. Betsy Anderson is a retired school librarian, and she would be the best person to do the job, if she is willing. On the other hand, perhaps she and Marie Larson could share the subbing duties. I'm sorry to bother you with this again, M.J. I don't think I've had this many subs or volunteers in all the years since I took the job as City Librarian."

M.J. didn't speak for an uncomfortable length of time, and when she finally opened her mouth, she looked and sounded petulant and angry. It was apparent that she still felt angry about the turn my life had taken – specifically, my marriage to James. I was concerned, because an angry M. J. could be a force to reckon with if she senses that I am holding back. She doesn't want to be left out of the information loop. I could tell that she had seen the marriage announcement in the Wednesday newspaper, even though she hadn't mentioned it -- yet. Her voice was snarky when she said, "I'll take care of getting staff for the library." And then she was silent for a few moments until speaking again. "I guess that congratulations are in order for the happy bride and groom. I suppose you're going on your honeymoon."

I wasn't sure of how much to tell her, but I had to say something. "Thank you, M.J. for the well wishes, and no, It's not really a honeymoon. I wish it were. Anyway, I have to go away for a while – James will be in and out of his office, but that information needs to remain quiet because of the case he's working on. If you really need to know of our whereabout, Dunivan knows everything, including the phone number where we can be reached."

M.J., cold and a bit surly, seemed to have difficulty with eye contact and her mouth was tight with anger. But, I knew she would do what I asked of her, because ultimately, M.J. was a professional when it came to her work. Grudgingly, she made notes for the substitute and volunteers, but I could see the jealousy on her face when James came looking for me. She slammed her notebook on the desk and marched down the hall, without a look back. I shrugged at James, and he just smiled, obviously understanding more than I had realized. We left the building hand-in-hand, and as we moved toward the rental car, he spoke, "Natalie, the metal box is still in the trunk of the car. Do you have the journal?"

"Yes, it's in my bag."

As we drove, I rehashed my discussion with M.J., trying to understand her feelings. Knowing that she was hurt and unsure of our future relationship, I reminded myself to show respect for our long friendship and to treat her gently. But, some changes are in order. Always feeling like a peacemaker, I usually agreed to what she wanted in nearly every situation, except for my work. That needs to stop. And there was another reality to face -- one that I had always blocked. There is no doubt that M.J. has deeper feelings for me than I have for her, and I'm not sure what that is all about. I was also beginning to wonder about her unreasonable anger and jealousy. Where did that come from? Finally, James spoke, breaking my train of thought.

"Before we drive to the Twin Cities, I want to go somewhere with access to tools that will allow me to open the box. We're going to my cabin on Lake Crystal, Natalie -- not Dunivan's."

Surprised, I said, "Cabin? I didn't even know you had a cabin."

James smiled a bit smugly and said, "Yeah, no one knows about it; none of the guys on the Coventry PD know, except for Dunivan. I got it as part of the divorce settlement five years ago. I just didn't want anyone asking to have guys' weekends that would involve fishing, boating, and alcohol. I bought it shortly after Laura and I were married, so we would have a place to stay when we visited my family in Coventry. She never liked it, and we rarely spent time there. Rustic log cabins and fishing just aren't Laura's thing. When it was agreed that Paige would live with me most of the time, she gave it to me --not really for me, but for Paige to enjoy, with the stipulation that it will belong to her when she turns twenty-five, or at a later time when she wants the ownership."

James went on to explain, "The truth is that Paige and I don't use it much, now that she spends most of her summers with her mother on the Cape. We mostly use it during weekends in the fall and spring and during mid-summer for two weeks. I like it best in October, when the lake is surrounded by fall colors. I'm not really interested in partying, but I want it available for spending time with my daughter, so I have kept it a secret. Only Dunivan knows about it."

That was so like the James that I had known, even in high school —— always serious and making sure that he did the right thing for the people in his life.

"We'll stay at the cabin tonight. Tomorrow, I'll have to go to work, but in the evening, we'll take off for the Cities and my parents' condo. Is that okay with you, Natalie? Do you have enough clothes and toiletries for a couple of days?"

I nodded, because I didn't know what else I could do. I had never been stalked before by a villain who most likely has murder on his mind, but I managed a smile, as I squeezed his hand. I still couldn't believe that a diabolical criminal would want to go after a small town librarian who had lived such a quiet, rather isolated life, unless it had to do with my newly discovered relationship to the Abbott family.

CHAPTER FIFTY-SEVEN

JUN E 27 – THE BOYS OF SUMMER

Natalie

It felt strange for me to be back at Lake Crystal. I didn't tell James that many of my early summers were spent here with Lydia and her brother Tice at the Abbott lake home.

Lake Crystal has been a major recreational area for local residents since the late 1800s. It is also well-known as a site of battles during the 1862 Sioux-/U.S. war. There are still arrowheads to be found by children digging in the dirt and sand.

The Abbotts had a lake house on the south end where the more expensive, larger cottages are located, along with the best natural sand beaches on Lake Crystal. The cottages are set on a rise high enough for a pretty view, but not so high that it takes more than a few steps to get to the sandy lakeshore.

As a child, The Abbotts allowed me to tag-along when they spent time at their cabin. Lydia didn't want to be without the company of a playmate. Between the ages of eight and thirteen, we swam, boated, fished, and dug for arrowheads in the sandy soil with her brother Tice. Whoever found the most arrowheads got to go to Olson's Pine Crest Lodge, the resort down the road, for a frozen Snickers Bar. The other -- the so called loser -- got to have a big, fat dill pickle from the large jar on Mr. Olson's counter. I was usually the loser, by my own design, but I liked dill pickles, so I was perfectly happy. Those were carefree childhood days, and I loved spending time here, because Helen, Lydia's raging mother, never came to the lake.

Ellsworth Abbott and his lethargic, neglectful second wife were supposed to be our caretakers, but Marian spent all of her days on the chaise in the cabin, with her books and pill bottles close at hand. Ellsworth often had to go back into town during the day to check on his businesses, so needless to say, we were pretty much on our own. Looking back, it was anything but a safe situation for two precocious children and a third, a servant's child, who did anything asked of her. Nellie, the very large second cook of Abbott House, came along to make our meals and watch us children, but she couldn't navigate the sand and rocky terrain to the beach. It's a miracle that none of us drowned in the undercurrents that Crystal Lake is known for.

Putting up with Tice was a challenge. I once found what appeared to be a rather small hatchet head, and it was immediately confiscated by Tice who always seemed to be aggressive when it came to weapons of any sort. He worked on it all afternoon, and by the next morning had turned it into a working hatchet, which he attached to his belt. After raiding Aunt Marian's makeup vanity for "war paint," he said he was going to look for "white eyes." When he didn't find any other children to torture, he decided that I, the head housemaid's daughter, would serve as an excellent captive and target of his practice throws. Before he could tie me to a gnarled, large tree, I screamed and ran faster than I knew I was capable of back to the cabin. Although I was obedient and docile in the presence of any Abbott, I never explored the lakeshore with Tice again. I truly believed that he would have thrown the hatchet at me. As children of the 50s, the movies of the era gave us an inaccurate template for playing cowboys and Indians, and Tice seemed unable to separate fiction from reality.

Things changed once Lydia and I became teen-agers. Our mornings at the lake were spent doing makeup and hair. In the afternoons, we perused the beaches in search of boys, so that we could experience the "summer romance" we had read about in teenage novels and saw in movies. I never found any boys that suited my fancy, nor did any seem interested in me. Ultra slim Lydia, however, with her sleek white hair and perfect skin, attracted the older boys. I felt dumpy, dark, and tongue tied, so I spent a good deal of time staring at the water and skipping rocks, as I waited for her to emerge from boat houses and the insides of canvas covered speed boats. Lydia never told me what she and the boys did, and I never asked. But for me, our carefree summer days of childhood fun ceased to exist, once Lydia began spending her time with the 'boys of summer'.

It was undeniable that things had changed, and once she went off to an eastern boarding school, our summers on the lake ended. I actually felt a sense of relief that I no longer had to tag along like a lackey while being expected to aid and abet her teen-age sexual exploits. I also no longer had to fear Tice's next homemade weapon, usually designed to be used on me. Spending my summers helping my mother at Abbott House and sitting in the gardens with a book were actually far less humiliating and much safer.

CHAPTER FIFTY-EIGHT

JUNE 27 – A STARRY NIGHT

Natalie

James' cabin, more rustic and less upscale than the Abbott's, was built in the 1920s and located on the north end of the lake on the small bluff. It had a moderate elevation from the water, and a lift had been installed to spare owners and their families the walk up the stone steps. The interior of the log cabin was full of "up north" charm with a large great room, kitchen and living area combined. There was also an open stairway to the three bedrooms and two bathrooms upstairs. The upstairs quarters were bordered by a balcony, visible from the center great room. If you sat in the living room, you could pretty much view the entire cabin from any angle. There was a door and stairway to the basement and a bathroom off a small hallway adjacent to the living area. The cabin needed some updating, but I found a good deal of charm in the rustic log interior and vintage furniture.

"I love this cabin, James. It's charming and feels like home. I'm so glad we're staying here tonight. Actually, would it be possible to stay longer?"

James responded to my question with a smile and said, "I guess so. No one knows we're here or even that we have any connection to this cabin. It might be a good thing. I can spend more time working on opening the box. I want to get it open tonight." He disappeared into the basement and returned with a hammer and a variety of other tools, including a sharp edged wedge, presumably to break the lock. His task wasn't easy, and he worked at it for about a half an hour, when I heard a sharp metallic sound.

"Success!" "It's open, Natalie!"

I turned around from my kitchen clean-up duties, and when the lid was raised and the contents exposed, confusion and shock were written on his face.

"I don't understand this, Natalie. Come here -- tell me what you think."

I looked into the box and was rendered momentarily speechless. "James, let's bring this over to the coffee table so that we can sit down and talk."

"We had better not touch anything, Natalie. This has to go to the state crime lab. I believe it's evidence of some sort, but I'm not exactly sure what."

Before we could discuss what we were thinking, trying to make some sense of what we saw, I instinctively knew what was in the box. "Babies, James. Marguerite Abbott's missing babies."

James began to examine the contents with a practiced eye. He had seen things I had never imagined, and his logic and expertise kicked in.

"You're right, Natalie, and they're quite well preserved, perhaps mummified, considering the age. The clothing looks like white linen christening dresses of some sort, now stained and rotting, and I can see tufts of wispy blond and brown hair still intact on the three tiny heads. The box has been lined with a satin fabric that has turned yellow and moldy, but surprisingly not excessively so."

James was very careful not to touch the tiny human remains, but it was apparent that lying on the yellowed, slightly decayed satin, were three tiny skeletal bodies, each appearing to be no larger than a very small doll. They had obviously been placed carefully, three in a row, with a small, bronze covered bible on one end. There was also a velvet box on the other end, with a photograph of Marguerite and Daniel Abbott set into the cover under glass -- presumably so the babies could have their family with them in death.

James said, "I have seen decomposed infants before, and these are probably the smallest -- but there is also something different about them -- something

I don't yet understand – maybe a deformity of some type." James looked at me and said, "How are you doing, Natalie?"

"I'm surprisingly okay, but I am exhausted. I can't make sense of what this is all about. Is this what Dewar was really after? It doesn't seem like something he would care about. Is there a panel underneath? Maybe we should go to bed now, and when we get up in the morning, something will enlighten you or me or both of us."

James said with a weary voice, "Yes, let's go to bed. As for taking the box apart to look for more evidence and clues, I would like the crime lab to do it. I don't want to damage anything. But I agree, there may be more than babies, pictures, and a bible in there."

After closing the box and placing it inside a larger cedar chest that was sitting in the closet under the stairway, he took my hand and led me up the stairs.

James and I made the bed with linens he had put on the closet shelf earlier in the summer. The bed was surprisingly comfortable, considering that the headboard was an antique ornate iron. When I commented, James said that he had replaced all of the mattresses. The only others who have ever been here were his daughter Paige and the cleaning service that takes care of opening the cabin before he arrives. Thankfully, the housekeepers were here earlier today, because the dust of his long absence was gone, and the place was spotless by the time we arrived.

James was in a rather pensive mood tonight and so was I. But something about the lake atmosphere, a fire in the fireplace and a crisp breeze coming through the window had loosened the knots of tense muscles in our weary bodies and created a cozy atmosphere inside. And then James said, "I want to show you something outside."

I protested a bit, "Oh, but I'm so warm and comfortable."

James insisted, "Wrap yourself in one of the cabin quilts and come with me. You won't be sorry."

Smiling with a trace of reluctance, I followed him, hand in hand, to the log swing overlooking the lake. James was right – what I saw was magical. The stars seemed to be hung so low that we could reach out and touch them. Cabins with lighted windows surrounded the lake and were like a painting, with the reflection of the moon on the water. The calling loons, looking for their mates, or in some cases, protecting their territory, were haunting with their cries. Despite possible lurking dangers, we kissed and laughed like teenagers on summer vacation. Charlie, following suite, began barking and running in circles, and when we ended up in bed in one another's arms, so did Charlie. At first, we thought that he could stay with us, but he wanted our constant attention. Finally, we had to put Charlie in the hall in his cushioned basket. After a bit of whining, he gave up and went to sleep, tired out by the lake air and playing fetch on the beach with James. We clung together beneath the quilts to throw off the nighttime lake chill, as the loons continued calling long into the night. Passionate and in love, sleep came after midnight.

The next day dawned with a blue sky and was everything a summer morning at the lake should be -- cool, crisp morning air, dancing blue waters, and a breakfast of bacon and eggs served on the porch. This was Minnesota at its summer finest. We were happy and joyous, and in our hearts, the world belonged to us. Feeling satisfied with our breakfast, James and I went back upstairs. After a long kiss goodbye, he left, and I fell back to sleep. I felt loved, safe, and happy to be alive. For a few hours on this lovely morning, I had quit thinking about Dewar.

CHAPTER FIFTY-NINE

FRIDAY, JUNE 28 - DANCING WATERS

Natalie

I awoke to the late morning sunlight streaming into the bedroom window. Sleeping so late is not like me, but I guess I am quite tired, and there are many reasons for that. After showering, I made the bed and pulled on a filmy white dress and a pair of sandals. The kitchen area of the great room smelled invitingly of coffee that James had made before he left for work. I filled the mug, grabbed my mother's journal, and walked down the steps to the dock and the Adirondack chairs. The water seemed to be dancing in the sunlight. The beauty of this place invigorates me. Maybe we shouldn't go to the Sullivan's condo in the Cities, I thought to myself. I'll ask James about staying here until it's safe to move back to Coventry. In any case, I had a task that I was eager to complete. I opened my mother's journal and began reading where I had left off while at the hotel.

CHAPTER SIXTY

GRACE LAPIERRE'S JOURNAL

December 8, 1941

The Abbott house is as quiet as a tomb today, because of the deaths of old Mrs. Abbott and my grandmother Anna. Mrs. Abbott was 89 years old. My grandmother was only 60.

Both bodies were removed from the house and taken to the funeral home -- Mrs. Abbott in a fine silver hearse and my grandmother in a station wagon with wood panels on the side. A practical coach for a practical woman. My heart is broken, and I have to figure out how to bury her.

June 15, 1942

I continue to live in the apartment at Abbott House, but I must move soon. It's clear that Helen, granddaughter of the now dead Mrs. Abbott doesn't want me there. There is an apartment above the newspaper office for rent, and I've paid a deposit. I'm eager to leave Abbott House, because I am afraid of Helen. I can tell that she hates me. She rages every day. After I learned that she had killed her father, I couldn't help but think that she could kill again.

July 15, 1942

I have now moved, but going home to my empty apartment every night makes me feel lonely. It's better when I am at work during the day, because I keep busy. I have just started going to movies again with the other hired girls from Morgan Street houses. Afterwards, we always go to the Sweet Shop for a hamburger and a coke and sometimes a soda or a sundae. I am trying to be strong, like Anna was, but I am still feeling very sad at losing her.

CHAPTER SIXTY-ONE

JUNE 28, 1991 – THE FAMILIAR STRANGER

Natalie

I stopped reading and focused on the sparkling water. It wasn't long before I was jolted out of my trance by an advancing shadow coming from behind. I first thought it was James, but as it moved closer, unhurried and with purpose, the reflection in the water told me it was not James, but a familiar and menacing presence. The scent that was present in Lydia's townhouse, and in my house, again penetrated my nostrils. And then it spoke, and I knew who it was. It was the voice of the angry man in Lydia's townhouse. It was the voice of the menacing man in Ragna Bergstrom's basement. That voice is now burned in my brain.

"Hello, Natalie. Do you remember the day I died?"

I was speechless and immobilized by the unexpected presence and his strange words. My eyes involuntarily looked downward into my mother's journal, as though not seeing him would make him go away. I turned my body around toward the sound of the raspy voice, but the sun hit me directly in the eyes, blinding me until I reflexively raised my right hand as a shield from the offending rays. Suddenly the field cleared, and my brain registered a name, along with fear. I knew who this intruder was before I could see him. But when I focused on the face, I felt a jolt of blinding terror, and I was speechless. The voice belonged to Dewar—the old man who lived across the street—the mastermind of so many deaths – Lydia, Ragna Bergstrom, John Bergstrom, and most likely Officer Dale Forbes. He is a cold blooded killer, and I am speechless, as well as terrified.

"You know, Natalie, it was very near here that I ceased to exist. In fact, it was in the boat house on Uncle Ellsworth's property about halfway around the lake. You know all about that, don't you?"

Still stunned into involuntary silence, my brain was rapidly attempting to retrieve memory to go along with the information that I was hearing. I couldn't comprehend what he was saying...ceased to exist...boathouse... Ellsworth. Who was this monster? The only nephew that Ellsworth had was Lydia's brother Edward, or Tice as he was known to family -- and he is long dead.

Dewar moved toward me, holding a gun in his claw-like hands. Charlie went crazy with fear. His protective instinct had kicked in, and he was barking and growling, as he tried to jump on Dewar's legs. Of course, Charlie didn't know that his protective instincts would not bode well for him.

"Pick up the noisy little beggar, my dear, said Dewar, and carry him to the boat house. Remember—I have this gun on you, so don't do anything stupid. I just want to give the little vermin a special treat."

I walked down the steps from the dock to the boat house and placed Charlie inside. Dewar followed and took a hypodermic out of his pocket, removing the orange cap from the needle. It contained a yellow liquid, and as he plunged it directly into Charlie's heart, I could only helplessly watch, panicked, stunned, and angry that this was happening. Charlie whined twice and then the convulsions began – and finally he was still. My heart was thudding in my chest. I heard the unintelligible sounds of disbelief coming from my mouth, and then Dewar told me to "Shut up!"

"Well, that's better," snarled Dewar with a smile. "The little beggar was much too noisy for his own good and mine. Now sit down by the window. We have some information to share – I with you and you with me. It's a perfect summer day for a good, long chat about family business, don't you think?"

I looked at Dewar, puzzled by what he was talking about. Chatting? Family business? And then he began to speak again.

"On second thought, I would rather have you read. Your mother's journal is tucked safely away in my coat pocket. She was such a kind woman, but even kind women can be untrustworthy. Take it out of my pocket -- carefully, and mind your p's and q's my little gypsy child." He laughed at me with disdain and condescension. Looking at you brings back memories of dark hair and flashing brown eyes, a little girl whose skin was always shiny from the heat of the kitchen, running through the house, book in hand, looking for a hiding place. You were a rather fat, sturdy little gypsy. I put up with you then, but now you're going to have to put up with me -- at least for a while. But don't worry. You're going to learn something about your mother, your father, and yourself, and possibly about me."

I moved toward him and cautiously pulled Mother's journal from his pocket. I felt the smoothness of the blue leather, as I slowly placed it in my hands. I thought to myself that I must have dropped it when he surprised me in front of the cabin. The things he was saying didn't add up to him being a stranger. After a brief silence, Dewar said in his raspy voice, " I'm looking forward to being read to, Natalie. Doesn't that sound cozy? ... like two teenagers stealing summer moments away from our parents who are in their chaise lounges, tipsy with afternoon cocktails. Oh, my dear, if only that could be. But of course, it's impossible. Before you read, you have to tell me where the metal box from the cellar is hidden."

I was dumbstruck, unable to act, until he stuck the gun in my mouth and threatened to pull the trigger. The shock of such a threat brought me back to reality, and I nodded.

Dewar looked at me and said, "I'll give you a choice. Can we have our chat now, Natalie, or would you rather read your mother's journal first? I have already read it, so it won't be news to me."

The only thing I could say was "I'll read. I want to read."

I didn't understand why Dewar would want me to read to him if he had already read it himself. This journal belonged to my mother, but perhaps there are passages in it that would relate to him, in some way unknown to me. And then it occurred to me after watching his unusual head movements and eye manipulations – Dewar's eyesight is so poor that he has difficulty seeing and reading. I doubted that he had read the journal prior to this moment, as he had claimed, but he definitely wants to know what is in it.

CHAPTER SIXTY-TWO

READING FOR MY LIFE - NATALIE

Grace LaPierre's Journal

September 22, 1945

I've spent three years going to the Sweet Shop on weekends, dancing, drinking cokes, and eating burgers and ice cream, all the while hoping to see Ted. I haven't forgotten anything about him, especially his smile and blue eyes. I am now twenty-seven years old and no longer young. Most likely he wouldn't be interested in an old maid.

Today the jukebox was playing, and I was doing the jitterbug with Susie when a glance in the mirror made my heart stop. There he was... very thin but still handsome ...walking through the doors with his charming crooked grin and twinkling blue eyes. He was with his friend who was still in uniform, but Ted was nicely dressed in khaki slacks and a blue shirt. They sat down in a booth, and when the song ended, Susie and I headed toward our booth. And then he noticed me. My heart nearly stopped when he walked over and asked me if I would dance with him. The next song was slow, a wartime song, "The White Cliffs of Dover." He pulled me close, and his hands were strong, but also soft and respectful. He said, "You're still here, Grace. I'm glad."

"Me too, I said."

We danced until the Sweet Shop closed at 10 p.m., and he asked if he could walk me home. Of course, I said "yes." We only had a block to walk to my downtown apartment, where I have lived alone since shortly after Grandmother Anna died. It wouldn't have been proper to invite him upstairs, but It was a nice evening, so we sat on the hard wooden steps leading to my apartment and spent another two hours talking.

I learned a lot about Edward Warner in those two hours. Everyone calls him Ted, a name that sounds friendly and good natured. It's a name that fits him well. He was wounded twice, the second time very badly and was missing in action for weeks. I could tell that he doesn't like to speak of the details of his time in the service, but I have heard that a lot of veterans don't. Two Twin Cities newspapers wrote an article about him and his service, and our local newspaper picked up the story. He was something of a war hero, leading a platoon and saving many lives by risking his own. That is something Ted would do.

Ted has been offered a job working for the railroad in Coventry, so he plans to stay. Before we ended our time together, he asked me to go to a movie with him the next evening. Of course I said yes, even though it was a Sunday and I had to be to work by 6 a.m. on Monday morning.

Sunday, September 23, 1945

It's very late, so my writing must be brief. Ted and I went to the movie, "I'll be Seeing You, "at the Hollywood Theatre. Joseph Cotton portrayed a soldier back from the war who was suffering from battle fatigue, and Ginger Rogers was a woman who was serving time in prison because she had gotten in with the wrong people. It was romantic, even if the two people were troubled.

Afterwards, we had a hamburger and a malt at the Sweet Shop, and he walked me home again. I could tell he wanted to come up to my apartment, but I said that I had to get up early tomorrow. "Okay. I'll be seeing you, Grace." He smiled and walked away. I started climbing the steps when I heard his footsteps coming toward me, I turned toward him, reached out my hand, and led him upstairs.

I am in love. The past month has flown by with dances at Valhalla and fall evenings at the pavilion on Lake Crystal. It seemed that the stars were hung in the sky just for us, and that we could touch them if we were able to reach just a little bit higher. Of course, my time with Ted is what has made it so wonderful. I love him, and I know he loves me too. We became lovers on our second date. I know that does not seem like something I would do, but being in love makes all the difference. He's coming tonight, but we aren't going out. He says that he has something to tell me. I'm hoping for a marriage proposal. I know he loves me. A woman always knows.

Much has happened since the last time I wrote in my journal, but there is little to say. Ted and Helen Abbott are now married. I didn't know they had been seeing each other until he came to my apartment a few days ago to tell me that Helen was pregnant. He said they dated only a few times in the spring, but he needed to take responsibility, even if he didn't love her. In fact, she scared him with her crazy moods. She wouldn't leave him or his parents alone. Helen drove her big fancy car to the farm looking for him nearly every day. Mrs. Warner, Ted's mother, had never met anyone like Helen before, and she warned him to be careful, but it was already too late.

Ellsworth called Ted to his office to tell him that he had to marry Helen because she was going to have a baby. Ellsworth said that he would have the state legally buy up his parents' farm, cheap, for the new crop experimental station if he didn't do his duty. His parents would lose money on their farm, and wouldn't have enough to live on in retirement. Ted had no choice, so he agreed to marry Helen, even though he isn't sure the child is his. Her baby is due in February. My baby is due in June.

Natalie

Speechless at the revelation of who my father is, I stopped reading. Lydia could be my half-sister, if her father was, indeed, Ted Warner. Her grandfather was my great-grandfather, so we were also cousins of some sort. And then I felt a hard blow to my rib cage. Dewar had kicked me. He was growing increasingly impatient and dangerous.

"Continue reading, you whore! Read!" The cold metal barrel of Dewar's handgun was pressed tightly to my forehead, and my shaking hand turned the page to the next entry.

"Yes, I'll read. Yes… Please stop!" It took a while to realize that the weak, trembling voice I heard was mine.

And so I read, trying hard to concentrate, and all the while thinking about James, saying a silent prayer that he would come and rescue me. But I knew this was a dangerous man who had no qualms about killing. I wasn't sure that James could save me and save himself, so I stopped wishing that he would come. While I read my mother's story, I began to create scenarios of self-preservation and survival in my head. I knew that I would most likely have to save myself from this monster, because no one but James knew that I was here. … and then I remembered that I had told another person, going against James' advice and my own better judgment, but she doesn't have any idea that I'm in danger. I had told M.J. that we were going to James' cabin, not Dunivan's. I did it on instinct just before I left City Hall. I was concerned that the substitute librarian might need some more information.

Again, I noticed that Dewar doesn't appear to have normal vision. He struggles with finding things and moving about. There must be something in Mother's journal that is of interest to him. In any case, he's a cold-blooded sociopath who has killed before with skill and without remorse. I'm just another expendable living creature -- and who knows how many other victims of his sick, diabolical mind have met their end at his hands. We know that some of them are in our community, but he may have also murdered others during his lifetime, if they got in his way.

I began to realize that I wasn't likely to get out of this alive, but I also knew, for the first time in my life, that I could kill. And so I continued to read, as I plotted my impossible escape. I also noticed that Dewar listened intently.

CHAPTER SIXTY-THREE

BIRTH

Grace LaPierre's Journal

June 14, 1946

Today I became a mother, and my baby girl is lovely. She's dark, like her father, and I hope she will have his twinkling blue eyes. My child was born at Coventry Municipal Hospital, with Doctor Ballantine attending me. It was a difficult birth, and forceps had to be used. She was dusky in color, but became pink right away when I held her and rubbed her body. She opened her dark eyes and looked straight at me, and I knew she would be a fine girl. Her name is Natalie Beret, after a beautiful child actress that I recently saw in a movie and my mother, whom I don't remember. Natalie Beret will make my mother Beret come to life for me.

Thursday, July 4, 1946

Today is the day that the Abbott House household workers are allowed to go to the lake to celebrate Independence Day. This has been the tradition since before Great-grandmother Anna came to live at the Abbott house as a maid in 1900. Now that I know what happened to her on this day, her rape at the hands of Thomas Abbott, I was glad that my baby is much too young for such an outing.

The story I told the Abbotts about the existence of Natalie is that I had been married briefly and secretly to a serviceman who came to town with one of Coventry's young soldiers. I put on the gold ring I bought at the dime store and showed it to them soon after I knew I was pregnant. I also made sure I wore it to the doctor's office for my first check-up. I told everyone I knew that my husband was killed in Germany when a bombed out building collapsed on him. ... another lie, but everyone in Coventry and Abbott House seemed to accept my story, or at least they acted like they did. I guess I was just another war widow to most people – there were so many of them. I continued to use my maiden name of LaPierre and also gave it to Natalie. I simply used the excuse that I wasn't married long enough to the young solder to take his name for a lifetime. Again, there was no comment. I don't like to tell lies, but I will do anything to protect us from Helen's murderous wrath. As long as she doesn't know that Natalie is her husband's child, we should be safe.

CHAPTER SIXTY-FOUR

GRACE'S JOURNAL –
HELEN'S INCONVENIENT HUSBAND

Natalie

I automatically stopped reading with the last entry, but my silence angered Dewar, and again I felt the toe of his boot dangerously close to my head. He seemed to hang on every word I read. "Do you think you're done, Bitch? Read!!"

August 31, 1948

Ted came to me about a week ago while I was alone in the Coventry library dusting books on my Saturday morning job. He said he wanted to meet with me after dark, away from Abbott House. I told him I would have to think about it, but I knew that I couldn't resist seeing him again. I have never stopped loving Ted.

A few nights later, after he watched Natalie sleeping in her crib, Ted sat in my living room and we talked. His blue eyes turned cold when he told me that Tice is definitely not his son. Ted and Helen hadn't slept together since shortly after their wedding. Today she finally told him the truth, thanks to her being more drunk and angry than usual. It seems that Tice is the result of a relationship between Helen and Ellsworth. Helen has had something going on with him since she was sixteen years old. She also said that she wouldn't sully the Abbott bloodline by allowing Ted to father her children. Helen told Ted that in 1945 any old war hero would do for a husband, even if he was from inferior stock. Before Ted left my apartment, he said, "We need to be together, Grace. I'll think of some way to get away from Helen and her family. There will be better days ahead for us." He told me he loved me and Natalie. and we kissed, hopeful for a future together. Before he left, he said, "I'll be seeing you, Grace," as he always has.

September 2, 1948

Ted is dead. He died when his car caught fire and burned near the Abbott's cabin on Lake Crystal. The Abbotts and their cronies in Coventry have spread rumors that he caused the fire himself because he was drunk and passed out in the back seat. They say his cigarette slipped down into the crevice between the seat and the trunk and eventually ignited the gas tank. But I know better than that. Ted never drank more than two beers, because it gave him a headache. His death is the work of the Abbotts. I am now afraid for myself and my baby girl. Helen has killed before and now Ted is dead. I must be very silent about who my baby's father is, or both of us could be in danger. Natalie must not ever know the truth of her father's identity. They are an evil family.

Natalie

The pages of Mother's journal turned blank, and it was obvious that she had finished putting her thoughts on paper. I was stunned by what I had learned, and my head was spinning with information. Mother was protecting me by keeping the identity of my father secret. She was terrified of Helen and what she might do if she knew that I was the daughter of her husband. Keeping the identity of my father from me and everyone else wasn't a selfish decision on her part, as I had once thought.

As I was fanning through the blank pages to the back of the journal, something fell out and onto the boathouse floor. It was an old photograph of my mother Grace and my father. I picked it up when Dewar was staring out the window and returned it to my mother's journal. He never saw it, thanks to his poor eyesight.

And then the silence was broken by Dewar. "Now you know who your father is, and the same is true for me."

CHAPTER SIXTY-FIVE

REVELATIONS

Dewar

"It's time... it's time for you to go, bitch. We must take a ride in the boat. Remember, I grew up here, so I know everything about this deep, dark lake."

Natalie

I shook my head wildly, foolishly hoping that Dewar would actually heed my protests. He responded with laughter in the face of my fear and then he spoke:

Dewar

"Did you know there are places in this lake where it's so deep and full of muck that it's almost impossible to find a body? With the proper weights, a body will never surface, and it's rumored that there are many of them buried in the silt bottom."

Natalie

Dewar tied my hands behind my back, gagged me, and attached lead weights around my waist. The terror inside, which I had been suppressing as best I could, swelled into a guttural sound from deep within my chest -- but it was quickly stifled by the hard back of his hand. I dropped like a dead weight to the floor hitting my head on the tongue of the trailer. And then Dewar spoke.

"Have you figured out who I am, Natalie?"

Natalie

I couldn't speak because of the gag, but I nodded 'no', which was the truth. What he was saying made no sense, and at this point, I didn't care who he was. I just wanted to get out of here alive.

Dewar

"You're not as smart as I thought you were, Natalie. I am Edward Tice Warner, son of Helen Abbott and Ellsworth Abbott, which has now been confirmed by your mother's journal. You know me as Dewar Renward. I'm surprised you didn't decipher the rather clever anagram of my name. If you jumble the letters again, you'll see that they can go back into place as "Edward Warner." As you probably gathered from your mother's journal, I am not your half-brother, even though your father was married to my mother. My sister Lydia is possibly your half-sister, but I doubt it. Mother Helen told me just before her stroke that she used your father to secure a marriage so that she could have Ellsworth's children without scrutiny. She and Ellsworth had been lovers since she was sixteen. And in fact, the old man was the love of her life. There was no incest, because Ellsworth was adopted. I guess I must concede that I am your cousin, since my great-grandfather Daniel Abbott is your great-great-grandfather."

Natalie

Tice is alive? I had gone to his funeral so many years ago. It never occurred to me that he was still alive in the person of Dewar Renward. I remembered his funeral and what looked like genuine mourning by the family. If the Abbotts could fake such a seemingly sincere display of grief, they were without humanity. No wonder Tice is so twisted.

Dewar

"You are probably wondering how I survived the boathouse fire when I was eighteen years old. Well, I'm going to tell you, and you will be the only other person to know of this, because everyone else who has had this knowledge is dead, as you will soon be yourself.

Natalie

Dewar seemed to have gotten lost in his own history, because he stopped talking and again went to the window, squinting as he looked outside. I continued to think of possible ways to escape his madness, and I began to realize that with the addition of the weights, he had left me no hope. Apparently satisfied that no one was outside, he started again.

Dewar

"The summer of 1967 is literally burned in my memory. Coventry being a smaller Midwestern city was beyond boring to my friend Cully and me. To make things worse, my mother had drastically limited my spending money due to my poor grades during the previous school term. To make ends meet, Cully and I began burglarizing homes of Coventry's wealthier citizens and fencing our loot in the Twin Cities. The profits were helpful, but being randy young men, we were also eager to find other activities,—namely girls who were willing to oblige our needs. After discovering that the big city had a red light district, we found some action, mainly in the persons of drug addicted homeless girls managed by a pimp named Johnny. We had little money for their services, but they were desperate. A restaurant meal

and a few dollars for Johnny's drug habit encouraged all kind of willingness. I guess you could say we took advantage of them. One hot summer day, we brought two of the girls and Johnny to Ellsworth's boathouse for an afternoon of fun. Pimp Johnny wanted to make sure we didn't steal what he considered to be his, so he came along. And that was the day I died.

"You remember, don't you Natalie? They buried me in the Abbott plot, alongside my so-called father—really your father. Only it isn't me in that expensive mahogany coffin. It's pimp Johnny that Cully and I picked up on the streets of Minneapolis. How ...why? Because my alcoholic mother Helen made a surprise trip to Ellsworth's cabin to retrieve a fucking bottle of especially fine and well-aged wine. Her interminable need for a drink caused Cully, Johnny and me to lose our lives to a madwoman."

"Hearing voices coming from the boathouse, Helen investigated by looking through the small window. Angered by what she saw, she began screaming and raging, the like of which I had never seen or heard before, even from her. She picked up an oar and attacked us. In the process, she knocked a gas can from a shelf... evidentially one with a loose cap. Panicked, we tried to cover our nakedness with our gas soaked clothes, but were able to get only half-dressed before the oar found its target on Cully's head. She knocked him unconscious or perhaps killed him on the spot. Mother dropped the oar and backed me into a corner with a spear used for ice fishing. I had no doubt that she would use it, and I would soon be impaled and gasping for breath like a dying fish. Johnny grabbed the spear from Mother, and in the melee, I heard a gunshot and the thud of a body falling on the floor. Ellsworth, who had driven my drunken mother to the cabin, was standing in the doorway of the boathouse, a gun in his hand, and Johnny was lying on the floor with a bullet hole in his head. He was clearly dead as a doornail. In the next instant, I felt my body explode with searing heat, and I realized that I was on fire. I never knew where the igniter came from: Mother's cigarette, her lighter, or the cigar that chronically dangled from Ellsworth's flaccid mouth. And then I heard my own screams, mixed with the chaos and insanity of the moment, and my instincts probably saved my life. I had enough presence of mind to reach for the trapdoor of the boathouse, and in an instant I was in the dark water beneath it, where scores of dead fish and entrails had

been disposed of for so many years. I lost consciousness when I heard the sizzle of my burning skin hit the water. As far as I know, the girls were never heard from again."

Natalie

Dewar, taking the time to again look outside, bought me more time, and I began to wonder. Was he hearing something? Was someone outside? James? I began to work harder on the gag and was able to push it out of my mouth and onto my chin, and in the next instant felt a stinging, brutal slap, and I lost consciousness. When I came around, I heard Dewar's croak, angry and berating me.

Dewar

"You never could behave yourself, even when you were a child. Always hanging around -- always annoying me. Sit up! I'm not done yet!"

CHAPTER SIXTY-SIX

DEWAR'S LAMENT

Natalie

I choked on the blood running into my throat, and Dewar began again, but not before I was gagged even more tightly than before.

Dewar

"Fearful of a murder scandal in the family and presuming that I would die of my burns, Mother and Ellsworth pulled me out of the water and allowed the boat-house to burn to the ground with Cully and a drug addicted pimp who calls himself Johnny inside. As they dragged me to lie beside Ellsworth's Lincoln, I could feel the skin come off my arms, face, chest, and almost everywhere. The only parts of my body that were spared were my buttocks and thighs. I went in and out of consciousness, as I heard them plot, throwing out ideas like they were dealing with a barbecued chicken. There was no attempt to call an ambulance."

"Ellsworth, ever the masterful businessman, devised a story to save his family's reputation and his own skin for killing Johnny. Their story was simple, but effective. They claimed that I, burned beyond recognition, was the pimp, and the other two bodies, dead and burned beyond recognition, were Cully and me. Cully was identi-fied with dental records and was buried in his family plot. With the assumption that the other boy was me, there is now an unknown man buried in the Abbott plot under

the name of Edward Tice Warner – my name. The ordeal proved to be too much for Ellsworth. He died of a heart attack a few days later. I didn't die, as expected, but was charged with my own bogus death and that of Cully. "

"After a year in a St. Paul burn unit, I pleaded guilty to the charges and served five years in prison. There was no use in claiming my true identity. No one would have believed an 'amnesic' pimp. Luckily, I was sent to a prison for inmates with medical problems, where I received free treatment and reconstruction, courtesy of the government. Although it was time well spent, I had lost everything, thanks to my insane, alcoholic mother. Look at me, Natalie – I haven't been human for nearly twenty-five years. My skin is like that of a one-hundred-year-old man, and it sheds constantly -- I'm sure you have also figured out that I am nearly blind."

"When I was released from prison, I was handed an envelope along with my belongings. I opened it and was shocked to find $1,000,000 in cash – no note – just the cash. I understood that it was a payoff – a strong incentive to disappear from the Abbott family forever, which I did – until my investments went bad and the money ran out. I was forced to seek the kindness of strangers – John Bergstrom for one. That's not his real name -- just the one we gave him, so he could come to Coventry and take care of his 'Aunt Ragna,' while he stalked you. Did you hear his footsteps behind you the night you took the metal box from Abbott House? No matter…he was an incompetent accomplice."

Are you wondering, Natalie, how I first found out about the fortune hidden in the cellar? There were always rumors, but I knew nothing until I forced it out of my elderly, drunken mother, causing her to have a stroke. The only problem is that she lied and said it was buried beneath the floor of the carriage house -- under the bricks. After extensive digging and searching with no sign of it, we had to move on to Lydia.

Natalie

Dewar moved to the shelving again and seemed to be searching for something. It's now obvious that he is nearly blind, because he seemed to have difficulty reading labels. I wondered if he was searching for a gas can or some other type of igniter. The thought of being burned alive terrified me, but no more than lying at the bottom of the lake with weights tied to my body. He stopped for a few minutes to take a pill from the container he carried in his shirt pocket and also pulled a small tube -- some type of cream-- from a shelf and rubbed it on his arms and face. I instantly recognized the smell. That was the familiar smell in Lydia's condo and my house -- it was the cream he puts on his skin. He also must have slept in the boathouse last night, the thought of which gives me cold chills. He was on the premises when James and I were outside looking at the stars and inside the cabin making love. He must have heard us talking, laughing, and loving. I felt sick at the thought of his voyeurism.

Dewar

I suspected that sister Lydia knew the whereabouts of the metal box. After making contact with her, she allowed me to have a room in her San Francisco townhouse – under duress, you could say. Unfortunately, the time I spent with her, after so many years apart, yielded no close bonding for either one of us. Family money often does that to siblings. We became increasingly wary of one another, and both of us were unwilling to share what was left of our family fortune. I believe she would have killed me had I not killed her first.

Before she died, Lydia put the finger on you, Natalie. She said that you had the answers I was looking for. She sold you out in a last ditch effort to save her own skin. Of course, it didn't work. And you, Natalie, complicated my plans for retrieving the remainder of the Abbott fortune from the basement, as did that fat policeman. I took care of him with a croquet mallet, a relic from more civilized days, and I will take care of you very soon. But first we must remove your gag so you can tell me what I need to know – the location of that illusive little box.

CHAPTER SIXTY-SEVEN

DARK WATER

Natalie

With the gag ripped off my mouth, I began to vomit swallowed blood onto the floor of the boathouse. Dewar was obviously growing impatient.

"*Where is it, you lying bitch? Where is the box?*"

I would have been happy to tell him of its whereabouts, but that was problematic. The last time I saw it was in the back of the closet under the stairway. As he kicked me, pulled my hair, and twisted my arms, I began to speak. "It's in the closet under the stairs. That's all I know. ...under the stairs... go look." ...and then he exploded.

"*Do you really think I'm so stupid? I've already looked in the closet. I saw your boyfriend put it in there last night when I looked through the window, and it's not there today. I know every move you made last night. Try again, Cousin Natalie, or I will likely decide not to wait for your confession to dispose of you. If you don't know where it is, your life is worth nothing to me... and believe me, it's not worth anything to you either, because your life will end immediately. I have worked much too hard for the fortune in the box to give up on it now. And you, Natalie, are the same uncooperative bastard child that you have always been.*"

There was nothing more I could say, because I didn't have the answer he was looking for. If I had the answer, there would have been no hesitation. I would have given it to him, although I knew he would have killed me anyway.

I have another reason to stay alive. I may be pregnant -- at the age of forty-five. I haven't yet told James, because I want to see a doctor first, just to be sure.

I tried to reason with Dewar, but once he understood that I knew nothing, his anger reached the point of no return, and he came at me with a fillet knife used for cleaning and preparing fish to be eaten.

"I could skin you alive with this you fucking bitch! One more chance to save yourself, and then I will gut you like a fish. Let me see...does one skin the fish before or after it's gutted?"

Dewar placed the knife on my collarbone near my windpipe and let it pierce the skin until the blood ran in rivulets between my breasts. I screamed in pain, and then -- without warning -- I heard a shot. At that moment, Dewar fell heavily on my body blinding me with the gray, stringy wig that was no longer attached to his head. He frantically reached for his missing hair, but his eyes were full of his own blood, the source of which I was unsure. He rolled off and fell unmoving to the floor. And at that moment, my eyes met those of James, who quickly began to attend to me -- perhaps too quickly. He cut the weights from my waist and the shackles from my hands, and I thought Dewar was dead. But, like the phoenix he is, he rose behind James, unnoticed and unexpected. With a force unusual for a man who appeared to be shot in the head, Dewar took a fishing spear from the wall and pushed it into James' back with a force I didn't know he still possessed. Dewar screamed, "Where is the box you Irish scum!"

James was gravely injured, but he managed to say, "It's locked away where you can't get it, and you'll never be able to get it, you murderous animal." Dewar raised the filet knife with both hands and aimed at James' heart. I reached for his police revolver lying on the floor, and pointing it at the monster, I pulled the trigger and watched the blood run from his neck. At that moment, the wailing sirens of police cars became deafening, and Dewar, eyes blazing, his wounded body full of the adrenaline that was keeping him alive, disappeared into the lake through the open trapdoor in the floor. In moments, the dark water had become still and silent, and he was gone. All that was left of him was his blood, as it mingled with the lake water beneath the boathouse. I turned my attention to James. I held him in my arms and whispered words of hope and comfort, and then I heard the sound of a boat's motor. Skittish to start, as if in protest, it finally screamed across the lake. Dewar...

"James, my love... Calling to him as I stroked his sandy hair, I watched the light in his blue eyes fade to a pale memory. The last thing he said before losing consciousness was my name, "Natalie – love you – not long enough."

I was still holding James, not sure if he was dead or alive, when I heard Detective Michael Dunivan's deep Irish brogue. "Sully — Natalie!" Dunivan's eyes met mine in a look of disbelief when the paramedics pushed us aside.

Dunivan held me to his chest and stroked my hair. I didn't speak until they took James away in the ambulance, but not before I saw the EMT shake his head at Dunivan, as though to say, *He won't survive.* When everyone was gone from the boathouse and the yellow tape was strung around the property, Dunivan finally let me go. I looked at this man who had endured too many losses of his own and too many vain attempts to drown his grief in beer and Irish whiskey, and I understood that he loved James Sullivan like a brother. When I found my voice and some of the courage that had been lost in Dewar's rampage, I said, "James can't die! I can't lose him. Our baby will have no father. It's all happening again -- generation after generation – women without men, children without fathers."

If Dunivan was surprised at my revelation, if he even understood my words, he didn't give it away, but stayed silent. Amazingly calm, he took my hand and said in his soft Irish brogue, "We'll keep him alive for your baby, Natalie. And we'll get Dewar. We have to get this evil man."

I pleaded with God for the life of my husband, but I knew that I had little control over James' fate. Nevertheless, I prayed silently for the first time in a long time, making a private bargain with God for James' life – a bargain that I will never speak of again.

Full of unanswered questions, I pulled away from Dunivan and asked, "How did James know that Dewar was at the cabin? He saved my life and the life of our baby. How did he know that I needed him?"

Dunivan said, "When M.J. didn't come to work today, and there was no call, one of the officers went to her house and found her tied up and barely conscious. When she was able to speak, she told us that you were in danger at James' cabin. Dewar had arrived at her home before dawn. He tortured her, and in his haste and greed, carelessly left her alive, but in pretty bad shape. She is in the hospital recovering from multiple injuries. It was lucky that you decided to tell her where you were before you left, because no one else in Coventry, except for me, knew that you were in danger or that Sully even had a lake cabin."

I thought for a moment, and realized that there was another side to this scenario. "And if I hadn't told her where we were hiding, she would have had nothing to tell Dewar, and James would not be mortally wounded."

Dunivan didn't reply to my comment. His only words were, "Natalie, let's get out of here."

"Yes," I said. "We need to go to James."

As we walked to the police car, I heard the search boats on the lake and the wailing of sirens on the surrounding roads. It seemed like a massive effort, but I held out no hope that Dewar would be found-- dead or alive. The search turned up only James' boat – empty and spinning in circles in the middle of the lake.

I pulled away from Dunivan and saw the dappled sunlight on the water, and I knew that Dewar, master of death and skilled navigator of Lake Crystal, would escape. He would slither into his own dark world, because he could. Such a monster is beyond intervention and redemption. Such a man is forged of an evil that normal people don't understand--evil that can exist among us without notice, until it is too late.

EPILOGUE

JUNE 1993

Natalie

As I stand in the kitchen of the cabin, looking out the window toward the beach, I see my beautiful girl playing with her sister Paige. At fifteen months, she is brave and fearless, tumbling and falling on the unstable sand with nearly every baby step. She is a lovely combination of both her parents, with dark curls and twinkling blue eyes. Her name is Anna Beret Grace Sullivan -- Anna B. as she is called by all who know her. Her big sister is cautious and solicitous of her determined little sister, so I don't worry about her safety. They adore each other.

After a one-year leave of absence from the Coventry City Library, I made the decision not to return. My daughter needs me, and I need to prepare myself for a new career that will take me out of the bubble that I had created and lived in for forty-five years. Twice a week, I drive to St. Paul where I attend law school. This is something I would never have had the courage to do before James came back into my life.

We returned to the cabin last summer with the expectation of preparing it to be sold, and surprisingly, we ended up living here for three weeks. Now there is no more talk of putting it up for sale. The sun dappled water, that seems to perform a joyful dance when we are here, has been a healing force.

At Paige's request, we have torn down the old boathouse and built a new one on a different part of the shoreline. The site of the old boathouse is now a colorful flower garden. Charlie's ashes were strewn where he lived his life, in the flower beds of my former home on River Flats. I miss him very much, but we will wait until Anna B. is older before bringing another dog into our lives. The next dog will be her dog, so she must be the one to choose a puppy.

James has had a long recovery. Yes, he survived the extensive physical trauma and is very much alive, thanks to the helicopter transport to a trauma center, along with the many donations of blood from the men on his force. James lost a lung and most of the blood in his body, and he has also been left with some mild paralysis in his left arm. He returned to his job after nine months of recovery and is still the finest Chief of Police in Minnesota -- and I have the best little family a spinster could have hoped for.

As for M.J., we are still friends, but with boundaries. She purchased my craftsman house and now lives there with Frank. M.J. has also undergone some rather surprising changes. She is now a blond, has lost thirty pounds, and no longer wears Birkenstocks. Surprisingly, the changes suit her. M.J. and Frank seem to be very happy together, and I expect news of a wedding in the near future.

That brings me to the innocuous appearing small metal box that led to multiple murders. James had taken it to the station after he left the cabin on that sunny, happy morning before Dewar intruded into our lives. The box was impounded and sent to the state crime lab for examination. That's why Dewar had not found it in the cabin during his desperate search.

What the crime lab found was completely unexpected. We knew about the dead Abbott babies, but no one knew what else old Daniel Abbott had placed in the secret compartment under the aged satin cushion. The babies were all afflicted with genetic bone malformations, something that Daniel Abbott was unwilling to accept, so he didn't allow them to live. Marguerite's babies now lie together in a tiny coffin in the Abbott plot.

As for the fortune that was so important to Lydia and her brother, Dewar/ Tice, it seems that in September 1919, Daniel Abbott had acquired some stock certificates from the Coca Cola company. At that time, the company had recently been purchased, and the new owner had put up shares for public offering. Mr. Abbott purchased 5,000 of them, paying $40 a share. There was also an envelope containing a note addressed to his mistress, Edna Howard, along with $100,000 in cash.

September 20, 1919

> *My Dearest Edna,*
>
> *I have always promised that I would take care of you as long as I lived and after my death. If I am gone, and you are reading this letter, the gift that comes with it should be in your possession, delivered by my faithful housemaid Tillie Johnson. I trust it will take care of you and our son for the rest of your lives. It is with gratitude and love that I bequeath these stock certificates to you, along with a sum of money in return for the years of devotion and love that you have shown me. Our years together have meant more to me than I can say. I am overjoyed with our love and the miracle of our son.*
>
> *All my love now and forever,*
> *Daniel Abbott*

Five days after writing this letter, Daniel Abbott died. Why didn't Tillie give Mr. Abbott's gift to Edna? The answer to that is a matter of record. According to her death certificate, Tillie, like Beret, died of influenza in October 1919, about two weeks after Daniel Abbott died of a massive heart attack. It's likely that she was incapacitated by illness and never had the opportunity to deliver the stock certificates and money to Edna before her death. On her deathbed, not knowing what to do, Tillie most likely gave the money and stocks to Ellsworth Abbott to deliver to his adopted father's mistress. Of course, Ellsworth didn't follow through, and instead placed them in the safest hiding place he could think of: the metal box in the crawlspace of the cellar. This selfish act ensured his financial security for a rainy day. Daniel Abbott had good reason for entrusting the delivery to Tillie and not to Ellsworth. He knew Ellsworth would betray him and Edna.

Today, in 1993, the stock certificates are worth a good deal of money. Legally, the contents of the metal box belong to the son of Edna and Daniel, or his heirs. The son would now be about seventy-eight years old. An extensive search has been taking place, but so far has not turned up any leads. Since there is no other legal claimant, I have been told that sufficient time has passed, as well as adequate investigative services, to designate me as the sole heir to the last of the Abbott inheritance — which at the time of Lydia's death consisted of only the contents of the metal box and the mansion itself. I'm ignoring the existence of the fortune that Daniel left for Edna – at least for a while. Being wealthy holds no appeal for me.

I sold Abbott House earlier this year for $1 to an organization that will provide shelter for women and children who have endured violence, rape, and threats of murder, or who are at risk of being abused. The sign on the gate says, "The Anna Grace House." It will be renovated and sustained in the same way that all women's shelters are supported, mostly with federal and state funds, but will need ongoing management to facilitate fundraising activities. I am no longer the occasional housemaid and caretaker for Abbott House, but I have been asked to sit on the board of directors.

About my father... he was here in Coventry all the time, in the Abbott cemetery plot. I am no longer a fatherless child, thanks to my mother's journal. Knowing who both my parents are has set me free, and understanding that my mother's motive was to protect me from Ellsworth and Helen Abbott takes me out of that restless prison and gives me peace.

Knowing that my father, Ted Warner, would not want to be buried with the Abbotts, I have had him moved to another location in the Coventry cemetery. He is now in the company of Anna, Beret and Claude, Grace, and when the time comes, he will be joined by James, me, and perhaps other family members. There is also a search for the unknown Johnny's family who was buried in Tice's plot. In the meantime, he has been moved from that location to his own gravesite. Tice's grave is now empty and waiting for him. The false tombstone has been removed. The day that Tice joins the rest of the Abbotts in their plot will be a good day.

I have learned another fact about myself. Lydia and I are not sisters, but we are cousins, according to the DNA testing that was done for settling the Abbott estate. It was revealed that Lydia and Tice had the same parents: Helen and Ellsworth Abbott. The test also showed that I have Abbott DNA, which, of course, is because my great-grandmother Anna was raped by Thomas Abbott in the year 1899. Though so long ago, the implications have been far-reaching.

James and I, our daughters Anna B. and Paige, live in the new condominium complex in Coventry -- a secure building. But today, we're at the cabin, where late afternoons are always serene and lazy. I've just heard a car pull up and a familiar voice call out. "Hi, I'm home. How are my girls!" It's the one I love, James Sullivan. We have created a joyful family, but we also live with a fear that we rarely speak of. Dewar/Tice's body was never found. Although it's doubtful that a human being could survive in a cold lake with such significant wounds, I know that he isn't a typical human, so anything is possible. We are vigilant and always will be for the sake of our family.

Dewar, a victim of his irrational, abusive mother's rage, became a killer without a conscience. He destroyed many lives, including his own. Dewar shared many of his evil thoughts as we spent that terrifying day together in the boathouse. His plan was to kill me, so he was careless with his words, but I listened well. There is one thing he said that has stayed with me, as he had intended. I replay it in my head much too often. "Beware of all things beautiful. Remember... Beneath beauty evil lurks well disguised." And I know that's the truest thing he said to me on that desperate day at the lake. Beauty is a perfect hiding place for evil. The perfect place to gather strength while waiting.

THE END